# Relocation Disclosure

By Kevin L. Bouyer

This book is dedicated to my father, Nathaniel Bouyer. Our family misses you dearly. Continue to rest in peace. We love you!

# Chapter 1

Jace's eyes widened in horror upon seeing Mr. Kincade's name appear on the caller ID. He picked up the phone, his heart pounding feverishly.

"Network support, Jace Valentine speaking?"

"Can I see you in my office?"

"S-sure. Be there in a minute."

Jace closed his eyes and tilted his head up at the ceiling. *Is this the day it finally happens*? he thought.

From day one, he felt uneasy when they hired the new network engineer. He was young, vibrant, and always up for the challenge when it came to helping resolve the company's technology issues, no matter what they entailed. Although Jace's interactions with him were always cordial, he felt extremely threatened by this newcomer who seemed to be the total package when it came to being considered a model employee.

Jace gritted his teeth, mentally kicking himself for not being more aggressive in his job search. Then he took a sip from his coffee mug, trying to clear the lump in his throat, and forged ahead, down the hallway, and toward the office where he tapped on the door.

"Have a seat. I wanted to discuss some upcoming changes to the firm," Mr. Kincade said in a deep voice to match his burly physique.

Jace sat with beads of sweat forming on his upper lip. He gazed out the massive window behind Mr. Kincade's desk, displaying a picture-perfect view of the Gateway Arch. The blended scent of coffee and Mr. Kincade's spicy cologne tickled his nose, almost to the point of sneezing. He pinched his nose and eased into the seat.

Mr. Kincade leaned back in his executive leather chair, emphasizing his protruding mid-section that had seen one too many beers. "I guess you're wondering why I called you in."

Jace cracked a meek smile and nodded.

"Let me ask you a question. How would you rate your decision-making skills during this past year?"

Jace scrunched his eyebrows. "I . . . I'm not sure what you mean by that."

"Well, we most certainly had our challenges this year with various technology issues, including the whole Y2K frenzy, which didn't turn out to be as frightening as predicted. I just want to know how you think you handled these situations and whether you were confident in the decisions you made to help get us through this past year."

Jace hesitated for a moment. "I did the best I could under the circumstances and would like to think I made all the right decisions."

Mr. Kincade tapped his right index finger on a folder sitting on his desk. "The reason I asked is because what I have in this folder may just be the biggest decision you'll have to make in quite some time." He slid the folder across the desk.

This was most certainly not the way Jace had expected to receive his walking papers.

He took a deep breath and opened the folder.

After reading the initial paragraph of the document inside, he looked up at Mr. Kincade. "Are you serious?"

Mr. Kincade smiled. "The company's been expanding, and we're in the process of opening a couple of new branches outside the St. Louis area. There will be a new office in Los Angeles and one in Albuquerque. As you can see, the office in Albuquerque is looking for a network support specialist who's willing to relocate and, well, that's where you come in." Mr. Kincade took a sip from his coffee mug.

"You've done an admirable job considering all the issues we did have this year, and you really stepped up to help our local office stay afloat. With all that said, I'm wondering if you'd be willing to relocate. We would hate to see you go, but we think your young apprentice can step in and take the reins if you do decide to leave. To sweeten the deal even more, the company will take care of the relocation costs, provide miscellaneous cash allowances, and assist you with finding a home in the area. There's also a good chance we can work out a pay increase to make up for any cost of living adjustments."

Jace rubbed his hands over his pants, wiping off the perspiration, as he felt a rush of heat flow from the pit of his stomach and up to the crown of his head. He loosened his tie. "It would be an easier decision if I were single, but with a wife and two kids—"

"I understand. I'm not expecting you to give me an answer today, although I do need to know in the next couple of weeks."

Jace stroked the side of his cheek, overwhelmed at the offer. "Let me talk it over with the family."

***

At the end of the workday, Jace was looking forward to sharing the news with his family. As usual, he bypassed the elevators and approached the door to the stairwell.

"You gotta be kidding me," he said in disbelief.

The stairwell was temporarily closed due to repairs needed for a water pipe leak.

Jace's heart rate immediately spiked at the thought of taking the elevator. With his ritual of taking the stairs every day, his coworkers assumed he was an exercise guru, having no idea of the real reason he avoided elevators.

He closed his eyes, gathering the nerve to press the elevator button. His hand shook upon pressing the button. Seconds later, a rush of air squeezed through the narrow slit between the double doors, signifying an elevator approaching. A chime sounded before the doors opened. Several men, dressed in business suits, moved back to give Jace room to board.

He bit his bottom lip, his pride and manhood telling him to get on, yet his legs would not comply.

"Are you getting on?" one of the gentlemen asked.

Jace mustered a nervous laugh. "I'm sorry. I forgot something in my office."

The men shrugged as the doors closed.

Jace softly tapped his head against the wall in frustration before taking a deep breath and summoning the courage once more to press the button. A minute later, another elevator arrived. This one was empty.

He closed his eyes and, with blind faith, stepped onto the elevator. He pressed the lobby button, saying a silent prayer before the doors closed and the elevator began its descent. He gripped the railing, glancing at the illuminated numbers.

"Eight . . . seven . . . six," he counted down, his voice trailing off to a whisper.

He dabbed his forehead with the back of his hand as sweat trickled from his pores and his mind struggled to stay within the boundaries of reality. The recessed lights beaming down from the ceiling felt like heat lamps, baking his skin on the hottest of summer days. He gazed at the walls, which, from his perspective, were closing in on him. He dropped to one knee, becoming dizzy as the sickening sensation of vertigo took hold. The elevator eventually shuttered, coming to a stop on the ground floor.

The doors opened, and two women immediately greeted Jace.

"Are you okay, sir?" one of them blurted out, looking at Jace's disheveled condition.

He took a deep breath. "Yes, I . . . I'll be fine."

They quickly moved aside as Jace walked by, looking as if he had just completed a five-mile run in his business casual attire. He plodded his way through the parking lot, getting stronger with each step, and pressed the button on his key fob to disarm the alarm to his beige Toyota Camry. After collapsing into the leather seat, he immediately arched his back at the shock of his sweat-drenched shirt pressing against his skin. He took a moment to inhale the sweet coconut scent from the air freshener before starting the car and turning up the volume to Kenny G's classic *"Songbird"* to calm his senses further.

He traveled west on Interstate 70, the sky displaying a dark orange hue as the sun descended beyond the horizon. The Mississippi River, which ran parallel to the highway for a short distance, sparkled with a myriad of blue, yellow, and white lights from the city's nightlife reflection. A multitude of tourists and locals lined the banks of the river, walking, cycling, or just sitting, enjoying the summertime twilight. Even with all the city's brilliance on display, Jace struggled to enjoy the nostalgic atmosphere. With his recent elevator ride acting as a blunt reminder, he was driving through an emotional minefield, brought on by a horrific event from the past that had changed his life forever.

After a forty-five minute commute, he pulled into the driveway of his three-bedroom condo, located in Maryland Heights, a suburb northwest of Downtown St. Louis. Faded wooden shingles covered the outside of the twenty-year-old condo, making it appear much older.

He shut off the engine and sat for a couple of minutes, tilting his head back against the headrest, attempting to unwind from the rigors of another day. He eventually exited the car and approached the front door.

Jace stood half a foot shy of six feet with a lightweight frame and lacked any substantial facial hair. He could have easily passed for a high school student, someone twenty-five years his junior. But a more detailed look at his face revealed someone quite the opposite. His square jaw and cleft chin prominently stood out on his face. Along with his neatly trimmed jet-black hair and molasses eyes, he was a rather distinguished-looking gentleman, despite his peewee stature.

He entered the house as his lanky, eleven-year-old daughter appeared. Her curly, ebony hair, and toothy smile, combined with her puppy dog eyes put her in the upper echelon when it came to measuring the cuteness factor.

"Hey, Ava," he said, pinching her cheeks.

He refrained from giving her the old-fashioned bear hug, noticing the stress-induced sweat from the elevator ride had left an odor. This was extremely unfortunate because there was nothing he adored more than getting a warm hug from his little girl. No matter how stressful his days at work might be, one squeeze from her, and everything was right with the world.

He proceeded farther into his humble abode with the sweet smell of baked apples filling the air. He placed his briefcase on a black, micro-fiber faux suede sectional that blended in perfectly with the rest of the contemporary decor and strolled into the Lilliputian-sized kitchen, struggling to hold the kitchenette set and four people comfortably.

With her back turned, his wife, Sarah, walked by the oven, unaware of his presence. She stood with her wiry frame on full display, along with her chocolate-colored hair, pulled into a frazzled ponytail. He cleared his throat to get her attention, and she turned around, sporting her usual baggy, gray jogging pants, protected by an apron, covered with a menagerie of faded food stains. She immediately glanced at her watch.

"Guess you didn't think to call and let me know you were running late?"

"Sorry about that. I had so much on my mind."

"I hope it wasn't another woman."

"What did you say?"

"You're not messing around on me?" she said, one eyebrow raised.

"Not this again. Why would you think I am?"

"Coming home late from work is how it usually starts."

He extended his arms and placed both hands on top of his head. "Please just stop being so paranoid. I'm not leaving you for another woman." He sighed, sitting at the kitchen table. "Can we just leave that subject alone and talk about what happened to me today."

She stared for a moment. "Okay. I'll let it go for now." She walked over, gave him a peck on the lips, and then immediately pulled back with her nose crinkled. "Did you forget to shower this morning?"

"No, but after I tell you what I went through today, you'll completely understand why I may not smell as fresh as I should."

"Please, do tell."

"For starters, would you believe me if I told you I had to take the elevator leaving work?"

Sarah looked on in disbelief. "No way. Why in the world did you do that? That's the last place on earth you need to be."

"I . . . I know. I had no choice. A water pipe burst and apparently flooded the stairwell."

"Did you make it out okay without an attack?"

Jace raised his arm and sniffed his right armpit. "From the way I sweated and now smell, the answer is a resounding no. Guess it's just something I have to live with."

He shook his head, clearing any further negative thoughts. "Enough about that. I have some other news to tell you."

"I'm all ears."

"Well, I received a nerve-racking call from the VP of my department this morning."

Sarah displayed a furrowed brow. "Jace, don't tell me you just lost your job. With me not working, we wouldn't be able to afford a pot to piss in."

"Wait, hold on a minute. It's not what you think. It was about a proposal to potentially relocate to Albuquerque."

"Albuquerque? We don't know anything about the city."

"I know. That's why I wanted to discuss it with you and get your thoughts."

Sarah grimaced. "That's a lot to throw at me now. I don't even know what to say."

Jace put his hand on her shoulder. "Don't worry; it hasn't even sunk in for me yet either. If it makes you feel any better, we do have a couple of weeks to think this through."

Sarah focused her attention beyond Jace and frowned. "Okay, but my thoughts should be the least of your concerns right now. I know someone else who's not going to want to hear anything about this."

Before Jace could reply, he peered down the hallway at his thirteen-year-old son. Ryan was a physically imposing young man, towering over the average boy his age. Unlike his father, he possessed a sturdy body frame. His curly, black hair rested in an uneven line across his forehead with a gang of pimples clustering around his cheeks and along the bridge of his nose.

"Hey, Dad. Guess what? You're looking at the new third baseman for my school's baseball team," Ryan said, proudly displaying the baseball cap on his head.

"Great," Jace replied in a lifeless tone.

"You don't seem too happy."

"Of course I am. I know how excited you were about trying out for the team." Jace playfully punched Ryan in the stomach. "You can tell me all about it at dinner."

Sarah waited for Ryan to leave the room. "This should be an interesting dinner conversation. You realize this was the first time he made the team after trying out a few times. Your son is not going to be happy when he hears what you have to tell him."

"Thanks for the vote of confidence. Besides, I never said we were moving."

"Good luck telling him that." She took a step back, distancing herself from Jace. "But before you even think about joining us at the dinner table, can you please do us all a favor and take a shower? The scent of apple pie mixed with your BO is not doing my nose any favors."

***

A half-hour later, Jace sat with his family at the dinner table.

"Dad, you should have seen me at baseball practice today. I was a one-man show. I had three hits, including a home run. One day, you and Mom will see me on TV playing for the Cardinals."

Ava rolled her eyes and laughed. "That was just practice, dummy. Let's see if you can do that in a real game."

"Shut up," Ryan replied.

Sarah glared at both of them. "Okay, kids, take it easy and finish eating your dinner."

A brief silence followed as Jace seized the opportunity.

"Hey kids, let me ask you a question. If you were working, and your boss gave you the chance to make more money, would you be excited?"

"Of course," both children replied.

"What if it meant you had to move?"

"Doesn't matter," Ryan said. "With the extra money, I could move to a rich neighborhood in St. Louis." Ryan paused, displaying a wide grin. "Wait a minute. Are you tryin' to tell me your boss is giving you a raise and we're going to be moving to a bigger house to live like kings and queens?"

"Let's not get carried away. Yes, there's a chance I could be making more money—"

"Yes!" Ryan cheered with joy.

"Not so fast. There's something else I need to tell you."

Ryan's enthusiasm quickly dissipated. "Oh, boy, I knew there was a catch."

"This would also mean we would need to leave St. Louis."

With raised eyebrows, Ryan asked, "Leave St. Louis? How far are we talkin'? Kansas City or Chicago?"

"Albuquerque, New Mexico."

"Albu—what?" Ryan said, coughing to expel the food particles that threatened to cut off his air supply. He sipped some lemonade to help clear his throat. "I don't even know how to spell it. Come on, Dad; are you serious?"

"Does it look like I'm joking?" Jace asked without cracking a smile. "Now, before you get too worried, this is just a thought right now. Me and Mom spoke about it briefly, and I wanted to get you and Ava's opinion."

"I wouldn't mind moving," Ava responded. "I think it would be fun moving to a new city."

With scrunched eyebrows, Ryan replied, "It figures you wouldn't mind. I'm the one who finally made the baseball team, and now I'm expected to just quit the team and move on? Plus, New Mexico doesn't even have a major league baseball team!" Ryan bolted from the table, running to his room.

"Ryan. Ryan!" Jace called out.

"I knew this was going to happen," Sarah said.

Jace let out a sigh. "That's okay. I'll wait until he

calms down before talking to him again."

***

Jace went to bed, hoping a good night's sleep would clear his head from the eventful day. However, he spent most of the night tossing and turning with an array of thoughts floating through his mind. The thought of leaving St. Louis unleashed a flood of mixed emotions. This was the only city he'd ever known, and attempting to adjust to a new city would be a challenge. On the flip side, a decision to relocate would allow him an opportunity to distance himself from the tragic childhood event that continued to consume his mind on a daily basis.

Born and raised in St. Louis, his life had taken a disastrous turn with the untimely death of his mother and brother. For this reason, he always believed moving to another city would help with the healing process. He never imagined thirty years after that fateful day he would continue to feel depressed whenever he saw the city skyline.

***

The sun rose on Saturday morning, the aroma of deep-fried country bacon waking Jace from his slumber. After a quick shower, he threw on a pair of faded blue jeans and sat on the edge of the bed with a V-neck shirt. He rubbed his hand against a pendant dangling from a chain around his neck. He pinched the heart-shaped locket with his thumb and index fingers and eventually opened it, beaming fondly at the picture inside. It was an old family portrait of Jace with his mother and older brother. He lifted his head to the sky, raising the minuscule picture toward his face, and gently kissed it.

"Happy birthday, Mom," he whispered.

He continued to get dressed and eventually made his way into the kitchen where Sarah and Ryan sat eating breakfast.

"Good morning," he said, not knowing if he would get a favorable response.

"Come get your breakfast while it's hot," Sarah said.

He sat in a frayed wicker chair, piling his plate with eggs, bacon, and toast. Silence overtook the room. He wondered if he'd interrupted a private conversation.

He turned his attention to Ryan, who sat quietly with his face buried in a bowl of cereal. "So, where's Ava?"

"She's still asleep," Sarah responded.

The room became quiet once more with only the soft tick from the clock hanging on the wall echoing around the room. Then, without warning, Ryan dropped his spoon in the bowl of unfinished cereal and stormed out of the kitchen.

Jace grimaced. "I see a night's sleep did nothing to change his mood."

Sarah shrugged. "You know your son. Somebody has to talk to him, and it ain't gonna be me."

He stood and took a few steps away from the table.

"Well, aren't you going to eat breakfast first?" she asked.

"No. Might as well talk with him now and get it over with."

Jace exited the kitchen and walked to the bedroom

door, knocking gently. "Can we talk for a minute?"

"Go away," Ryan said from beyond the door.

Jace twisted the knob, but it was locked. "Come on; we go through this all the time. Being quiet is not going to make the issue go away."

"It will for me."

Jace gently tapped his head against the door. "Can you at least hear me out, and then decide if you want to talk to me or not?"

He received no response.

"I never said we were moving to Albuquerque. My boss just gave me the offer. I never accepted it. That's why I brought it up during dinner. It's going to be a family decision, which means your opinion counts."

Jace waited patiently for some feedback.

"I feel kind of stupid talking to a door. Can you just open it so we can talk face-to-face . . . man-to-man?"

After a few seconds, the bed squeaked, followed by the shuffle of feet across the floor. A soft click followed.

Jace twisted the knob and entered, finding Ryan sitting comfortably on his bed with his back against the wall, tossing a baseball in the air. Jace pulled a wooden chair from under the computer desk and sat down. He stared at Ryan for a few seconds.

"Do you honestly think I'm trying to pull you away from the one thing you love?"

Ryan continued tossing the ball without looking and replied, "Yup."

"And why would I do that?"

Ryan finally made eye contact. "I don't think you want to know the answer to that."

"Try me."

"Have you ever been to one of my baseball tryouts?"

Jace thought for a second. "No, that's because your tryouts were always during work hours. I couldn't take off. I'm always busy at work."

"So, you couldn't have left a couple hours early one day to watch me?"

"I doubt it. There's always problems at work, and if there's a major issue, I need to be there."

"I guess a major issue at work is more important than a major issue with me?"

Jace took a deep breath, trying not to take Ryan's bait and get drawn into an all-out debate.

"Well . . . no, I didn't say that." He leaned forward. "A major issue to me is if you were hurt, or got into a fight, or was sick."

"Oh, I get it. So my dream of making the baseball team isn't included."

"I didn't say that, either." Jace threw his hands in the air. "What do you want me to do? Will an apology help?"

"No. It won't change anything."

"Okay, so back to my question: what do you want me to do?"

"You can promise me we're not moving to Alburque or whatever the name of that place is."

Jace strolled over to the bed, sitting on the edge. "If I never told you about the relocation offer, would you still be mad at me?"

"Maybe."

"Come on. Everything was fine until I told you at dinner. You never told me before about being upset because I didn't make your tryouts."

Ryan put his head down, squeezing the baseball. "I don't have to tell you. You should know."

"Don't gimme that nonsense. I know you, and if something's on your mind, you have no problem letting the world know."

Ryan's face softened.

"I . . . I can't make any promises now about moving because I honestly don't know. It's probably a good idea if we all visit the place to see what life is like there."

Jace grabbed the ball from Ryan.

"Think of it this way. Let's say you were the owner of a baseball team, and there was talk about moving your team to another city. Wouldn't you want to visit the city first before deciding to move your team?"

Ryan nodded.

"This is the same concept. We're the owners, and Albuquerque is the new city. If we don't like it, we don't move. It's as simple as that. Can I at least count you in for the trip?"

Ryan shrugged. "Guess I have no choice. You won't leave me here by myself."

"Thatta boy," Jace said, extending his hand for a firm shake.

# Chapter 2

The plane arrived at Albuquerque International during the evening. They entered the hotel an hour later. Palm trees, cascading waterfalls, and ancient Native American sculptures populated the massive hotel lobby. Jace marveled at the glitz and glamour, but only hoped he would be just as impressed with the rest of the city.

After checking in, he followed the family to the elevator bank and slowed upon approaching.

"Um . . . I'll meet you upstairs," Jace said, his voice edged with tension.

Jace opened the door and ascended the stairs, gritting his teeth with feelings of anger shrouding his mind. Here he was, the man of the house, the breadwinner, the protector, afraid to ride the elevator with the rest of the family.

Although he hated feeling vulnerable, he concluded this was something he had to live with for the rest of his life. He thought it might fade away in time, though his recent elevator ride at the office had proven that theory wrong. His phobia was here to stay, and there was nothing he could do about it. He grimaced at the harsh reality and continued to climb until he reached the fifth floor where he reunited with his family in front of the room and opened the door to their living quarters for the next few days.

Two queen size beds were pushed against the wall, parallel to one another, with a desk splitting them apart. A clean, cotton potpourri scent circulated the room.

Jace approached the window and pulled apart the curtains. An electronic keyboard of lights flickered in the distance, illuminating the city skyline. He nodded, excited at the possibility of calling this place home. However, as quickly as the smile crossed his face, his cheeks relaxed, and his lips leveled off. He sighed heavily, doing his best to temper his excitement. He hadn't even seen the city during the day and had no clue what surprises the night could be hiding.

He yawned. A good night's sleep was what he needed. Time to relax and clear his mind for the busy day ahead.

He turned to see Ryan laying on the bed with his arms stretched out.

"Now this is what I call living," Ryan said.

Sarah smiled. "Someone's mood has changed since we left St. Louis."

Jace put his luggage on the bed as he proceeded to unpack some items. "Let's unwind and get to bed as soon as we can. It's already late and we need to get up early tomorrow to meet the tour guide."

***

The following morning, the phone rang as Jace finished a cup of coffee.

"Hi. This is Sabrina Newman, your tour guide for the day. I wanted to let you know I'm parked out front of the hotel. You can come down when you're ready."

A short time later, Jace walked across the parking lot with the family on his heels and a slight breeze ruffling his clothes. He squinted, focusing his eyes on a forest-green Econoline van with the words "*SW Tours*" printed on the side. A young woman leaned against the van, dressed in navy khakis and a buttoned-down, white-collared shirt. She stood with an air of confidence as her shoulder-length, coal-black hair glistened in the sun, along with her caramel-colored face, highlighted by a welcoming smile and a deep set of dimples embedded in her cheeks. A pair of sunglasses rested on top of her forehead.

"You must be Sabrina," Jace said.

"Yes. It's a pleasure to meet you."

Jace introduced the family.

She pointed to the van. "Hop in and let's get started. We have a lot to see."

Jace gazed out at the vast land. The cobalt blue skies were a perfect backdrop to the open desert environment, surrounded by reddish-brown mountains off in the distance. Apache plumes, desert marigolds, and juniper trees were scattered about. The buildings, which were few and far between, displayed classic southwestern themes—thick adobe walls trimmed with varying degrees of stucco and plaster. Some properties were surrounded by acres of ranch land with horses grazing on sparse grass patches. The air was saturated with the scent of sagebrush and pine trees. The night was indeed hiding something—something that by no means needed to be hidden.

Jace continued to marvel at the breathtaking view that reminded him of a Wild West theme. He imagined at any moment, a stagecoach would pass them by.

"Where you folks from?" Sabrina asked, interrupting Jace's daydream.

"St. Louis," he replied.

"Never been there. I heard it's a beautiful city. Hopefully, after this weekend, you'll see that Albuquerque has a lot to offer, also. Our first stop for today will be downtown. This will give you a taste of our city life." She handed Jace some tourist brochures. "And if we have time later, we can take a ride down our famous Route Sixty-Six. Sit back for now and enjoy the scenery. And, if you have any questions while we're riding along, don't hesitate to ask."

A few minutes of silence passed as Ryan and Ava stared out the window at this strange new land.

"How long have you been living here?" Sarah asked Sabrina.

"Funny you should ask. It'll be exactly ten years tomorrow."

Sarah nodded. "So, on a scale of one to ten, how would you rate your living experience?"

"I'd say about a nine. The only reason I wouldn't give it a ten is because of my first couple of weeks here. I had finished college in Tucson and decided to move here. I figured I had a better chance of getting a job here based on my degree. I accepted a job offer downtown and moved into an apartment not far from here. A few days later, the apartment building caught fire and destroyed everything. I had nothing left but the clothes on my back."

"Were you in the building when the fire started?"

"Luckily, no."

"I'm sorry to hear that. Must have been a horrible experience," Sarah said.

"Yeah. As we say here in Albuquerque, I was bit by the Jeffries Jinx."

Jace's eyebrows scrunched in confusion. "Jeffries Jinx?"

"It's a local term we use to describe anyone who runs into a string of bad luck."

"And how did they come up with the name Jeffries?"

"From what I've been told, the name originated from a businessman named Robert Jeffries. He was a successful entrepreneur here in Albuquerque decades ago. His businesses began to crumble after experiencing a string of bad luck, and he was forced to work minimum-wage jobs to support his family. It became such an embarrassment to him and his family that he eventually moved, and I guess the rest is history."

Jace nodded, feeling content with his new knowledge of local folklore.

***

They continued to drive while Jace focused his attention up ahead. A community of single-family homes came into view. Some were constructed of brick, while others were surrounded with seamless vinyl siding. Well-manicured bushes and decorative stones were sprawled across the intriguing landscape. The freshly paved roads leading into the complex added to the welcoming curb appeal.

*"Granwin Estates. Edgewood's newest development,"* he read from a colossal sign posted at the entrance.

"Beautiful, isn't it?" Sabrina responded.

"Do you know anything about this complex?"

"It's been under construction for a while, but I think they're finally finished."

"Do you know if it's possible to tour any of the homes?"

"I think there's a local realty office not too far from here. We can swing by later today to see if they have any information."

***

They arrived in Downtown Albuquerque, absorbing the city life. They drove by the New Mexico Museum of Natural History and the Albuquerque Museum of Art, along with a quick pit stop at Old Town Albuquerque. Jace was impressed with the office buildings and modern architecture surrounding the Albuquerque Civic Plaza. The tour also included a scenic ride past the University of New Mexico and a glimpse of Isotopes Park, a minor league baseball stadium, no doubt of special interest to Ryan.

They left the downtown district and came to a sudden stop in the middle of a traffic jam. An assortment of flashing lights flickered in the distance about a mile up the road. As they crept closer, intertwined in a heap of metal were a semi-trailer and a family sedan. A closer look revealed the car wedged under the trailer portion of the truck. Shards of glass littered the road, along with broken wooden crates from the truck's cargo. A hoard of emergency personnel surrounded the car to try to free the passengers that were trapped under the truck's trailer.

Jace stared at the scene in disbelief. The carnage brought back painful memories. He briefly closed his eyes and drifted off to that tragic day.

*He could see his brother in the back seat, still strapped into the seat belt, bleeding profusely from the neck. A jagged piece of projectile glass from the back windshield had severed an artery. Up front, his mother's body dangled halfway out of the windshield. Although she had died on impact, her legs still moved with a slight twitch.*

*Jace felt the blood running down the side of his face, but he couldn't move, trapped in the seat belt from the impact with the tree. He yelled for help, to no avail. The walls of the steep embankment, in which the car rested, muffled his screams. He was trapped, forced to look at the dead bodies of the two most important people in the world to him.*

*He clawed at the seat belt with all his might, trying to set himself free, but it didn't budge. At times, he gasped for air, struggling to get enough oxygen in the confined wreckage of the car. After a couple of hours, he stopped screaming, struggling, and all other efforts to free himself. He made up his mind life wasn't worth living without his mother or brother. He peacefully closed his eyes, waiting patiently for his last breath.*

Jace batted his eyelids, getting rid of the horrible daydream. He reached for his chest, gently rubbing the middle, where the pendant rested. He opened his misty eyes when Sarah started rubbing his back in comfort. They eventually passed the chaos and continued to their next destination.

***

A short time later, they pulled into a dirt-covered parking lot off the main road, approaching a cream-colored, one-story building. They parked next to a faded blue Honda CRX, with no other vehicles in sight.

"I'll only be a few minutes," Jace said upon exiting the van.

He walked up a few stairs and onto a wooden porch.

"*Winchester Realty*," he read aloud the sign hanging above the door. He twisted the knob, opening the door.

A brawny gentleman with his back turned immediately came into view. A black ponytail dangled halfway down his back. He sported a blue, collared shirt with beige khakis. He turned, revealing a bulldog face that would intimidate most people. Squint lines were drawn under his crescent-shaped eyes, along with a neatly trimmed goatee surrounding his protruding lips.

"Hello, sir," the gentleman said. He smiled, displaying an ample gap between his top front teeth. "Welcome to Winchester Realty. How can I help ya?"

Jace hesitated for a second, looking beyond his mammoth frame, focusing on a tantalizing female specimen sitting behind the desk. Her nut-brown, silky hair flowed along each side of her face, coming to a rest on her shoulders. Raven-colored eyes, surrounded by a thick set of eyelashes, were the perfect centerpiece to a face devoid of any skin blemishes.

"Oh . . . hi," Jace said, embarrassed by his apparent gawking. "I . . . uh, wanted to know if you had any information on the new housing community down the road."

"Of course we do. You came to the right place," the man said.

He edged toward Jace with his hand extended. "The name's Malcolm Winchester."

Jace's nostrils were immediately greeted by the stale odor of cigarette smoke. He shook the man's hand and introduced himself before focusing his attention back on the female behind the desk.

"Hi. I'm Maria," she said with a foreign accent.

Malcolm turned to Maria. "Can you do me a favor and get Jace some water? Just want to make him comfortable while we talk."

"Oh no. That's okay. I'm not thirsty."

Malcolm nodded. "What type of info are you looking for?"

"Anything I can get my hands on about the Granwin community down the road. I'm just visiting from out of town and scouting the area for a possible relocation."

Malcolm glanced at Maria once again. "How about grabbing some brochures along with a pamphlet about Granwin for Jace."

She scribbled something on a sheet of paper before standing and walking by the cabinet against the wall.

Jace did his best to tame his wandering eye, although

he couldn't help himself. She strutted across the floor, about five-foot-seven, wearing a powder blue, floral-printed business suit. A tropical mixture of mango and coconut lingered in the air. Jace couldn't tell if it was body lotion or perfume—a pleasant scent either way. Her voluptuous sway hypnotized him for a moment. He blinked, suddenly aware of his drooling episode. He darted his eyes back to Malcolm, who sat with a half-smile on his face.

"I can imagine, with your interest in the homes, you probably have a family."

"Yes. They're outside waiting."

Maria approached Jace with several brochures while stretching out a trembling hand as she passed them to him. A slip of paper jutted out from the middle of one of the brochures.

"Where you from?"

"St. Louis."

Jace looked at Maria, who returned his gaze. She immediately diverted her eyes to the brochures in his hands.

"Good ole St. Louis. Been there once. It's a beautiful city. I'd like to formally welcome ya to Albuquerque, the land of enchantment. There's no finer place to raise a family," Malcolm said, sitting on the corner of Maria's desk. "I must tell you right now, you just stepped foot into the finest real estate business this side of town. Granwin Estates has been a hot commodity lately, and there is a large assortment of properties on sale in the community. I'm sure we can find something that suits your needs and fits your budget."

Jace nodded. "I'm definitely interested in seeing what you have available."

"I'll tell you what, there are some model homes you and your family can tour. It should only take about an hour of your time." He paused, glancing at his watch. "What's your schedule like today?"

"I'm with a tour guide who's showing us around town. Not sure what she has planned."

"Fair enough. Normally, I would have one of my agents give the tour, but since you and your family came from such a long way, I'd be willing to personally do it myself."

"Sounds good to me."

"Great! If it's okay with your tour guide, give me about an hour to finish up some work, and then you can meet me back here and we'll get started."

Maria focused her eyes on Malcolm. "Maybe you should go now. I'll be okay here until you get back."

"Don't think that's a good idea. I'd rather wait until the rest of the team gets back instead of leaving you here by yourself. Besides, we don't want to intrude upon Jace's tour guide schedule. They may have something planned for the next hour."

Maria offered no reply and focused her attention back down at some paperwork on her desk.

"See you back here in an hour," Malcolm said before waving his hand to get Maria's attention. "How about showing Jace some of our western hospitality and walk him to the front door?" Malcolm glanced at Jace and smiled.

"Just in case you didn't know, the south isn't the only place that can offer exceptional hospitality."

Maria stood as Malcolm sat comfortably on her desk.

Jace exited the office before turning to wave goodbye and found Maria trailing close behind. She glanced over her shoulder for a quick second then turned to Jace, motioning to the brochure.

"Did you read the note," she whispered.

Jace looked down at the brochure before extracting the slip of paper sticking out and turned to the tour van with all eyes focused on him. An awkward moment of silence followed. Without looking at it, he promptly folded the paper and stuffed it in his pocket.

"I . . . I don't think it's a good time now. Gotta go. My family's waiting."

Maria opened her mouth to say something then stopped as Malcolm approached the front door.

"Everything good here?" he asked, looking at both Jace and Maria.

Maria quickly waved goodbye to Jace before disappearing inside.

Jace backpedaled away from the door and displayed a halfhearted grin at Malcolm before returning to the van.

"Change of plans. We have a date in about an hour to tour the homes." He turned to Sabrina. "If it's okay with you?"

Sarah cut her eyes at Jace with a grimace and mumbled, "Looks more like you have a date."

Jace turned to Sarah. "I didn't hear you. What was

that?"

She glared at him. "Nothing. We'll talk later."

Sabrina interrupted, "Since we have an hour to kill, how about a bite to eat? I can take you to one of my favorite spots."

***

A short while later, they arrived at a Mexican restaurant, squeezing into a booth. A pendant light, shaped in the form of a sombrero, hung over the table. The aroma of spicy tacos and sizzling beef fajitas filled the air.

Sabrina fixed her attention on Sarah. "Are you okay? You haven't said a word."

Sarah flashed a wooden smile. "I'm fine. Just hungry."

After ordering food, Jace excused himself from the table and walked toward the restroom. Upon entering, he immediately reached into his pocket and pulled out the folded note from Maria. He couldn't help but blush at the anticipation of reading it. *Maybe a phone number or some other form of contact information? The women are fast around here.* He had no intention of following through if it was a one-on-one invitation; he was just thrilled to know a middle-aged man like himself could still attract a beautiful young woman. He took a deep breath and unfolded the note.

*Please don't leave me alone with him. I'll explain later.*

Jace blinked with surprise. Then he bit his bottom lip, mentally kicking himself for not opening the note sooner. His ego also took a blow, as this note had zero to do with her being attracted to him.

He folded the note and stuffed it back in his pocket. There was nothing he could do at the moment. He could only wait until they returned to the office, hoping nothing had happened to the young lady.

He closed his eyes, attempting to calm his nerves. He didn't want to return to the table appearing overly anxious. He arrived back at the booth, doing his best to hide his anxiety. The food eventually arrived as he joined in the conversation and played along as if everything was status quo. He normally would have been concerned with Sarah's intuition—she could read his facial expressions like a book—but throughout the entire lunch, she hadn't looked at him once.

***

An hour later, they returned to the office and entered the parking lot with no other cars in sight.

Jace's heart rate quickened. "I'll be back."

Sarah cleared her throat. "I'm going with you."

He turned to Sarah. "I'll only take a minute. There's no need for you to go, also."

She replied emphatically, "Oh yes, there is."

He sighed, sensing the jealous demons floating to the surface of Sarah's mind. Upon further retrospect, he couldn't blame her. Up until he'd read the note, he'd assumed Maria was interested in him as well. Although, this was not the time nor place for him to explain the contents of the note.

Offering no further resistance, Jace exited the van with

Sarah trailing closely behind. He neared the entrance, his hand trembling ever so slightly as he reached for the doorknob. The door opened, revealing an empty office.

"Hello?" he said, receiving no response in return. Jace stood by the door, reluctant to take a step inside.

Sarah nudged him in the back. "Are you planning to go inside?"

He hesitated before eventually complying. He surveyed the area, looking for a bell to tap or anything else to make noise and indicate their presence.

Miscellaneous documents and brochures were scattered about Maria's desk, giving no indication she had left for the day.

"Anybody here?" he called out. Only the humming from the air conditioning vents could be heard.

He checked the time. "I swore he told me to come back in an hour."

He approached Maria's desk, carefully analyzing the folders and papers that were scattered about. He circled the workstation and peeked under the desk.

"What do you think you're doing?" Sarah asked. "I swear you're going to get yourself into trouble one day. Always snooping around, looking for things. You missed your calling. You should have been a detective. What are you looking for, anyway?"

"Nothing," he said, tapping his fingers on the desk.

Sarah offered a suspicious glare.

He would be foolish to try to deny her false beliefs, especially with her intuition in high gear. He figured this was as good a time as any to show her the note and calm her jealous fears.

He reached into his pocket but immediately stopped when one of the back doors swung open.

"Sorry to keep you waiting. I was in the bathroom," Malcolm said. He extended his hand to Sarah. "And you must be Jace's better half."

She hesitated to shake his hand.

"Don't worry; my hands are clean."

Sarah reached out for a fist bump instead.

"Give me a minute to gather my stuff. My truck is parked out back. You can follow me to the development."

Jace felt obligated to ask about Maria but resisted the urge. He didn't want to rouse Sarah's suspicions any further.

Minutes later, a black Chevy Silverado with tinted windows emerged from the rear of the office. Sabrina shifted in gear and followed. After only a short distance in pursuit, it was apparent Malcolm didn't care much for the speed limit. Jace looked at Sabrina with concern as she sped along, struggling to keep up. She kept both hands on the steering wheel and, at times, swerved around several curves to keep pace. She eventually caught up and stayed within a reasonable following distance until the drive ended at the entrance of the complex.

She immediately pulled alongside the pickup truck. "I hate to see how fast you drive when no one is following you."

He extracted a cigarette from his mouth. "Please

forgive me. I honestly didn't realize a female was driving. The name's Malcolm."

Sabrina stared at him intently. "What does a female driving have to do with anything?"

He laughed. "Sorry if you took that comment the wrong way. I'm just here to show the Valentine family these beautiful homes. Maybe they'll appeal to you, too. By the way, you never told me your name."

"Ms. Newman."

"How about a first name?"

"You can just call me Ms. Newman."

He glared at her for an instant before proceeding into the development.

As they entered, a splash of desert marigolds colored both sides of the road. Driving further, a beautiful row of houses became visible, each one displaying a unique landscaping style. Some of them showed off a country theme with front porches surrounded by flower gardens. Others showed off a more contemporary theme with rows of spiraled-shaped bushes and lights lining the walkway. The driveways leading to the attached garages were wide enough to fit two cars with room to spare. The ride came to a halt before Malcolm led them into the driveway of one of the model homes.

"As you can see from the outside, everything is new from top to bottom. The roof, gutters, windows, doors, the list goes on and on. The lawns, bushes, and trees were all recently planted. The driveways are extra wide and newly paved with motion detector lights above the automatic garage. Also, if you look out on the curb, there's a mailbox to match the color and style of the house."

They followed Malcolm beyond the front door and into a massive foyer with decorative floor tiles and cathedral ceilings. To the right, a cascade of sunlight filtered in from a grand bay window, highlighting the spacious living room.

"Simply beautiful, isn't it?" Malcolm said. "And this is just the beginning. Follow me into the kitchen."

Granite countertops with an oatmeal glaze finish highlighted the L-shaped kitchen. Several wrought iron dinette lights hung over a half-moon-shaped island, sitting in the middle of the room. Slate gray ceramic tiles crisscrossed along the floor.

"The kitchen is a modern marvel. There's enough space in this room to fit ten people comfortably. There's plenty of counter space with dual sinks and sliding doors leading to the backyard deck. There's also plenty of room to fit a large oven, refrigerator, and dishwasher." He eyed Sarah. "That gives Mrs. Valentine plenty of elbow room to work when cooking some of those delicious meals for Mr. Valentine after he puts in a hard day at work."

Sarah shrugged and smiled halfheartedly, while Sabrina looked at Malcolm with a withering stare.

Jace could only imagine it was pure coincidence that Malcolm assumed Sarah was a stay-at-home mom; a bold and contentious assumption, nevertheless.

Jace focused on Sarah and Sabrina, doing his best to read their faces as an uncomfortable silence followed. He could feel the tension growing in the air and didn't want

Ryan or Ava to experience any unnecessary adult drama.

"Hey, Ryan, why don't you and Ava go out on the deck to check out the backyard," Jace said.

"Whatever you say," Ryan replied.

They both exited.

"I apologize, Mrs. Valentine, as I realize my comment may have been taken out of context. I just come from an old-school family," Malcolm replied.

Sabrina cleared her throat out loud.

"Apologies to you, as well," he said.

They continued into the dining room and eventually made their way onto the backyard deck where Ryan and Ava had made themselves at home. The rectangular wooden deck spanned roughly two hundred square feet. Both ends of the deck contained a set of stairs, leading to the backyard lawn. A few evergreen shrubs populated the fenceless yard, along with an ocean of lush green grass. Off in the distance, a lake highlighted the scenery, the water rippling from the gentle breeze. Several other houses bordered the other side of the lake.

"Hey, Mom! Look at this yard," Ava said. "A perfect place for an afternoon picnic."

"Picnic?" Ryan replied with a scowl on his face. "Forget about a lousy picnic. We could use this space to build an outdoor pool or even a baseball field."

Ava frowned. "That's all you think about is baseball. There's more to life than just baseball. You need to wake up and smell the coffee."

Ryan arched his eyebrows in anger. "Shut up!"

Jace pointed at them both. "Hey, kids, relax. You know better than to act this way around company.

"Why don't you follow me, Ryan, so we can get a closer look at the lake?" Jace knew from experience that the best way to cool this sibling rivalry was to separate them.

"Anything to get away from her."

Sabrina stepped forward. "Don't worry about it, Jace. I'll take him. I can use some fresh air right now."

Ava folded her arms. "Can I go, too?"

"Not if you're going to keep fighting with Ryan," Jace said.

"Okay. I'll be good."

Sabrina departed with the kids in tow.

"Sorry about that. I think we're ready to continue the tour."

"Don't worry about it. No harm done. I know all about family fighting," Malcolm said.

He waved his hand across the yard. "As you can see, the backyard is extremely spacious. We're standing on a solid oak deck that's been stained with a protective coating to prevent termite and water damage. The lawn was recently planted, along with the trees." He pointed to the lake. "And that is the pride and joy of this backyard. A lake fully equipped with paddleboats, and its natural wildlife of fish and geese. So, what do ya think so far?"

"Looks great," Jace said.

Sarah remained quiet, getting a questioning look from Malcolm.

"You haven't said one word since the tour started. Any

thoughts?"

"Not at the moment. Just a lot to take in right now."

Malcolm laughed. "I can understand if you're speechless. Most people are when they see this." He placed his hand on Jace's shoulder.

"I can tell you have a taste for the finer things in life. Now, I know the one thing on your mind is how can we afford a house like this?"

Jace nodded, looking at the price on the listing.

"All you need to do is come to my office where I can crunch some numbers and see if it fits your budget."

"Wait a minute," Jace said. "We don't want to rush into anything now. This is only the first house we've seen. We need to look around the city some more before committing to buying a house."

"That's understandable. I'm not trying to rush ya, but if you decide to buy a house in this development, you need to act fast. I'm receiving plenty of interest each day from potential buyers. I wouldn't want you to miss out on an opportunity like this."

He glanced at his watch and handed Jace his card. "Sorry, didn't realize it was this late. Need to run to the office for a meeting."

Jace motioned for Sabrina and the kids to return. They all eventually followed Malcolm to the front before he departed.

Sabrina displayed a pitiful look of appeal. "I apologize for my less-than-friendly behavior on the tour. I don't have much of a poker face, if you couldn't tell."

Jace laughed. "Don't feel bad. I can see how Malcolm may have rubbed you and Sarah the wrong way."

"It's just that I'm extremely sensitive when it comes to anyone who displays male chauvinist views. It's a long story. Tell you about it another time."

***

A few hours later, they pulled into the hotel parking lot.

"Hope you enjoyed the tour," Sabrina said.

"Absolutely. We have plenty to think about once we get home," Jace said. He stared at Sarah. "Right?"

"Yeah," she replied with no discernable expression.

Sabrina winced, making eye contact with Sarah. "I'm sorry if you didn't enjoy the tour. I tried my best."

"Oh no, it has nothing to do with you or the tour. I think you did an excellent job," Sarah said.

"Thanks. I was beginning to get worried." She handed them a card with her contact information. "Please give me a call if you decide to move out here. I'll be the first to knock on your door with a housewarming gift," Sabrina said as she departed.

Jace walked into the hotel lobby, following Sarah, who shuffled several steps ahead of him.

Ryan tapped Jace on the shoulder, pointing down the corridor. "Can me and Ava check out the game room?"

He handed them a few bills. "Make sure you both come back to the room in an hour."

Sarah continued to walk toward the elevator lobby without stopping. Jace proceeded to take the stairs up to the fifth floor. Her silence annoyed him most of the day; however, looking at it from her perspective, he understood. He opened his wallet and extracted the note with every intention of discussing it.

He entered the room to see Sarah sitting on the bed in total silence. He stood in front of her and immediately placed the note in her lap. She continued to stare, beyond Jace, apparently not interested in him or the note.

"Don't you want to read it?"

She immediately grabbed the note without looking at it and crumbled it into a tight ball before throwing it on the floor. She cut her eyes at him, her arms crossed and eyebrows furrowed. "You have some damn nerve!"

He took a deep breath before retrieving the note and smoothing it out with his hands. A part of him wanted to laugh at her ridiculous reaction, but he refrained, knowing this would only agitate her further. He gathered himself and said, "I figured you wanted to see what she wrote."

"It's too late now. You knew this was bothering me the whole day. If you had any plans to show me, why didn't you do it sooner?"

"Did you expect me to interrupt Sabrina or Malcolm's tour to discuss it?"

"Why not?"

"Because I didn't want to put our business out in front for everyone to see. I figured it was best to wait until we were alone. And here we are."

She looked away, rubbing her forehead. "I'm done talking for now. I have a massive headache and can't think straight.”

Jace let out a hefty exhale. He had noticed recently that Sarah's attitude had changed for the worse. He surmised some form of depression might have been setting in due to her inability to hold down a job because of her health issues. And if you combine this attitude shift, along with her jealous insecurities being on high alert at this moment, he realized there was not much he could do at this time to get his point across.

Offering no further response, he folded the note, stuffed it in his pocket, and walked away to fight this battle another day.

# **Chapter 3**

At the end of another business day, Malcolm exited the realty office, driving west on Interstate 40. He hoped he wasn't being too overbearing in trying to sell the home to that lovely family from out of town. He also hoped his asinine comment in the kitchen didn't distract the couple and ruin his chances for a sale. Although, in retrospect, he understood his propensity to sometimes speak before he thought would always drop him in the middle of these uncomfortable situations, especially with women. He promised to try to work on improving his interactions with women, though it had no doubt been an extreme challenge.

He drove another ten miles before exiting onto a secluded road and turning onto a private driveway. A short distance up ahead, a single-story ranch house came into view. The cream-colored, vinyl-sided house with pine green trim stood all alone. Several slats within the shudders surrounding the windows were loose, almost to the point of dangling. The window frames were worn as bubbles of paint formed, some completely cracked with paint chips flaking off. The front yard landscaping didn't fare much better, as the hedges lining the front of the house were misshapen, with branches protruding at odd angles.

He pressed the remote for the two-car garage, watching the door slowly rise. He pulled beside another vehicle sitting idle in the garage—a 1965 Ford Thunderbird convertible. The car was in pristine condition, from the glossy winter-white exterior to the shining chrome Thunderbird emblem resting proudly on the front hood.

He exited his pickup, patting the hood of the antique car as he walked by, and then opened a metal door, entering a utility room. A water heater and gas furnace were located on the right and diagonally across were an oversized washer and dryer.

He strolled into the living room, with a forest green suede sectional becoming the focal point. The battered furniture was scarred with several burn marks from cigarette ashes that floated to the surface at one time or another.

A sable brown Burmese edged its way toward him.

"Hi, Sunshine," he said, stroking the cat on the nape of its neck.

He reached for his stomach, as a dull ache that had been bothering him off and on for most of the day, became more intense. He grabbed his briefcase resting on the sofa and pulled out a small brown bottle before walking down a narrow hallway and into the kitchen. The vinyl-tiled floor unleashed several squeaking noises upon entering.

He flipped the switch, a fluorescent light flickering before steadying and illuminating the kitchen with a soft blue hue. White laminate cabinets surrounded black appliances nearing the end of their life. He walked over to the sink and grabbed a glass from the cabinet before filling it with water and eventually swallowing a white capsule he'd extracted from a medicine bottle resting on the counter.

***

A short while after watching TV, his stomach began to bubble in a gaseous fury. He drank another cup of water with sweat trickling down the side of his face. Hoping to cool off, he unbuttoned the collar on his shirt, but it didn't work as he continued to sweat profusely along his back and neck.

He stumbled forward and made his way to the bathroom located in the hallway. He fell on his knees in front of the toilet and, with one large heave, expelled the contents of his stomach. He coughed, struggling to catch his breath, and stumbled back onto his feet before rinsing his mouth and wobbling his way back to the sofa. The pain eventually subsided, allowing him to relax until his head snapped back and forth with drowsiness. He eventually nodded off.

***

There it was again, the yelling and screaming coming from behind the door in the far corner of the hallway. The smell of alcohol circulated all around him.

He took a step down the hallway then another, making his way to the awful noises. But, with each step he took, the hallway expanded as the rooms moved further and further out of reach.

He stopped and turned to his right, facing a door. He reached and turned the knob, the door creaking open, revealing a well-kempt bedroom. A twin bed, a desk, and a dresser were all that furnished the room. There was no sign of anyone.

He focused his attention on a lone closet door, hearing

a muffled cry. He opened it, pushing aside the rack of hanging clothes to see a boy crying, cowering in the corner. He knelt, comforting the boy with a hug, shielding his ears from the banging and screaming that continued beyond the walls. He heard the bedroom door swing open and listened for footsteps echoing across the floor, edging closer to the closet.

The hanging clothes were violently pushed aside as a hand suddenly gripped the back of his neck. His head snapped forward, waking him out of the dream.

# Chapter 4

The flight arrived back in St. Louis close to midnight. The taxi ride from the airport to the house added another hour to the seemingly endless trip. Exhausted from jet lag, Jace shoved the unpacked luggage into the corner of the bedroom and collapsed onto the bed next to Sarah, who had already fallen asleep.

He awoke the next morning, rolling over to find the bed empty. This was unlike Sarah, who normally would still be asleep. He sniffed, smelling the aroma of percolating coffee beans. He made his way into the kitchen to see Sarah sitting alone, sipping a cup.

"What are you doing up so early?"

She removed the coffee mug from her lips. "I couldn't sleep."

He had a hunch this was still related to the incident with the note. He eyed Sarah cautiously and contemplated the best approach to bringing up this note fiasco a second time.

"What's on your mind?"

She grimaced. "I should be asking you that question."

He sat, joining her at the table. "Okay. I'll tell you. Obviously, the whole relocation idea is floating around in my head."

"And?"

"I'm wondering what you and the kids think of

Albuquerque."

"And?"

"I was also thinking about the note the young lady at the realty office gave me. Are you now interested in knowing what she wrote?"

"I already know."

"Did you finally read it?"

"No. I don't have to. Did you call her yet?"

He shook his head vehemently. "No, but—"

"Are you planning to?"

"No. Can I just tell you—"

"Am I not sexy enough for you? Am I too old? Do you want to trade me in for a younger woman?"

"Of course not. Can I please talk about—"

"After thirteen years of marriage and the birth of your two children, you're thinking about cheating on me, if you haven't already."

He raised his hands in frustration. "Can I please get a word in without being interrupted?"

Sarah stretched out her arm with an open palm toward Jace. "I'm done talking."

He slammed his fist on the table. "Fine. Just stay right there."

He exited the kitchen and returned after a minute. With the note in hand, he shouted, "Please don't leave me alone with him. I'll explain later."

He tossed the note on the table in front of her.

"If you don't believe that's what it says, read it your damn self."

Sarah dragged the note directly in front of her to get a better view. She read it and immediately placed her head on the table. "This is what she gave you?"

"Yes."

She laughed, putting her head back down. "I feel like a complete ass."

"Will you get mad if I agree? You're getting all worked up for nothing. These jealous episodes are getting out of control."

"I'm trying, but . . . it's still hard for me." She stood, hugging Jace, no doubt embarrassed by her behavior. "Please forgive me. I'm sorry."

Jace gave her a gentle squeeze and nodded. "Apology accepted."

She read the note again. "What do you suppose this means?"

"I don't know. She seemed nervous the entire time I was there."

"Why didn't she just tell you instead of handing you a note?"

"She tried when I was leaving, but Malcolm came out and she ran back inside."

"Was there anyone else in the office?"

"No." He pondered for a few seconds. "I hope nothing happened to her. I'd feel really guilty if it did." He stuffed the note in his wallet. "I'll hold on to it for a while."

"Don't you still have the number to the office?" she asked.

"Yeah."

"You can always call later to see if she picks up."

"Good idea."

He sat at the table. "Now, on to the next big question. What did you think about Albuquerque?"

She took another sip from her coffee mug. "It was nice."

"I detect a but."

She shrugged.

"Seems to me you were enjoying it up until the note exchange."

"I was."

"So talk to me. Can you picture us living there?"

"Not really."

"Can I get more than a two- or three-word answer?"

Looking down at the table, she replied, "If you want me to be honest . . . I don't think I can do it. I don't want to move."

"Why?"

"St. Louis has nothing but good memories for me. This is where my happiness in life began. I can't just up and move now."

"All I'm asking right now is to think about it. Keep an open mind. Aren't you curious to know what it's like to live in another city?"

"No. Not really."

"Oh, come on, Sarah. This could be an opportunity for me to start a new life and leave all my past troubles behind."

"Did you just say *me*? An opportunity for *me* to start a

new life?"

"I don't think so. If I did say me, I meant to say us."

"That's a damn shame. You're only thinking about yourself. What about my feelings—or the kids?"

"Well . . . I meant to say us." He grimaced. "Come on; let's not start another argument. As far as I know, there's no law saying we need to stay in St. Louis for the rest of our lives." He paused before continuing, "Besides, I think if I don't accept this relocation assignment and stay where I am, they'll probably let me go, anyway, and have Mr. Perfect take over my job."

"Well, we don't know if that's true or not, but I can tell you one thing, I'm not moving for your selfish reasons."

"Do you think I'm that selfish to not even think of you and the kids with such a major decision like this?" He shook his head. "You know what? I think we should just end this conversation for now because I see where this is headed."

***

Later that evening, Jace returned home from work. For most of the day, he thought about what Sarah had said. Although he hated being called selfish, he came to the conclusion she was right. He had become so wrapped up in the possibility of leaving St. Louis that he had overlooked the feelings of the most important people in his life.

A grin came across his face as he grabbed his laptop case and walked inside. He opened the door to find Sarah and the kids sitting on the couch, looking through some pictures they had taken on the trip.

"Hey, Dad. Take a look at these cool pictures," Ryan

said.

"All the pictures came out perfect except the last one. There's a picture Ms. Newman took of us with that big real estate dude, and she mistakenly cut him out of the picture," Ava said with a slight chuckle.

"It may not have been a mistake," Jace replied.

"He didn't deserve to be in the picture, anyway," Ava said, her lips curled up in disgust.

"Why do you say that?" Jace said.

"I think he was a creep. There was something about him I didn't like."

"I thought he was cool," Ryan said.

Anticipating retaliation from Ava's lips, Jace turned to her and covered her mouth with his hand.

"Let's not start anything, kids. I know where this will end up."

Sarah continued to look at the pictures without saying a word.

"Since we're on the subject of Albuquerque, we need to discuss what we want to do," Jace said.

"I'd rather stay in St. Louis," Ava said.

"Why?" Jace inquired.

"I don't know. The museums and zoo were nice, but everything else was a little boring to me."

Ryan laughed and said, "That should be perfect for you. A boring city for a boring person."

Ava returned a cold stare. "Shut up, Ryan. You were the one complaining like a baby that you didn't want to go because of your stupid baseball. Now you're in love with the place, and all because you saw that stupid baseball field."

Ryan's face grew flushed. He gripped the sofa pillow behind him with every intention of flinging it on a collision course with Ava's face.

Jace grabbed Ryan's arm. "Hey! What the hell is wrong with you? Don't even think about throwing this at your sister." He glared at both of them. "You two can't agree on anything. Instead of fighting all the time, you need to appreciate the time you have with each other. If there's one thing I learned in life, it's to appreciate the ones you love before it's too late. Now do me a favor, and go to your rooms and think about that!"

They both jumped off the sofa, storming toward their bedrooms. Without saying a word, Sarah followed suit, leaving Jace alone in the living room.

"Are you kidding me? Hey, where are you going? I didn't mean for you to leave, too."

She ignored him and continued into the bedroom, closing the door.

"Great. Now the whole damn family is upset."

He waited a few minutes before approaching the bedroom. He attempted to twist the doorknob, which didn't budge.

"Can you please let me in, Sarah, so we can talk?"

He received no response.

"First Ryan and now you. Being on the other side of a locked door is becoming a weekly event for me." He knocked gently. "I'd much rather talk to my wife than a closed door. Can you please act like an adult and open the door so we can talk?"

Still no response.

"Would it help if I told you I'm sorry for what I said this morning? I was being selfish, and I feel bad about it."

A few seconds elapsed before he heard the knob click. He cautiously opened the door, keeping an eye out for any shoes that may come whizzing by his head. Then he entered, spotting Sarah sitting up in bed, in deep concentration. He closed the door, keeping his distance.

She looked up. "Apology accepted."

He breathed a sigh of relief. "I know we got side-tracked with the Ryan and Ava meltdown, but we need to make a decision. It's fine to have the children's input, but the ultimate decision is going to come down to you and me."

She crossed her arms. "You already know my feelings."

"Yes. And I respect it, though I need to know why else you wouldn't think about a chance for us to have a better lifestyle. To get ahead in life, sometimes you need to take chances."

"I'm not sure I'm willing to take this chance."

"I think we all got a good taste of what life would be like in Albuquerque. Nice houses, schools, neighborhoods, and not to mention a potential pay increase. What else would it take to convince you to take a chance?"

"I just don't have a good feeling about the place. Don't get me wrong, everything was fine during our visit, but that was only for a short stay. It was too good to be true. The grass isn't always greener on the other side."

"I see your point, but are you going to let your woman's intuition make the decision or the realization of what we saw with our own eyes? The city was beautiful, and the houses were unbelievable. How can you let something like this slip through our hands?" Jace said, doing his best impersonation of a politician trying to convince voters to see it his way.

"Realistically, we can't afford those houses. I'm also not too comfortable with purchasing a house from a rinky-dink real estate company that can't afford a paved parking lot."

"I already checked the better business bureau, and he's legit. He's been in business for over ten years with very few complaints."

"So?"

Jace realized, no matter what he said at this time, she would find a way to shoot it down.

"Okay. Let's make a deal. We go over our budget and come up with a price range we can afford. I'll research other similar homes in the area, and we compare those prices to Granwin Estates. Will you then consider a change of heart if the prices are within our range?"

"Can't make any promises."

Jace did his best to control his grin, thinking he had made a dent in Sarah's armor.

# Chapter 5

The red light flashed, as it always did when a message was left. Maria did her best to ignore it and thought about running out of the office for an early lunch. However, that would only delay the inevitable. She knew who had left the message and had no desire to play it back.

She immediately deleted the voicemail without listening and reluctantly dialed an extension.

"Yes?"

"Can I please see you in my office for a minute? I have another assignment to give you."

She hesitated. "Um . . . is it okay if you come out here? I'm kind of busy."

"It'll only take a few minutes, and I promise it will be well worth your time away from the desk."

She put her head down, breathing deeply to relax her anxiety. She reached for the top button on her blouse, making sure it was snapped, before standing, and walking toward the corner office. She appeared at the door.

"Come on in and have a seat."

She hesitated for a moment before sitting.

"I'd like to apologize for what happened the other day when we were alone in the office. I had no right to invade your private space. I hope I didn't make you too uncomfortable."

Maria met his eyes briefly then looked away with a

cursory smile.

"I'd like to do two things for you. First, I wanted to let you know I'll be giving you the raise we talked about, and second, I'd like to treat you to lunch so we can discuss the details."

***

An hour later, they left in Malcolm's Silverado.

He turned on the radio, giving Maria a sidelong glance. "What do you have a taste for?"

"I don't know. It doesn't matter."

"How 'bout we keep it simple? A burger and fries?"

"That's fine," she said, reluctant to make eye contact. She sat, slouched in the passenger seat with arms folded in her lap and legs together.

A brief moment of silence followed as Kenny Roger's "*The Gambler*" emanated from the speakers.

"So . . . when was the last time you been to Mexico?" he asked.

"Um . . . maybe ten years."

"That's a long time. Don't you have any family back there?"

"My aunt, uncle, and a few cousins."

"What about your parents?"

She hesitated for a moment, her eyes immediately glazing over with moisture. "I lost contact with them about five years ago."

"What happened?"

"My father was sick, and my mother tried to get him to another town with better medical care. After leaving their

58

village to get help, they disappeared and I haven't seen or talked to them since."

"Have you thought about going back to find them?"

"Yes, I tried once but was unable to find them."

"Sorry to hear that. If it'll make you feel any better, I lost contact with my parents over thirty years ago. Although, the reason for my separation was a little different than yours. So, I definitely know what you're feeling."

They parked in front of a local diner on Route 66.

"I think I depressed you enough," he said. "Let's go inside and chow down."

Maria opened the door, stepping through a time warp, dating back more than fifty years. Black and white checkered floors were complemented by tabletops of the same design. Turquoise decor accents, red fluorescent borders along the walls, and a red jukebox, shaped with the front end of a classic Chevy, completed the 1950s atmosphere.

She followed Malcolm to a booth in the corner. A waitress, wearing a white mini skirt, with red chiffon trim and a polka dot scarf, approached the table. She took their orders and then departed with a touch of cinnamon spice lingering in the air.

Malcolm sniffed. "They sure know how to whet your appetite."

Maria sat quietly, staring at the table, fumbling with the salt and pepper shakers.

"It's okay. I'm not going to bite you. Loosen up a little. Now, on to the reason we came here. As promised, I've monitored your work habits over the past few months, and now that your probationary period is over, I want to let you know a raise is in your future. You've proven yourself to be a loyal worker."

"Thanks."

"We just need to take care of a few minor details before your raise goes into effect. I was thinking about a five percent increase. How does that sound?"

"I'd like that," Maria said, looking pleased with the offer.

A few minutes later, the waitress returned, holding two hamburger platters, surrounded with steak fries and a sliced pickle. Maria grabbed the ketchup and poured a generous amount on her burger.

"Can I see that when you're done?" he asked, holding out his hand.

She passed the bottle, and as she transferred the ketchup to him, he ran his fingers across the back of her knuckles. She quickly let go, dropping the bottle onto his plate with a portion of ketchup spilling onto his white cotton shirt.

She covered her mouth with her hands. "I'm so sorry."

He poured some water onto a napkin and dabbed the stain. "Excuse me," he said, and departed for the restroom.

She took one bite of her hamburger and grimaced. Her appetite had disappeared, replaced with an uneasy feeling in the pit of her stomach. She had no idea what type of mood he would be in once he returned.

A moment later, the bathroom door opened as he

returned. A faded streak of ketchup marked the middle of his shirt. "Does it look bad?"

She shrugged.

"Just for this, I'm going to have to knock a few percentage points off your raise."

She looked at him with her eyes wide open.

He chuckled. "You have to learn not to take my jokes seriously."

***

An hour passed before they left the diner. Although happy with the news regarding the raise, Maria was eager to get back to her desk, amongst her coworkers, and to more familiar surroundings. She realized her anxiety wouldn't subside until she was free of any further one-on-one contact with him.

She stared out the window as they sped along, approaching the office, but instead of slowing to make the turn, he continued cruising, beyond the entrance.

"Wait. Where are you going?" Maria asked.

"I need to make a quick stop at the store for some cigarettes."

"You can drop me off here. I don't need to go with you."

"It'll only take a minute."

He drove another couple of miles before turning onto a desolate dirt road. Maria's heart pounded at a frantic pace, sensing something was terribly wrong.

He peered at her with no discernable expression. "This is a shortcut."

They soon came to an abrupt stop in the middle of a sea of dirt and desert vegetation surrounding them from all sides.

"W-what are you doing?"

"This is one of the minor details we need to take care of before I can give you a raise."

Maria swiveled her head from left to right. "There's nothing out here."

"Exactly. Nothing but you and me."

Her breath quickened, hoping this would be revealed as some kind of joke yet realizing with each passing second that she had a serious problem brewing.

"What do you want from me?"

"Come on, Maria. You know what I want. It's all about giving and receiving. I give you the raise, and I'm looking to receive something in return."

"P-please, can we just go back to the office?"

"Sure, right after I receive my gift for being so generous to you."

Her entire sense of reality went numb. *Is this actually happening?* she thought.

She briefly closed her eyes, weighing her options. This most certainly wasn't her first fishing expedition, and she was tired of being the bait. It always started with a nibble at first, and then an exploratory bite, followed by an all-out feeding frenzy. And this scenario would likely be no different, though the shark circling her this time was much larger than her previous encounters.

If she resisted further, she had no idea what he was

truly capable of, and he definitely held the upper hand when it came to the strength factor. On the other hand, there was no way she would let this aroused behemoth take advantage of her. She opened her eyes, darting them around the area, looking for a way out. Then she took a deep breath, turning toward him.

"Okay. What do you want me to do?"

"I knew you would come around. Why don't we start with a kiss?"

*As predicted, here comes the nibble first.* She recoiled at the thought of getting anywhere close to this man's lips.

She glanced outside, wondering if opening the door and jumping out into the desert landscape would be the safer option. She hesitated with that approach, however, realizing there were at least a few miles between their current location and the office, and that would be a brutally long walk, especially considering the daytime heat. In addition, there were all types of desert critters out there she would potentially need to contend with. She decided to let instinct take hold and see how far that would get her.

She swallowed hard, wondering if she could go through with this outlandish request. *Maybe he'll be content with one kiss, and this would all be over.* As much as she wanted to believe that, her woman's intuition vehemently disagreed.

Throwing caution into the wind, she clenched her fists and leaned in his direction as he closed his eyes. Upon approaching his face, she could smell the cigarette smoke, buried deep in the recesses of his lungs, escaping from his nostrils as he exhaled. And if that wasn't enough of a turnoff, his purple lips were complemented with a host of cracks and crevices, no doubt suffering from extreme dryness.

She came within a few inches of his lips and suddenly changed course, shifting her mouth toward his right cheek, filling her mouth with saliva, and promptly ejecting the fluid onto his face.

His eyes shot open as a glob of Maria's liquid DNA slowly oozed down the side of his cheek.

*What the hell did I just do*? That was not what she had expected when she'd agreed to let her instinct take over. Now she was fair game to whatever retaliation Malcolm could muster.

She instinctively jumped back, waiting for a slap, a punch, or an all-out barrage of four-letter words. However, to her surprise, none of those actions came to pass.

She studied him as he glared at her for a second and used his sleeve to wipe away the saliva sliding down his face. Then he grabbed the steering wheel with both hands as he closed his eyes.

Without looking at Maria, he said, "I'd suggest you open the door and get out."

She fumbled for the door handle and opened it before jumping out. She backpedaled away from the truck.

Malcolm made brief eye contact but didn't say anything before driving off, leaving her engulfed in an enormous dust cloud.

She frantically brushed herself off. "*Usted idiota!*" she

screamed.

She stood in the middle of this ocean of dirt, wearing her crisp, clean business attire, clearly dressed for the wrong occasion. She looked down at her wedged heels and wondered how on earth she could walk across this rugged terrain of dirt and rocks without twisting her ankle. She was in total disbelief that he had left her alone in the middle of nowhere, like a pile of trash.

She took one step, and then another as her ankles wobbled, trying to stay balanced. After walking for a few minutes, she squinted up ahead, following the faint sounds of a vehicle approaching in the distance. She found it hard to believe this secluded area would have any vehicular traffic.

She stopped in an instant and clutched her bag as Malcolm's Silverado came into view. She prayed he wasn't coming back for more mischief.

He pulled alongside with the window down. "Please accept my apology. I was wrong. It was completely stupid on my part to do what I just did."

Maria continued to stare forward, not the least bit interested in making eye contact or listening to his sorry-ass excuse.

"There's no way I can leave you out here alone. Please hop in and I'll take you back to the office."

In an instant, any anxiety or fear Maria had felt dissipated into a cloud of dust, replaced with a sudden rush of anger.

She lifted her head, cutting her eyes at him. "How the

hell do you think I got here in the first place?"

Malcolm shook his head. "I had no choice. I figured it was best to just drive away and collect my thoughts. Didn't want to do anything I would regret later."

Maria's forehead wrinkled in confusion. "And you don't regret requesting a kiss and whatever else in exchange for a raise? And leaving me out here alone in the middle of nowhere?"

"I swear I didn't plan this."

She kept quiet, too upset to continue talking. Then she turned and took a stride away.

"Now common sense says there's no way you can walk three miles back to the office without passing out from exhaustion." Malcolm leaned over to the passenger side and opened the door. "Please, Maria, I'm begging you to get in so I can take you back safely to the office. I promise to behave like a gentleman."

Although she knew he was right, her pride and ego prevented her from immediately following through with his offer. If she did get into the truck, she wasn't boarding without insurance.

She looked down to the right and then left before spotting a softball-sized rock. She picked it up and stared back at Malcolm.

"So, is this your form of protection?"

She nodded.

"Okay, if that's what it'll take for you to get in, then so be it."

She boarded, gripping the rock tightly while keeping

her eye on Malcolm. She rested the rock on her lap, careful to cup the rock with both hands to avoid any dirt from rubbing off on her dress.

The vehicle lurched forward as Malcolm pressed on the gas. "I must say, this is somewhat uncomfortable with you sitting next to me with a rock in hand, ready to knock my block off. But I get it and have no one to blame but myself."

He cleared the dirt-covered terrain and pulled onto the paved road, heading east toward the office.

"I truly apologize with all my heart for what just happened. I lost my mind, and I'm truly sorry."

Maria remained quiet while continuing to grip the rock.

"If it'll make you feel any better, I still plan to give you a raise. Instead of five percent, why don't we make it ten?"

Although Maria's face held firm on the outside, she couldn't help but feel a sense of intrigue and excitement on the inside. A ten percent increase was appealing, but at what cost? Or was this just another ploy to regain her trust?

Malcolm glanced over. "Aren't you going to say anything?"

She continued to look straight ahead, with no discernable expression.

"Well, the offer is there if you decide to take it. I simply ask you don't tell anyone about what just happened. It'll just be our little secret."

A few minutes later, they arrived back at the office. Without saying a word, Maria exited the truck, tossed the rock aside, and walked over to her car. She collapsed into the seat and eyed Malcolm walking into the office as if nothing happened. She contemplated whether or not to call the police and report the incident, yet she had no proof anything had happened. No physical confrontation had occurred and there were no bruises on her body, just his word against hers. She realized alerting anyone of what had just happened would most likely wipe out her chance of getting that hefty raise, and she was in no position to pass on extra money, especially being behind on her rent, as well as an assortment of other bills.

She grimaced at the thought of respecting Malcolm's wishes and keeping this a secret. She didn't want to burden her mind with making such an immoral decision, but at the same time, money talked. And, in this case, it was shouting from the mountaintops. Walking back into Malcolm's office and agreeing to keep this a secret would most certainly mean defeat. Not only for herself but for any proud and confident woman who would have never returned after what had just happened. However, she couldn't resist—she needed the money desperately.

Against her better judgment, she decided to entertain his offer and accept the embarrassment and humiliation that would accompany her as she walked back through his doors, hoping on a wing and a prayer his offer wasn't another hollow promise.

# Chapter 6

Becoming impatient with the automated system, Jace drummed his fingers on the desk. This was the third local realtor he had attempted to contact, and none of them offered any additional information about Granwin Estates, other than what he already knew from his tour with Malcolm. He'd also been in contact with a resource at the home relocation services provided by his company, but there were no other communities that matched up with what Granwin offered.

He pulled out the business card from Winchester Realty and dialed. After pressing zero for the operator, he anticipated hearing a female voice on the other end, preferably one with a foreign accent. Instead, another young lady greeted him.

"May I speak to Malcolm," he asked.

Moments later, Malcolm responded, "It's great to hear your voice again, Mr. Valentine. I can only hope this is good news."

"That depends."

"On what?"

"Me and my wife talked things over and, to be honest, we're not sure if we can afford—"

"Say no further. I already know what you're going to say. The model I showed you was a mid-level priced home. If you're looking for something more economical, there are houses on the other side of the lake going for fifty less. Of course, they're a little smaller."

Jace's eyes lit up with excitement. The price was still slightly above his range but within reach, depending on how much he could get for the condo.

"Let me talk it over with my wife a little more. I'll get back to you."

***

Later that evening, Jace arrived home from work, and entered the kitchen, where Sarah was putting the finishing touches on the evening's meal.

"Hi, sweetheart," he said enthusiastically.

Sarah's face remained unchanged, unaffected by the positive energy Jace was dishing out.

"What's that look for?" she asked.

He proceeded to give Sarah an affectionate hug and kissed her on the lips. "A man can't come home and be happy to see his wife?"

"I haven't seen you this happy since our honeymoon. Did we hit the lotto?"

"No. But it could be the next best thing."

"Did Ryan and Ava sign a peace treaty?"

"No. Although that would be something to rejoice about."

"Okay. I give up."

"I spoke with Malcolm today about the price range for the houses."

"And . . .?"

"How does three-fifty sound?"

"I thought—"

"Yeah, me, too. He said the listing we saw was for a mid-level home. He can get us a smaller house on the other side of the lake."

"So, why didn't he tell us while we were there?"

"We never had a chance to discuss any pricing in detail."

"I'm still not convinced. I think he's just a fast-talking salesman, trying to get all the money he can from us. There's has to be a catch."

"I don't know, but I already planned everything out. We can put a large down payment on the house if we sell the condo and—"

"There you go again, making decisions on your own and not thinking about the rest of the family."

"I'm sorry. I'm just so excited. I think this is a chance of a lifetime. Where else can you find homes like that for such a low price? Besides, didn't you say you would change your mind if we found out the houses were affordable?"

"No. Don't put words in my mouth. I said I couldn't make any promises. Just give me a little more time."

***

The next morning, Jace sat in the kitchen, finishing off a bagel before going to work.

Sarah entered, sitting at the table, running her hands through her unkempt hair. She looked at him with bloodshot eyes.

"Doesn't look like you slept much," he said.

"Nope. Had a lot on my mind."

"Any further thoughts on the move?"

She sighed. "I don't know what to think anymore. I still don't like the idea, but . . ."

Jace waited with bated breath.

"You win."

"Are you trying to tell me you agree to move?"

"Yes," she mumbled.

"Can you say that a little louder, dear?"

"Yes, Jace!" she uttered with the body language of a prizefighter who had just lost a championship fight.

"I'm speechless," he said, giving her a bear hug. "I'm honestly surprised you came to a decision so quickly."

"Yeah, me, too. I just kept thinking about what you said about maybe losing your job to Mr. Perfect. I can't imagine the guilt I would feel if you listened to me and we stayed in St. Louis, and then you eventually got the ax."

Jace continued grinning from ear to ear. "You won't regret this decision in the least bit. There's so much to do. Where do we begin?"

"How about letting Ryan and Ava know."

"Good idea."

He called out to them as they raced into the kitchen.

"Guess what?"

"Are we putting Ryan up for adoption?" Ava asked.

"No, let's be serious for a moment. We're moving to Albuquerque!"

***

Jace relayed the news to Mr. Kincade. This began the marathon relocation process that included selling the condo and purchasing a home at Granwin Estates. Within a matter of a couple of months, they successfully found a buyer for the condo and settled on a purchase price for the new house. Jace was overwhelmed by the amount of time and effort it took to complete the process. After filling out mounds of paperwork, writing a stack full of checks, working with real estate lawyers, and flying to Albuquerque for the closing, Jace's relocation dream became a full-fledged reality.

The night before the move, Jace and Sarah packed away the last few boxes of clothes.

"We're coming down the home stretch. A few more boxes, and we'll be done," he said, sounding exhausted.

"Yeah," she responded with her head down.

He walked over, massaging her shoulders. "Are you still worried about the move?"

"A little," she said, avoiding eye contact.

"It's okay to be nervous. This is a major change in our life, but I'm sure it'll work out for the best."

She wiped the tears that suddenly flooded her eyes. "You don't know how hard this is for me. I have nothing but good memories here. We got married . . . the children were born here."

He gently embraced her before looking into her eyes. "Go ahead; let it out. It's okay to cry. It's natural for you to feel this way. Think of this like your first day as a freshman in high school—you had no friends, most of the kids were bigger and older than you, you didn't know how to get to your next class, and you felt completely out of place. But, after a while, you met new friends, could find your way to class with your eyes closed, and you no longer felt like a stranger."

Sarah sniffled, wiping a tear from her cheek.

"I think you understand where I'm coming from," he said, kissing her on the forehead. "Now, let's get some sleep. The movers will be here early in the morning, and we've got a long drive ahead of us."

***

After a sixteen-hour drive, they arrived in Albuquerque, entering Granwin Estates and pulling in front of their new residence.

Jace walked up to the ivory-colored front porch. An old-fashioned swing chair dangled from the roof of the porch. He opened the door to their new twenty-two-hundred-square-foot house. He strolled through the foyer, across the parquet floors, while the echoes of his footsteps softly reverberated off the walls. He entered the living room, illuminated by the sunlight streaking in from the massive bay window. He proceeded through the hallway and into the kitchen, the layout just as he remembered from the tour, although somewhat smaller. He ran upstairs and inspected the bedrooms.

The movers unpacked the assortment of furniture and boxes from the truck. Miscellaneous items were unloaded and placed in the basement. The move was now completed, and a new chapter in Jace's life opened.

# Chapter 7

The following morning, Sarah woke up to an empty bed. She found a note on the bathroom vanity from Jace.

*Be back soon. Just exploring the new surroundings.*

He acted like a kid on Christmas morning, excited by all the new toys. Except, in this case, a new city. She only hoped she could grow to like this city half as much. For now, her guard remained up, still pensive about the whole relocation idea. She'd promised herself to give it a chance and realized, with any change, there were adjustments in the beginning. She most certainly had enough tasks to keep her mind off any negative thoughts at the outset. A multitude of unpacked boxes awaited her in the basement.

***

Later in the morning, with sweat on her brow and aching hands, she stepped away from the tedious task of unpacking and strolled out to the lake with Ryan and Ava. She swiveled her head from left to right, marveling at the size of their new backyard which, in her mind, was probably the best thing about the move up to this point. She had never thought she would own a lakefront house.

Seeing a flock of geese floating on the calm water, she sighed, allowing her cautious feelings to ease for a moment. *Maybe this won't be so bad after all.*

"This is pretty cool," Ryan said, tossing a few pebbles into the water.

Ava walked closer to the edge of the lake. "This water smells funny."

"I don't think it's the water, and it sure ain't me or Mom," Ryan said with a devious laugh.

"Okay, you two. You've been doing good up until this point. Let's keep it that way," Sarah said, attempting to prevent another squabble.

She inhaled, agreeing the water did have a slight stench.

She looked to the right, scanning the perimeter of the lake, and spotted a few dead fish, washed up on the land. She directed Ryan and Ava's attention to the source of the smell.

"There's your answer."

She twisted her neck to the left, revealing more dead fish.

"Hey, neighbor," someone shouted from behind.

She turned to see a tall figure standing on the grass by the deck.

She walked up to get a closer look, focusing on a familiar figure.

"Hi," she said, wondering what Malcolm was doing in the yard.

"I came by to see how you were making out. I rang the doorbell, but nobody answered. That's when I heard ya in the back."

"We're doing fine. Still in the process of unpacking."

"That's understandable." He paused, scanning the backyard. "Where's Jace?"

"He's out running a few errands. He should've been back a while ago. I hope nothing happened."

"I'm sure he's okay."

He reached into his pocket to take out a pack of cigarettes, extracting a stick before stuffing the pack back into his pocket. He placed the cigarette between his lips, raised the lighter, and then immediately stopped, eyeing Sarah.

"Do you mind if I light up?"

"Doesn't seem like I have a choice. You got this far, might as well keep going."

He focused beyond Sarah, watching the kids by the lake. "Seems like they're enjoying themselves." He pointed to the wooden pier off in the distance, with a few paddleboats anchored to a pole. "Feel free to take the boats for a ride. It's one of the advantages of owning a lakefront house."

"Thanks." She focused her attention on the water. "Speaking of the lake, I think you should know, there are some dead fish that washed ashore. It might be a good idea to have it cleaned up because it's starting to smell."

"There should be a number for the company that handles the lake in your welcome packet. They can clean it up if it already hasn't been reported. If you don't have the number, let me know and I'll find it for you." He puffed on his cigarette. "That's the benefit of hiring Winchester Realty as your agent. Most agencies will sell you a house, get their commission, and never talk to you again. My company, on the other hand, will sell you a house and help you out with any initial problems you may have. You can think of us as a one-year warranty for your home."

"I like that."

He laughed. "Most people do." He blew smoke into the air. "See, I'm not so bad after all. This is just one of the many things you learn about me as we get to know each other."

# Chapter 8

*What's Malcolm doing here?* Jace thought, pulling into the driveway and noticing the black Silverado parked in front. He walked inside and into the kitchen but didn't see anyone. Then he heard voices in the backyard and proceeded onto the deck.

Malcolm turned. "Look who's back. Trying to find your way around town?"

"Yeah. Got a little lost, but it was worth it. Learned a few shortcuts."

"What do you expect? You only been here a couple days. It'll take some time to get used to the area," Malcolm said.

"And to top it off, almost had an accident."

"You need to watch some of these people on the roads out here. They can drive a little recklessly."

"Thanks for the warning." Jace laughed. "The last thing I want to do is get bit by the Jeffries Jinx my first week out here."

Malcolm scrutinized Jace's face. "Jeffries Jinx?"

"Oh, I'm sorry. I thought everyone around here knew about it."

"It's not that I haven't heard of it before, I'm just surprised you know anything about it since you just moved here."

"It's . . . it's just something I heard in passing." His

face flushed in embarrassment. "Forget I even mentioned it."

Malcolm shrugged and glanced down at his watch. "Got any plans now?"

"Nothing besides unpacking."

Malcolm turned to Sarah. "Do you mind if I steal your husband for an hour? Wanna show him around town so he knows where he's going next time."

"Fine with me."

Jace followed him to the Silverado. He sat in the passenger seat, closing the door behind him. He scrunched his nose at the mix of pine-scented air freshener and cigarette smoke.

The leather interior, combined with the sunrays, heated the truck cabin to an uncomfortable temperature. Malcolm turned on the air conditioner and pulled away.

Jace focused his attention on a pet collar dangling from the rearview mirror.

"That belonged to my first true love," Malcolm said.

Jace remained silent, utterly confused.

Malcolm laughed. "Let me clarify. It was my cat, Oscar. Had him for most of my childhood. He was with me for twelve years before he passed away."

A few seconds of silence followed.

"What does a family man like yourself enjoy doing?"

Jace shrugged. "Besides working and spending time with the family, not much else."

"I'm sure you have at least some hours on the weekend to yourself."

"It doesn't seem like it."

"We need to change that. All men need time for themselves, time to hang out with some buddies for a little male bonding."

"You're probably right."

"I know I'm right. When's the last time you sipped some brew and visited the local booty bar?"

Jace blushed, thrown off guard by the question. "To be honest, I don't even remember."

"Stop depriving yourself. I can tell you're a man who enjoys watching beautiful women. Kind of like my sexy little secretary, Maria."

*Now we're getting somewhere.*

"What about her?" Jace asked.

"Come on. You make it sound like she's no big deal. I saw the way you were looking at her when we first met. And to tell you the truth, I don't blame you. That's why I hired her. What man wouldn't like being around an assistant like that? Funny thing is, not only is she pretty, but she turned out to be a damn good worker."

Jace was relieved to get confirmation she still worked at the realty office, and apparently was unharmed. Whatever happened that day hadn't been a life-or-death emergency, but he still needed to dig deeper and find out the reason for the note.

"Is that how you hire your female employees? Based on looks?"

"Why not? The look factor should always be taken into consideration. You act like you wouldn't do the same thing."

"If I want a successful business, I wouldn't. No matter how good she looks, she still needs to be able to perform her job duties, and if she can't . . . it's time to go."

Jace cringed at his response. Not because he didn't believe in what he'd just said, but more so because he'd always been insecure with people thinking of him as a goody two-shoes, the perfect gentleman, Captain Moral, who never did anything wrong. But, he did have some skeletons hanging out in the closet that could testify against his complete innocence.

He braced himself for Malcolm's reaction, which would no doubt feed into his insecurities.

Malcolm laughed. "I can't believe you're saying this with a straight face. You need to loosen the belt around your waist and live a little. You're definitely a different breed from the men I know. Or is this just how the men out in St. Louis operate?"

Jace's face grew flush. He felt like a school-aged boy being teased by his peers for bringing an apple to school for the teacher.

Jace shrugged. "I can't speak for other men in St. Louis, but that's how it is with me."

"You need a little eye candy in the office to keep the stress levels down," Malcolm said. "Who knows? If you're lucky, maybe you'll get a chance to unwrap the candy."

Jace narrowed his eyes with suspicion. "Is that your goal?"

"Isn't that the goal for most men?" He shifted his eyes

in Jace's direction. "You mean to tell me, if you were alone with a pretty lady and had the opportunity to see some skin, you wouldn't take advantage of that?"

"If you're talking about my wife, then of course." Jace turned with an inquisitive look. "Would you?"

Malcolm laughed. "There's no collar around my neck. I can do whatever I damn well please."

Jace pondered for a moment, still needing further details about his relationship with Maria. If there ever was an opportunity to be nosy and straight to the point, this was it.

"Have you had a chance to unwrap Maria's candy?"

Malcolm cut his eyes in Jace's direction. "Don't you think that's getting a little too personal?"

"I'm not the one who brought the subject up."

"Well, I'm going to need to plead the fifth on that one."

Jace shook his head with a few seconds of silence following.

"Enough about that, Jace. Let's move on to the reason why you're riding shotgun with me. What do you want to see around town? I can show you the local supermarkets, bars, restaurants, and whatever else your heart desires."

"Doesn't matter."

"I'll tell you one thing I desire now—another smoke. Do you mind?"

"No. As long as you can crack the windows."

Malcolm pointed to the glove compartment. "Can you do me a favor and open it? I should have a pack in the corner."

Jace pulled the tab as the glove compartment swung open, followed by a black gun hitting the floor between his legs."

"What the hell?" Jace said, raising both feet in a panic.

"I'm so sorry. I forgot that damn thing was in there. Don't worry; it's not loaded."

Jace offered Malcolm a critical squint, looking for a damn good explanation as to why this gun came tumbling out of the glove compartment.

"Guess you're wondering why I have a gun in the car?"

Jace nodded.

"It's simply for protection. There are some crazy people in this world."

*And you're one of them.* He remained still, eyes wide open, clearly uncomfortable with the presence of the gun.

"Do you see a cigarette pack?"

"No."

"How do you know if you don't look?"

"I'm not moving until this gun is put away, and I'm not touching it."

"It's harmless with no bullets."

Malcolm shook his head, pulling off onto the shoulder of the road. He reached down to the floor and grabbed the gun, placing it back into the glove compartment. He pushed aside the mess of papers that were scattered about.

"Damn. I thought I had a pack in there." He closed the compartment. "If you don't mind, let's swing by my office.

I should have a pack there." He patted his chest. "Need to have my daily allowance of carcinogens."

***

After arriving at the realty office, Jace waited in the truck as Malcolm ran inside. He took a deep breath, closing his eyes to relax his senses, still uncomfortable with the thought of a gun sitting in the glove compartment, just a few feet away from him.

He opened his eyes upon hearing the front door open. Malcolm's self-proclaimed eye candy stepped out, bypassing the truck without looking, and sauntered across the lot, nearing the faded blue Honda parked at the far right. This was his chance.

"Hi," Jace said.

She turned, clearly startled. Then she flashed a halfhearted smile, waved meekly, and continued walking.

Jace struggled to think of what else to say to get her attention.

"Nice day, huh?" he said, mentally kicking himself in the butt at his sorry attempt to strike up a conversation.

She opened her car door.

"Not sure if you remember, but we met a few months ago," he said.

"I don't remember. I meet so many people each day. Sorry to cut you short, but I only have an hour for lunch."

He tapped his foot in a nervous fit. He couldn't think of what else to say.

She sat in her car and reached for the handle to close the door.

Jace hopped out of the truck and approached. "Wait!"

He rifled through his pocket, grabbed his wallet, and pulled out the note, thrilled he had decided to keep it. He displayed it for her to see. "Do you remember this?"

She squinted. "Where did you get that?"

"You gave it to me."

Her eyebrows furrowed. "I have to go," she said, slamming her car door shut, her pleasant demeanor fading by the second.

"Hold on a minute. I know this is probably not the best time to talk about this, but I can do my best to help if you need it."

She avoided eye contact and started her car. "I'm good. I don't need any help," she said, shifting her car in gear.

"So, why did you give me this note? Something must be going on."

Without saying anything further, her car lurched in reverse.

"Wait!" Jace shouted.

She drove out of the parking lot at about the same time Jace heard laughter in the background and turned to see Malcolm standing by the front door.

"I thought you were a married man."

Jace stuffed the note in his pocket. "I am."

"I didn't hear the conversation, though it seems to me you were trying to help yourself to some candy."

Jace frowned at the comment. "It's not what you think."

"That's what they all say." He smiled. "Keep trying.

Maybe she'll give in. And don't worry; I won't tell your wife."

# Chapter 9

Jace arose early the next morning, looking forward to enjoying his last couple of days home before starting his relocation assignment. He poured a cup of coffee and strolled out onto the deck to admire the lakefront view. It didn't take long before he noticed an acrid smell in the air as a stiff breeze blew in from the lake. He immediately covered his nose before walking onto the grass and lifting the garbage can tops on the side of the deck, but they were empty. He squatted below the deck, looking for any dead animals, but found nothing out of the ordinary. He walked the perimeter of the house, searching for answers to the sickening odor. He made a concerted effort not to inhale too deeply, though it wasn't working as his stomach struggled to stay calm.

He poured the remainder of his coffee onto the grass and then approached the lake with his shirt pulled over his nose. With each step, the stench became worse. He noticed some debris floating on top of the water. After a couple more steps, he spotted a flock of dead geese, floating aimlessly. Some were washed up along the land, intermingled with a slew of dead fish. An unnatural brown tint covered the surface of the lake. He backpedaled away from the water and hustled back into the house.

A while later, he peeped through the kitchen patio door as a group of environmental agency vehicles converged on the lake. A portion of the lake was roped off with yellow tape securing the area. A small crowd of neighbors had gathered, surveying the scene.

Jace stepped onto the deck and lifted his shirt over his nose to protect against the stench. He approached the scene, noticing no one else covering their noses. He uncovered his nose, breathing in a small sampling of air, which no longer carried that heavy stench. He joined the inquisitive group and watched several men in green hazmat suits bag the dead geese and fish.

"What a shame," someone said from a short distance away.

Jace stared at the scene, oblivious to the chatter surrounding him.

"What do you think happened?" the same voice echoed again.

His peripheral vision caught a glimpse of someone staring in his direction. He blinked, clearing his mind from the trance that had temporarily consumed him. He turned to the left, focusing on an older gentleman with thinning gray hair, slicked back over his scalp, and a neatly trimmed mustache of the same color.

"I'm sorry, sir," Jace said in a sincere tone. "I didn't realize you were talking to me."

The older gentleman smiled, a web of squint lines forming around his eyes. "Don't worry, young man. I think we're all in shock by this." He extended his hand. "The name's Mr. Aderlee."

Jace introduced himself.

"Any idea what happened?" Jace inquired.

"No. I was asking you the same thing."

Jace shrugged. "The lake seems to be polluted with something. I was out earlier this morning, and the smell was horrible." He took a deep breath. "It's not as bad now."

Mr. Aderlee chuckled. "I know what you mean. I had to close all the windows in my house to keep out that horrible smell. I think the wind direction must have shifted."

Jace looked around at a few of the houses surrounding the lake. "Which one is yours?"

Mr. Aderlee pointed to the house on the right.

"Well, nice to meet you, neighbor. Didn't realize you lived next to me."

Mr. Aderlee turned, looking at Jace's house. "Is that one yours?"

"Yes," Jace replied.

"When did you move in?

"A few days ago."

"It's been about a month for me and my wife." Mr. Aderlee said. "I was the one who convinced my wife to come out here in the first place. She wanted us to retire in Key West and live in a beachfront house." He waved his hand toward the lake. "This isn't exactly a beach, but I figured a lakefront house would be just as nice. Boy, was I wrong. I think she's ready to wring my neck after this mess."

"Sounds like you and me are in the same boat. I also had to convince my family to move out here."

A brief moment of silence ensued, both men focusing on a man who appeared to be taking water samples.

Mr. Aderlee extended his hand. "Sorry to cut you short, but I need to get back to my wife. She doesn't get around all that well these days. See you around, neighbor."

# Chapter 10

Jace was eager to welcome Sabrina to the house. He hadn't seen her since their initial visit to Albuquerque, and she'd been a wealth of knowledge through various phone conversations, offering advice and suggestions throughout the moving process. As promised, she arrived with a bottle of Ruinart Brut Rose and a small, neatly wrapped house-warming gift. They sat at the dinner table, enjoying the meal Sarah had prepared.

"This is delicious. It's not often I get a chance to eat a home-cooked meal. I'm always eating out. I think most of the restaurants in the area know me by first name," Sabrina said.

"Glad to hear you like it. I'm just happy you didn't lose your appetite with that smell lingering in the air outside."

"I didn't smell anything."

"That's good. Guess the breeze is not coming in from the lake at the moment," Jace said.

"What's wrong with the lake?" Sabrina asked, stopping midway from bringing a fork full of food to her mouth.

"There was this horrible smell coming from the lake yesterday. I found some dead geese and fish floating around. Thankfully, a crew was there the same day to clean up the mess. We thought that was the source of the smell, but we were dead wrong—no pun intended. We've been smelling the same odor off and on throughout the day," Jace said.

"I hope they find out what's causing the smell. That's the last thing you need after just moving into the house," Sabrina said.

"You got that right," Sarah said, shaking her head. "There's usually something that doesn't go as expected when you first move into a house, though I didn't expect this."

A few minutes later, Ryan scooped up the last bit of food from his plate. "Sorry to eat and run; I've got a computer game to finish." He jumped up from the table and made his way upstairs.

Ava soon followed, excusing herself to go watch TV.

"It must be fun being young," Sabrina said. "You have time to do leisurely things. By the time I get home from work and eat dinner, it's lights out for me."

Sarah turned to Sabrina. "How far do you live from here?"

"I live in an apartment about twenty-five minutes from here."

"Ever thought about owning your own home?" Jace said.

"Been there, done it. And I have no immediate plans to do it again."

"Why? I think owning a home is a great investment," Jace said.

"I used to live in a three-bedroom house, not too far from downtown. But the house wasn't the problem; it was my marriage. The worst mistake I ever made. Don't get me wrong; I think marriage is a great institution, only when you find the right person." She took a sip of her champagne. "I, unfortunately, did the opposite and found the absolute wrong person for me. We divorced after a year."

"So soon?" Sarah asked.

"He became mentally abusive. He was very controlling and thought I should do all the housework, but he had no idea who he was messing with." She displayed a sheepish grin. "That would probably explain my behavior during the tour. I put up with the mental abuse for a while. I'm sure you probably don't believe this, but I wasn't as strong-willed back then. That all changed one day when that fool tried to hit me. All bets were off after that. I turned around, grabbed the nearest thing to me, which happened to be a glass lamp, and smashed it over his head." She chuckled. "That was the last time he raised his fists at me."

"And you have a sense of humor about this? I'd be pissed," Sarah said.

"I have no choice. It's all part of the healing process. I learned this from a nonprofit organization that I joined to help abused women." She flashed a sheepish grin. "I feel like I'm talking to a psychologist. I find it easy to talk to you guys."

"Are you still part of the organization?" Jace asked.

"I guess you can say that. I'm not involved as much as I once was, but I volunteer when I can."

Jace stared with probing eyes. "Is the organization only limited to dealing with spousal abuse?"

"No. We've helped people in all different types of abuse or harassment situations, from mental, to physical, to sexual." She offered Jace a critical squint. "It sounds like you may know someone who needs some assistance."

He rubbed his chin. "As a matter of fact, I think I do."

# Chapter 11

Sabrina parked in front of the realty office, taking advantage of leaving work a bit early. She was not accustomed to traveling to a potential client's home or, in this case, place of business for a first-time meeting. Most clients initially contacted her via phone with abuse allegations before scheduling a face-to-face meeting. However, this meeting was different.

She followed Jace's hunch that someone needed help yet had no evidence or claims of any abuse, besides the note Jace had shown her and his conversations with Malcolm. Although this alone would normally not be sufficient to pique her interest, she felt compelled to follow through with Jace's suspicion, especially after her first and only uncomfortable encounter with Malcolm. As far as she was concerned, his Type-A personality, mixed with his male chauvinist display, were enough warning signs. And these were signs from her experience that couldn't be ignored.

She sighed at the thought of disturbing someone at their place of business to discuss a personal matter. To make things more challenging, she didn't have much of a plan in mind on how to approach this situation—the true definition of winging it.

"Okay. This should be interesting," she mumbled, exiting the car.

Entering the building, she spotted several people

walking around the office. She scanned the area, carefully looking at each individual for a match from Jace's description as well as relying on her memory from when she had briefly seen this woman during her initial tour with the Valentine family. Still unsure of herself, she scanned each employee's desk within her view and focused on the name tags. Her eyes locked onto a desk just a few feet away from her.

She waited her turn as the young lady assisted a customer. Minutes later, she approached the desk, looking at the woman's name tag, confirming her target had been found.

"Welcome to Winchester Realty. How can I help you?"

Sabrina stood mesmerized at the flawless face before her. It reminded her of the airbrushed faces that adorned any one of the countless fashion magazines. The same type of face that could attract a great deal of male attention, whether wanted or unwanted.

"I hope you can help," Sabrina responded. "Someone recommended I come here and thought I may be of some assistance."

"Are you looking for a job?"

"Uh . . . sort of."

"We do have some openings for an administrative assistant and a real estate agent. Is this something you would be interested in?"

Sabrina nodded emphatically.

Maria reached into her desk and then handed Sabrina a folder. "If you don't mind, can you sit at the corner desk to fill out this application? Include your resume and return it to me."

Although Sabrina didn't have much of a plan at the outset, this gave her an idea. She proceeded to the corner desk and reviewed the application.

"Here goes nothing," she mumbled.

After including her name and cell phone number on the application, she proceeded to write the following:

> *I know you don't know me, but I received a tip from a mutual acquaintance that you may be in need of some assistance. Please call me, and I can give you more details on what this is all about.*
>
> *Regards,*
> *A concerned friend*

Sabrina couldn't help but laugh at the irony. Here she was, leaving a cryptic note for Maria, in response to the mysterious note she had left for Jace.

Sabrina purposely sat for a few more minutes to give the illusion she completed the entire application.

After a short while, she returned to Maria's desk, handing her the folder. Maria took it and, without looking, placed it in the corner of her desk, on top of some miscellaneous papers.

"Aren't you going to look and see if I'm at least qualified?" Sabrina asked.

"I'm sorry, I'm not the one who makes the hiring decision. I'll give this to my boss when I see him."

Sabrina opened her mouth to speak but hesitated after hearing a familiar voice at the back of the office. She looked up and spotted Malcolm talking to an employee in the back.

Before she could look away, he glanced up, locking eyes with hers. Much to her dismay, he approached.

"Well, this is most certainly a surprise. And how can we assist you today? Looking for a home perhaps?"

Sabrina shook her head without uttering a word.

"Are you looking for someone else interested in purchasing a home?"

Sabrina followed with another headshake.

Malcolm rubbed his goatee. "I'm all out of guesses. Please do tell me the purpose of this visit. The suspense is killing me."

"Just discussing a personal matter," Sabrina blurted out, not knowing what else to say. She immediately focused her eyes on Maria, who remained busy sorting through some paperwork on her desk, apparently not interested in joining the conversation.

Malcolm took a peek at his watch. "If I'm not mistaken, four p.m. on a Tuesday is still well within business hours. Now you should know better than to come around here to discuss a personal matter at this time."

She hated the thought of agreeing with this man, yet she knew he was dead right. Lord knew, if the shoe was on the other foot, she would have grabbed any person disturbing her at work by the collar and personally dragged them out of the office.

Offering no further resistance, Sabrina asked, "What are your business hours?"

"Nine to six," Malcolm said.

Sabrina glanced at Maria, giving her a cordial smile before departing. She exited the office, and before she could open her car door, she turned to see Malcolm had followed her outside, standing at the entrance.

"Are you checking up on me to make sure I'm leaving the premises?"

"Nope, just coming out for a quick cigarette break and to offer a piece of advice." He tilted his head and blew a puff of smoke in the air. "If you had any thoughts of waiting until business hours were over before coming back, I would cancel those plans."

"Why? According to you, business hours are over after six, which would be fair game for some personal chatter."

"I never said that."

"Well, that would be a logical conclusion for anyone I know following our conversation."

Malcolm smirked. "Problem is, I don't want you trespassing on my property, no matter what time it is."

Sabrina gritted her teeth as whatever little patience she held on to quickly exited stage left. "And what will happen if I decide to come back?"

"Let's just say I have the sheriff's office on speed dial and would have no problems calling."

Sabrina nearly laughed before sitting in her car with the door partly open. "That's a damn shame. You can't handle your battles without calling the sheriff for help?"

Malcolm's eyes narrowed. He exhaled another puff of smoke into the air. "I must admit you have a lot of spunk. Not accustomed to seeing that in a woman."

Sabrina turned on the ignition and closed the car door. She proceeded to roll down the window. "You apparently need to expand your horizons with the women you meet. You'd be surprised how many women can hold their own against someone like you."

With smoldering eyes, Malcolm said, "I've had enough needless chitchat with you. If you don't leave my property in ten seconds, time to make a call."

Sabrina shook her head. "You can save your call to the sheriff's office." She shifted her car into drive and lurched forward for an instant before hitting the brakes. She turned to Malcolm. "You know what they say. Never send a boy to do a man's job. Guess which one you are? I'm thinking the former."

She put the car in gear and pulled away from the parking lot, eyeing Malcolm in the rearview mirror. "Not today. You're messing with the wrong one," she mumbled while shaking her head.

She pulled onto the main road with a shot of adrenaline coursing through her veins, thinking of a promise she had made to herself some time ago.

She immediately flashed back to her less-than-stellar year of being married and the tension that had come about from dealing with her so-called husband. Her skin would crawl whenever his monstrous ego would reveal itself in the form of a chest-beating maniac, thinking he owned her mind, body, and soul. Thinking he could tell her what to do, how to do it, and when to do it. She had vowed, after the divorce, that she would never let any man make her feel less than the strong-willed, independent, brilliant-minded, and soul-nurturing woman she was born to be.

She turned on the radio, looking for any good music to soothe this negative energy that had suddenly invaded her mental space. She stared straight ahead, disgusted with Malcolm's poor timing to interrupt her conversation with Maria and circumvent her ultimate plan. However, she also realized she was at fault for being careless enough not to think of an excuse to grab the folder on the way out, especially since there had been no guarantee Maria would even lay eyes on what she had written. Now it was all about playing the game of chance.

She hoped Maria took a look at the bogus job application before Malcolm had an opportunity. If the latter occurred, he would have every right to begin his investigation as to what had initially prompted the note.

Sabrina gritted her teeth at the ominous possibilities. Not only would she be a suspect in his investigation, but this would also put Maria directly in the line of fire, and the worst part was she wouldn't even see it coming.

# Chapter 12

Malcolm watched as she finally left the premises, speechless, embarrassed, and angry at the same time after what had just transpired. He couldn't recall the last time a woman had challenged his manhood.

He took a deep breath, gathering his ego that had been shattered in an instant. He entered the office and stormed straight to Maria's desk.

"Can I see you in my office?"

Maria followed as he held the door until she entered.

He closed the door behind her and sat on the corner of his desk. He pointed to the vacant chair a few feet away from him. "Have a seat."

Maria complied and sat with her head tilted down at the floor.

"Where do you know her from?"

"I don't know her."

He grimaced. "Don't play stupid with me. I'll ask you again. Where do you know her from?"

"I . . . I swear. I don't. She just came into the office and started talking to me."

"About what?"

"She was looking for a job."

"Is that what she told you? How come she didn't mention this when I asked?"

Maria shrugged.

"Sounds to me like someone is lying," Malcolm said, scratching his goatee. "Well, if she was looking for a job, I imagine she completed an application and left her resume. Did she?"

"Yes, it's on my desk. Do you want me to get it for you?"

Malcolm paused for a moment. "I have a meeting in a few minutes. I can grab it later." He pointed to the door. "You're free to go. We'll continue this another time."

She approached the door, and as she grabbed the doorknob, he whistled to get her attention.

"By the way, don't let me find out you're lying about not knowing her. If I see you and her together anywhere, you and me are going to have some serious problems."

# Chapter 13

Sarah stared out the patio door, shaking her head. The lakefront, once the highlight of the backyard oasis, had been transformed into a contaminated moat, surrounding the castle they called home. It had been a few days since the foul water had appeared, yet it seemed like weeks.

She watched as the trees bordering the lake gently swayed from a slight breeze. A breeze that, at one time, offered a refreshing filter of air through the house. A breeze that had now been confined to the outdoors, cut off by the airtight windows and doors, sealed shut to block out the sickening odor.

She took a deep breath, her frustration becoming a catalyst for another migraine. She sat at the kitchen table and closed her eyes, before eventually nodded off at the table.

A short while later, Sarah felt a tap on her shoulder. She opened her eyes to see Ava.

"Hi, Mom."

Sarah cleared her throat. "Didn't expect you home so soon. Is this what time the bus is supposed to drop you off after school?"

Ava shrugged. "I guess so."

"So, how was your first day at school?"

"Okay . . . I guess."

"That doesn't sound too encouraging."

"It's hard when you don't know anybody."

"It was only your first day. You have plenty of time to make friends." Sarah peered into the empty hallway. "Where's Ryan?"

"Oh, he went upstairs to his room."

"Since when does he walk in and not say hello to his mother?"

"I don't think he wants to talk now."

"Why?"

"It's probably better if he tells you."

Sarah walked up the stairs, approaching his bedroom door.

She knocked. "Ryan? You okay?"

"Yeah, I'm fine."

"Can I come in?"

"If you want."

She opened the door, finding Ryan lying facedown on his bed.

"What's the matter? Are you sick?"

"If you want to call it that."

She sat at the edge of the bed and gently rubbed his back. "What else can I call it? Did something happen at school today?"

"Everything was fine. I'm just a little tired."

"Being silent like this is not going to help. Can you please turn around and tell me what happened."

Letting out a sigh, he slowly turned around.

Sarah winced, looking at his left eye, surrounded by a myriad of black and blue marks.

"Who did this to you?" she screamed.

"I got into a little fight. It's nothing. The bruise will go away."

"Fighting on your first day of school. What's wrong with you?"

"But it wasn't my fault. Blame the guy that was messing with Ava," Ryan said, putting his face in the pillow.

"Are you trying to tell me you were protecting your sister?"

"Yeah, something like that."

Sarah displayed a massive grin. "So . . . you do love your sister after all."

Ryan shrugged.

"I'll be right back. Let me get some ice for that eye."

She ran downstairs into the kitchen. She stared at Ava who was sitting, eating an apple.

"You should be proud of your brother for trying to protect you."

"Yeah," Ava said nonchalantly.

"Did you at least thank him?"

"No. Not yet."

"Are you planning to sometime today?"

"Yeah. I'm going to do it right now," she said, grabbing the bag of ice Sarah prepared.

She walked up the stairs with Sarah trailing and knocked on the door.

"Come in, Mom."

Ava entered.

"Oh, it's you."

"I came to bring you this for your eye."

"Thanks." Ryan gently placed it on his eye.

Ava swung her arms back and forth. "Um . . . I wanted to thank you for what you did today."

"No problem."

"You didn't have to step in. I could have handled him."

"That's what big brothers are for."

She bent down to hug him. "I'll leave you alone so you can rest." She slowly exited the room. Seconds later, she stuck her head back in and said, "By the way, next time, try not to block any punches with your eye."

They both laughed.

Sarah stood by the doorway, hoping this would be a turning point in their sibling rivalry.

# **Chapter 14**

Jace returned home from his first day of work, excited by the opportunity to start fresh with new coworkers, take on new job responsibilities, and have a chance to explore the Downtown Albuquerque area.

He entered the kitchen, and found Sarah at the table, reading a magazine. The countertops were empty, devoid of any food.

"Any leftovers for me?"

She pointed to the refrigerator without looking up.

He walked to the fridge to prepare a makeshift meal. He gave Sarah a slow, appraising glance, confused by her quietness. "Aren't you going to ask how my first day of work was?"

"How was it?" she said with little enthusiasm.

"Sounds like you wouldn't care much even if I told you. What's the matter?"

She placed the magazine on the table. "I'll start with the good news. Your son did something courageous at school today. I'll let him explain when you go upstairs to see him. In the meantime, we need to talk."

"This doesn't sound good."

"I took it upon myself to make some calls to see who can help with getting rid of that smell from the lake. I didn't talk with anyone but left some messages."

"Good. Hopefully, we'll start getting some answers."

Sarah folded her arms and shook her head. "I'm letting you know right now that I can't spend another day trapped in this house with the doors and windows shut. The weather is beautiful, and we can't even enjoy a nice, refreshing breeze from the outside."

"How about taking a walk somewhere away from the lake?"

"Where? I don't know anybody I can visit. Besides, I'd feel funny walking around aimlessly by myself."

"Maybe you can call Sabrina, and she could take you out on one of her lunch breaks."

"I can do that, but what if I just want to sit on the backyard deck and enjoy the outdoors?"

"That's still possible. It just depends on what direction the wind is blowing."

Sarah grimaced. "What's wrong with you? How come you're so nonchalant about the situation?"

Jace put his head down to gather his thoughts. "I know you're frustrated, and I am, too. We just need to stay calm and put things in perspective. Sure, I'm upset we can't enjoy our backyard, but I'm sure the community is doing all it can to get this resolved. Believe me; the last thing they want to do is let this problem linger and attract bad publicity. As a matter of fact, it may already be too late because I saw a news van roaming the streets as I was coming home."

He walked over to Sarah and massaged her shoulders. "I'm confident we'll hear something tomorrow."

"And what if we don't?"

"Then it's time for plan B."
"Which is?"
"Whatever's necessary to get the answers we need."

# Chapter 15

The following day, the doorbell rang, jarring Sarah out of her daydream. She sat on the living room sofa, hoping her expected guest had arrived. She had taken Jace's suggestion and called Sabrina for a lunch date.

She squinted through the peephole, spotting a young woman standing on the porch with a cameraman directly behind her. Sarah backed away from the door and peered through the living room window to see a news van parked outside. She sat back on the sofa, ignoring the unexpected guests. After a few minutes, she peered out the window again, noticing the van had left. She collapsed back onto the sofa and eventually closed her eyes.

A short while later, she awoke at the sound of the doorbell ringing again. She peeked out the window once more to see a midnight blue luxury car parked out front. She couldn't tell if it was a BMW or Mercedes—an eye-catching car either way. She focused her attention on the porch and spotted Sabrina.

She opened the door, giving her a welcoming hug. "What happened to the tour van?"

Sabrina laughed. "I hope you didn't think that hunk of junk was mine. Once I'm done with my tours on the weekend, that thing goes right back to the lot." She pointed to the car. "This is my real baby."

Sarah boarded the car and sunk into the beige, leather

interior. She looked at the dashboard, which resembled something out of an airplane cockpit. She glanced over at the center of the steering wheel, displaying the BMW logo.

"Which BMW series is this?"

"It's a five. Was hoping to get a six series, but my bank account furiously protested against that idea. To be honest, my bank account protested against the five series, but I just couldn't resist buying it. You have to excuse me. I suffer from CTBB, commonly known as champagne taste on a beer budget."

Sarah chuckled. "What do you press to make this thing go?"

"It's no different from any other car. All you need is the gear, the pedal, and both eyes on the road."

Sarah turned her neck from side to side, eyeing the many bells and whistles that populated the interior cabin. "If I could only convince Jace to buy a car like this. I keep trying to tell him to live a little and get something that excites him. And I would say this qualifies."

Sabrina laughed. "Good luck with that. Maybe he'll come around one day."

Sabrina shifted in gear and nudged forward before a news van came to a screeching halt in front of them, blocking her path.

Sarah grimaced at the unexpected guests returning.

A woman approached with a microphone and a cameraman following.

"Excuse me. Do you think we can speak with you for a moment?" the young lady asked.

"No, thank you," Sarah politely declined.

"It'll only take a minute of your time."

Sabrina turned to the lady and took a deep breath. "As my friend said, we're not interested in talking and would appreciate it if you can move your van so we can leave."

"I don't want to cause an argument; I just have a couple quick questions about the lake."

Sabrina glared at the woman and displayed a less-than-enthusiastic smile. "I'm trying my best to be polite, although my patience is running thin. I understand you have a job to do, but this is not the time or place for us to answer your questions. Now, if you'll excuse us, we need to go."

Sabrina put the car in reverse, allowing enough distance to speed around the van, leaving the young woman and her cameraman standing in the middle of the street.

"Sorry about that, Sarah."

"Don't worry. I've been trying to avoid them, anyway. They've been snooping around the neighborhood recently."

Sabrina grinned. "Sometimes I wonder why you still want to hang out with me."

"What do you mean?"

"It seems like whenever we get together, someone is ruffling my feathers and testing my patience. Nothing like a deep breath and a smile to help keep a level head when your patience decides to run for cover." Sabrina laughed. "I'm really a nice person once you get to know me."

"Stop it. I'm sure you are. I wouldn't be going out to lunch with you if I thought otherwise."

"Thanks. So . . . what do you want for lunch? If you

don't mind, maybe we can go back to the Mexican restaurant I took you guys to when we first met."

"Sounds good to me."

***

They arrived, finding a table for two.

"Thanks for getting me out the house. I needed the fresh air," Sarah said.

"No problem. Speaking of fresh air, have they figured out the problem with the lake?"

"No. Still waiting, and that smell is getting on my last nerve. I guess, if I had a job to get me out of the house, it wouldn't be so bad."

Sabrina took a sip of water. "Not to get in your business, but how come you're not working?"

"Long story. I'll give you the short version. Back in my early days, before I married Jace, I use to be a computer programmer at a bank in St. Louis. After we got married and the kids came along, I decided to be a stay-at-home mom for a while. When I attempted to go back to work, I kept getting these horrible headaches. The doctors said I had some type of stress-related migraine disorder, or something like that. They gave me all types of different medicine, but nothing helped. I figured my health was more important than work, so I've been home ever since."

"Oh. I'm sorry to hear."

"I tried starting a small home business, but it didn't work out. I feel like such a lazy bum. Sometimes I wonder why Jace is still around and hasn't run off with a younger and more ambitious woman."

"Stop putting yourself down. It's not your fault your health is preventing you from working. Besides, Jace is doing what every honest, caring husband should do."

"Which is?"

"Honor his marriage vows and stay with you through sickness and in health, for better or for worse. You should be happy. The only thing my ex-husband honored was our divorce decree."

They both laughed.

Sarah took a bite of her chicken quesadilla and then said, "Enough about my sorry life. How are things with you?"

"I'm doing fine. Too blessed to be stressed."

"Any luck with the detective work Jace gave you?"

"Oh, you mean the assistant at the realty office?"

"Yeah."

"Let's just say I screwed up royally on that assignment."

Sarah stopped chewing momentarily. "I'm afraid to ask what that means."

"Well, I'm usually one to plan out things beforehand, but for whatever reason, I decided to go to Maria's office to see if I can at least give her my contact information to call me. I figured slipping her a note with my name, cell number, and a cryptic message to call would do the trick. Problem is, I didn't think this through." She took a sip of water and then continued, "She didn't know me from a hole in the wall, and here I am, thinking she would immediately trust me and be curious enough to call me about who knows what. And of course, that hasn't happened."

"Sorry, it didn't work out like you planned."

Sabrina placed her hand on Sarah's forearm. "And that's not even the worst part. I ended up disguising my note in the form of a fake job application, thinking Maria would take a glance at it before I left, but once again, that never happened. And now there's a good chance Malcolm may see the note before she does, and he didn't seem too happy while I was there." Sabrina sipped the last bit of water in her glass. "I wouldn't be surprised if he tries to call me to ask about the note."

"You didn't think to take the note with you before you left?"

"I was completely distracted since Malcolm literally kicked me out the office and warned me not to come back. I did try calling the office to speak with her a few times and could never get her on the line."

"You poor soul."

"I'll be okay. I'm more worried about Maria." Sabrina pointed her finger at the ceiling. "Oh well, nothing I can do now but leave it in God's hands. I have my fingers crossed and trying my best to think positively this will all work out."

# Chapter 16

The parking lot showed no signs of life as Maria rolled to a stop, well in advance of business hours. She proceeded with her daily routine of opening the office, and preparing for another day. She inserted the key into the front door knob and twisted clockwise, a quarter turn, listening for the lock being released, but that familiar sound never occurred. She tried again, the key stopping midway and not budging any further. She twisted the knob and pushed. To her surprise, the door swung open.

She instinctively reached for the light switch against the wall and then snatched her hand back after noticing the lights beaming brightly. She wondered if someone had forgotten to lock up the previous night, which had never happened throughout the time she'd been employed at the office.

She backed away from the door and proceeded to her car. She reached for her phone, dialing Malcolm's cell.

"Are you calling out sick?" he asked before she could say hello.

"No. I'm already at the office. The door was unlocked and the lights were on. Did you forget to lock up last night?"

"Of course not."

"Well, I think someone broke into the office. I'm not going in until you get here."

A brief moment of silence followed.

"What if I tell you I'm already here?"

Maria hesitated, confused at the comment.

"Why don't you disconnect the call and come see me in my office? We need to talk again."

A sudden sense of dread consumed Maria. Ever since the incident, she had promised she would never be alone with him again, not unless someone else was present in the office, and at this time, all other employees were nowhere close to arriving.

She finally responded. "We can talk, but only if you come outside."

He disconnected without saying anything further.

Maria started the car, feeling more comfortable with the engine running. She tapped her fingers on the steering wheel, wondering why he had arrived at the office so early to meet with her. He had been in a decent mood the day before, and she couldn't think of any mistakes she had made with her work assignments yesterday that would warrant this impending conversation, which didn't appear like it would be pleasant based on Malcolm's tone.

He opened the front door and stepped outside, approaching with a folder.

"Any idea what's in this folder?"

Maria shook her head. "No."

Malcolm opened the folder, took out the sheet of paper, and stretched his arm closer to Maria's face so she can read.

Maria read the note and displayed a questioning glance. "What is this and why are you showing me?"

"Don't you think you should be enlightening me on what this is? This is the so-called job application your friend, who you claim you don't know, left a few days ago."

"Okay, but I don't know what this means."

"Well, she did say she was there to discuss personal business with you, so I imagine you have some clue as to what this is about. Or maybe I'll just reach out and call her myself to get some answers."

"I've never seen her in my life and have no clue why she wrote this note. Besides, do you think I would have volunteered to bring you this application if I knew this is what she wrote?"

"At this point, it doesn't matter. I swear, Maria, if you don't start talking and letting me know what the hell is going on—"

"I'm sorry, but I—"

"Did you tell her or anyone else about our secret?"

"Of course not," Maria said, attempting to control the quiver in her voice.

"Is this how you treat the man who gave you a chance? I gave you this job even though you had little experience. I gave you a raise, as promised. After all that, you should at least have the common courtesy to tell me the truth."

"I am! I don't know what else to tell you."

Malcolm let out a massive sigh. "That's it. No more Mr. Nice Guy. Until you start talking, your raise is being revoked and you're going back to your original salary."

"But—"

"But nothing. The next thing out of your mouth better

be you giving me a confession about this note."

Maria struggled to keep the tears from cresting her eyelids. Her fight-or-flight response raced in overdrive as she couldn't think straight. There was a thin line between love and hate, but at this moment, the opposing emotions teetering the line for Maria were fear and anger, and the pendulum quickly swung in anger's direction.

Her face grew hot with rage, tired of being strung along like a puppet on a string, controlled by promises of money. At that instant, she regretted ever going back into his office and accepting his crooked deal for a raise.

She gritted her teeth and peered at Malcolm with squinted eyes. "*No mas.*"

"Excuse me?"

She reached into her bag and grabbed her work ID. She extended her arm.

"What's this for?"

"As they say in my country, *dejo*!" She dropped the ID to the ground.

"Are you quitting on me?" he asked as he tilted his head down, following the ID as it hit the ground.

Maria immediately focused on the sheet of paper that Malcolm continued to hold in his hand. During his moment of distraction, while watching her ID hit the ground, she reached out and snatched the paper from his hand, throwing it onto the passenger seat. Then she quickly shifted the car in reverse, her tires kicking up a puff of dust in her haste to leave.

"Hey, what the hell are you doing?" he yelled as a

cloud of dust briefly enveloped his massive frame.

Maria put the car in drive and peeled away from the parking lot, listening to Malcolm's inaudible screams of defiance until they eventually faded. *Now how does it feel to be choking on a cloud of dust?*

She pulled out onto the main road, feeling like the getaway driver of a massive bank heist, and no doubt now considered an outlaw in the eyes of Malcolm.

# Chapter 17

Jace felt a nudge on his shoulder. He turned over, squinting through his heavy eyelids to see Sarah sitting up in bed.

"Did you hear that?"

"Huh?" he said, still halfway between consciousness and his personal dream world.

"There it is again."

He rubbed his eyes and tried to gather his senses. He listened more intently but only heard the deluge of rain pounding against the house.

"It's just the rain," he mumbled. "Go back to sleep."

He turned around, on the verge of nodding off, when he heard it, something other than the rain. His eyes shot open.

Sarah whispered, "I knew I wasn't going crazy."

He sat on the edge of the bed, listening for the unsettling creaking noise he'd heard seconds ago.

"Sounds like it's coming from downstairs," she whispered.

His eyes darted around the room. "Can't be anyone in the house because the alarm would have sounded." He looked at Sarah. "You did set the alarm before you went to bed, right?"

"No. I thought you did it," she said, her voice edged with tension.

His heart rate quickened, horrified at the possibility of an unexpected guest prowling through the house. He bent forward and reached under the bed, pulling out the second and only other option of security—an aluminum bat. "Stay here."

He shuffled his way, approaching the bedroom door, and peeked into the hallway, which showed no signs of life. He inched his way to the top of the stairs, standing silently, waiting to focus in on the sound. After a few seconds, he heard the weird noises once again.

He thought about turning on the hallway light, hoping it would scare the intruder away, but he didn't want to announce his presence.

He gripped the bat and made his way down the stairs, one step at a time. He descended the stairs far enough to peek down the hallway and into the kitchen. Although the lights were out, the streetlamp outside illuminated the hallway, just enough to spot someone's shadow disappearing into the kitchen.

Jace's palms grew clammy, maintaining a vice-like grip on the bat's rubber handle. He was deathly afraid of guns, though this would have been a great time to have one.

He peeked into the hallway once more before continuing to the foot of the stairs. As he slowly put his weight on the last step, he disturbed a squeaky floor joist, letting out a sound loud enough for the intruder to possibly hear.

In a panic, he tiptoed his way into the living room, hiding behind the sofa. He peeked beyond the sofa and spotted the intruder standing in the hallway near the steps. The person remained motionless, facing the living room. Jace had no doubt in his mind the intruder had heard him.

The shadowy figure walked into the living room, about ten feet away from him. The person seemed oblivious to him hiding behind the sofa. If he was going to do something, this was his chance.

With all the courage he could muster, he jumped out from behind the sofa and tackled the mysterious figure. He wrestled the intruder to the ground and grabbed the person by the neck. He raised the bat, ready to strike.

"Dad—wait!"

Jace's act of aggression took a sudden detour.

"Ryan? What the hell are you doing?"

"I heard some noises," Ryan said, his chest violently moving up and down.

Jace focused his eyes on Ryan, who was laying on the floor, helpless, with nothing to defend himself.

"What were you going to do if it was an intruder? Scare them off with bad language?" He helped Ryan off the floor before hearing the creaking noise once again.

They both froze, their eyes transfixed with horror upon realizing neither of them had been the source of the noises.

"Sounds like it's coming from the basement," Ryan whispered.

Jace gripped the bat once more as they both edged their way to the top of the basement stairs. He flicked on the light switch, listening out for any sudden movement. He figured, if somebody was there, they would have scurried away from the light.

They slowly descended the stairs. Outside of a few remaining unpacked boxes in the basement corner, an intruder would not have many places to hide.

Jace leaned forward, peeking in the middle of the basement to make sure no one was standing out in the open. With nobody in sight, he focused his attention on the three boxes in the corner. Two of them were pushed up against the wall; the third stuck out about three feet from the wall, making it a perfect place for someone to hide behind.

Jace looked around and spotted a pair of Ryan's sneakers in the corner of the floor. He reached, grabbing one, ready to launch it by the box. He carefully aimed in the direction of the boxes, waving his arm back and forth, mimicking the motion of throwing a dart. He released the sneaker as it hurtled toward the box. A soft crash resounded from the corner. He listened for any further movement, but it remained quiet.

He figured the space was only large enough to fit one person and, with Ryan by his side, they had the person outnumbered. Of course, if the person brandished a weapon, that would even things out.

Jace looked at Ryan as he motioned to charge the box on three. Jace raised his hand in the air, counting down. They rushed the box, Jace wielding the bat like a madman with Ryan following close behind. Jace swung the bat with all his might. A large thud followed, and his intended victim turned out to be the old sneaker he had thrown.

"So . . . if there's nobody down here, what was making

that noise?" Ryan asked.

Jace scanned the room further. He focused in on the wall by the washer and dryer, containing several cracks branching out in no particular pattern. He pressed his fingers against the wall, feeling for any soft spots. *Maybe a possible water leak?* He walked behind the water heater, shutting off the water valve for precautionary measures. The creaking noise persisted off and on as Jace attempted to locate the source. It appeared to be coming from beyond the walls.

"I heard of a new house settling, but this is ridiculous," he said.

He struggled to remember if some of these cracks had formed before this evening. He'd been in the basement numerous times to unpack and didn't recall the condition of the walls at that time.

He panned around, viewing the other walls, which showed no signs of damage.

He turned to Ryan. "Go get the camera."

Minutes later, Ryan returned and handed the digital camera to Jace, who proceeded to take pictures.

"Someone's got a lot of explaining to do," he said, intending to pay Malcolm a visit.

*****

The following morning, Jace peeked out the bedroom window, expecting to see the house floating on a river of water. He was elated to find no flooding in the backyard, but something else did concern him by the edge of the lake.

The torrential rains from the last twenty-four hours had

increased the water volume in the lake, causing it to rise, spilling over onto the edge of the property line. At one time, the wooden dock stood several feet above the lake, but it was now partially submerged in the murky water.

Jace looked on with concern. He still hadn't heard from anyone regarding the lake that now encroached on his property.

He grabbed the digital camera, taking several more pictures.

***

Jace arrived at the realty office during the early afternoon. He stepped out of the car and meandered around several areas of mud.

As he stepped around the soft soil, he spotted a small metal object protruding from the earth. He kneeled and extracted the object, shaking off the excess mud, revealing a metal clip with a work ID attached. It showed a familiar female smiling. He carried the ID into the office, intending to return it to the rightful owner.

"How can I help you?" a woman sitting at the front desk asked.

"I was looking for . . ." He paused, looking at the ID. "Maria Ortiz."

"You mean the woman who normally sits here? She's not here now. I'm just filling in."

"Do you know when she'll be back?"

"You need to talk to the boss about that."

Jace slipped the ID into his blazer pocket.

"Is Malcolm available?"

"Unless you have an appointment, he won't be available for most of the day."

"It's important I speak with him."

"Sorry, sir. I can take a message and have him get back to you."

Jace pulled the camera from his pocket. "Do you mind if I show you something?"

She shrugged.

He pulled up the pictures and scrolled through the photos on the minuscule screen. "Have you ever seen a new house look like this?"

The woman glanced over the pictures. "Hard to tell looking at this small screen. What am I looking at?"

"These are cracks that suddenly appeared on my basement walls last night."

"Okay, sir, I don't know what you want me to tell you."

"How about letting me see Malcolm so I can show him."

"Sorry, I've been instructed to take messages. I can't disturb him now."

Jace rested both hands on the desk and leaned forward. "Look. I'm on my lunch break. I don't have much time to waste. To make a long story short, I purchased a home from Malcolm a month ago and, as you can see from the pictures, I'm having some issues with the house. Now with that said, I suggest you call his office and tell him Jace is here to see him, or I'll just march back there and invite myself into his office."

The woman blinked with surprise before fumbling for the receiver.

A minute later, Malcolm appeared. "This better be a good one, Jace, because I really don't have time to chat now."

Jace turned the digital camera screen in Malcolm's direction. "Here take a look at these pictures."

Malcolm squinted, looking at the screen. "So, what's the problem?"

"I'm no structural engineer, but I find it very concerning my basement walls look this way after only living in the house for one week."

Malcolm motioned his hand for Jace to follow him to his office. As Jace followed, Malcolm closed the door behind him.

"Do you want to see more pictures? I have plenty to show."

"No need for me to see anymore. It's just a natural occurrence with a new house."

"The walls damn sure shouldn't look like that after only a week of living there."

"I guess you failed to realize the construction of your house was completed months before you arrived. It's not out of the ordinary for a new house to start settling within that timeframe."

"Not when most of these cracks appeared last night during the rain storm."

"Impossible."

"I figured you wouldn't believe me, which is why I

took the pictures."

Malcolm eyed the pictures once more. "They were probably there before last night and you just didn't notice."

"Believe me; I would have noticed. I've been in the basement every day since we moved to unpack boxes, and I don't recall seeing anything like this."

"I don't know what else to tell ya. Monitor the situation and let me know if it gets any worse."

Jace threw up his hands in disgust. "That's it? You gonna push me out the door without any help or suggestions?"

"What else do you want me to do? I can give you a recommendation for a structural engineer to inspect your house, but I think that's a waste." He paused for a second. "If you're looking for a suggestion, how about this one? Give it a few more months for the house to completely settle then patch up the cracks with some joint compound and paint over it. Problem solved. Now, if you'll excuse me, I have some work to finish."

"You think this is some kind of joke? For all we know, my house could be on the verge of collapsing, and this is the sorry-ass suggestion you give me?"

"Let me tell ya something. I've been in this business for over twenty years and have seen it all. Believe me when I tell you these houses at Granwin were built from the finest quality material. Barring an earthquake or some other natural disaster, these houses will be standing for the next five generations."

Jace laughed sarcastically. "So you want me to ignore

what happened last night? Sweep it under the carpet and forget about it?"

"I think that's a great idea, because you wasted enough of my time now."

Jace took a deep breath and gathered himself before speaking. "You're disappointing me. I would have thought, after all these years in business, you would know how to treat your customers."

"I certainly didn't build my business by treating my customers badly."

"And you won't keep this business much longer by treating customers the way you just treated me."

Jace turned without saying another word and exited the office.

# Chapter 18

A few days had passed since Maria had relinquished her duties at the realty office. A part of her regretted that daring move, but she couldn't morally live with the fact of selling her soul to Malcolm and being constantly manipulated by the promises of money. With no severance coming in, and the real possibility of not qualifying for unemployment insurance, the need to inject some type of cash flow into her bank account became critically real. This need for money was even more important considering her time working at the realty office, and the short stint with the pay raise, had done little to improve her financial circumstances. She was already behind on her rent and utility bills and received several threatening shut-off notices from the electric company. Even worse, if she didn't come up with enough money to pay her back rent, the threat of being evicted loomed large.

She entertained the idea of delving into the world of payday loans but knew that was an absolute death trap for anyone trying to dig themselves out of a financial crater. Her financial situation teetered on disaster, yet she could only take it one day at a time and hope the storm clouds would eventually part, revealing a rainbow leading her to a pot of gold.

After days of desperately searching, she successfully landed a job as a cashier at a newly opened gas mart. The pay was minimal, but having the option of starting work immediately without much experience necessary sealed the deal.

The gas mart was located off Route 66, between Chelwood Park and Downtown Albuquerque. A twenty-foot high neon sign stood at the entrance of the station reading, "*Gas-n-Go*." Two self-service islands, along with an air pump station, were located on the outside. Within the gas mart, there were four aisles containing an array of merchandise—potato chips, cookies, candy, over-the-counter medicines, magazines, and other novelty items. In the back of the store, against the wall, stood a refrigerated beverage section. Up front, behind the cashier, there were several shelves containing cigarette and other tobacco-related products, along with a carousel of scratch-off lotto tickets.

Her first day on the job didn't come stress-free, as expected, attempting to learn how to operate the register and, at the same time, remember the store policies and procedures.

Late in the afternoon, she finished with a few customers, roughly fifteen minutes before her shift ended. She had shadowed a seasoned employee for most of the day and was now left alone for the last few minutes of her shift. The person working the next shift had not arrived yet.

She peered through the window—no cars in sight. The gas pumps were all empty of vehicular traffic, and the store was eerily quiet. Only the soft humming sound from the refrigerated soda section could be heard.

When her shift had ended, there was still no sign of her coworker. She had been instructed during the brief orientation to wait until her shift relief arrived before departing. She kneeled behind the counter to retrieve her personal belongings, patiently waiting.

As she crouched, she heard the squeaking of brakes out front. Then she heard the familiar door chimes, notifying her someone had entered the store. She finished packing her bags and rose to her feet, eyeing a man with his back turned in one of the aisles. Then she stared out the window at a black pickup truck parked out front. Her heart throbbed uncontrollably, realizing who it might be. She focused on the license plate for confirmation, which immediately dropped her in the middle of a frightening scenario.

The customer turned around, prompting her to instinctively hide behind the counter. She never thought, or at least hoped, she would see Malcolm again. And to make things worse, she was alone in the store with him.

To the left of her, the front counter bumped up against the wall, making it impossible for customers to see behind it unless they purposely leaned over. However, in sharp contrast, the view to the right of the counter was wide open. Any customer standing in the first aisle would have a clear view behind the counter.

She followed the rhythmic sounds of his footsteps, tapping across the tiled floor. She heard one of the doors to the refrigerated soda section open and close. Seconds later, she heard the ruffle of potato chip bags, located in the second aisle. She was all but certain he would walk into the first aisle and see her cowering behind the counter.

She wiped the sweat off her forehead, anticipating what to do. She knew she couldn't stay hidden behind the counter forever. So, she said a quick prayer, seconds away from facing her worst fear when she heard the door chimes.

"Good afternoon, sir. I'll be with you in one minute," a young lady said.

A tidal wave of elation flowed through Maria's body, ecstatic to hear what appeared to be her shift relief.

The young lady came around the counter and flinched at the sight of Maria resting on her knees. Maria made eye contact with her while making a gesture to be quiet. The young lady did her best to stay calm, acting like there was nothing out of the ordinary.

Maria remained hidden while the young lady rang up Malcolm's items.

"Thank ya very much. You have a good evening," he said.

Maria shuttered at the sound of his voice.

She heard the door chimes, indicating he left. She glanced up at the woman with a sheepish grin.

"It's a long story. Thanks for keeping things quiet."

"Okay," the young lady said, shrugging in confusion.

Maria peeked to make sure his truck had departed before grabbing her belongings and bolting out the back door.

# Chapter 19

Jace reached into the closet, sifting through his tie rack, searching for one that matched his navy blue khakis and white-collared shirt to complete his business attire for the day. He grabbed a white and blue tie, patterned into a collage of interesting shapes. He wrapped it around his neck and proceeded to tie the knot under his collar before suddenly stopping to rub his back, which had developed an annoying itch over the past couple of days.

He turned to grab his shoes, resting by the foot of the bed. He flinched, not expecting to see Sarah standing in the doorway. With her arms folded, she unleashed a wicked stare.

"We need to talk," she said.

"About what? Is everything okay?"

"No." She gritted her teeth, and opened her folded arms, revealing Maria's work ID.

A sudden rush of adrenaline heated Jace's internal core upon being reminded of the ID he had forgotten to leave at the office. He couldn't understand the cruel swing of fate that would leave his wife of all people to find the ID.

"Where did you find that?"

"It fell out your blazer pocket."

"Oh."

There were days when absolutely nothing went right, leaving Murphy's Law in complete control. This unexpected turn of events indicated Murphy had Jace by the neck, with no plans of letting him go. He found himself hemmed in a corner, and although he had nothing to hide, convincing Sarah at this point would be next to impossible. He had to choose his words carefully.

"Well? What do you have to say for yourself?"

"I found it in the parking lot at the realty office yesterday."

"Don't give me that bull. You expect me to believe that?"

"It's true. I was going to give it back to her, but I found out she wasn't in for the day, so I kept it."

"Why didn't you just leave it with someone at the office?"

"I . . . I don't know. I was going to . . . I guess I became distracted when I started talking." He winced after making that comment, which lacked any semblance of confidence and credibility. It was flimsy at best and just set him up for an all-out assault.

"I'm not falling for it this time. You did a good job fooling me with the note, but this is a different story," she said as her eyes flooded with moisture. She walked over to the bed before sitting down and wiping her tears.

He looked up at the ceiling and sighed. "What do I need to do to show you I'm not cheating on you? Just name it and I'll do it?"

"It's too late for that now. You might as well come clean and tell me everything."

He sat down next to her, attempting to plead his case

further. "There's nothing to tell because nothing is going on."

She turned her back and remained silent. Jace sat in disbelief. A part of him wanted to laugh at these outlandish accusations, but he was mindful of Sarah's fragile state of mind and suppressed the urge.

He placed his right hand on her shoulder. She quickly stood to distance herself from his touch.

"Please believe me when I tell you I'm not seeing this woman. And if you don't believe me, I can pick you up during my lunch break, and we can take a drive to the office to see for yourself."

She remained quiet and strolled over to the closet, putting on a pair of sneakers. He was distracted for a moment upon hearing Ava screaming and banging on a door in the hallway, most likely another fight with Ryan.

He turned his attention back to Sarah. "Where you going?"

"Why should you care?" She exited the room.

He followed her into the hallway as Ava pounded on the bathroom door, screaming at Ryan. He watched as Sarah ignored the chaos and walked downstairs.

He closed his eyes, shaking his head. "Can I please catch a break this morning?" he mumbled.

He approached Ava. "What's going on out here?"

"Ryan won't let me in the bathroom," she said with her face flustered.

"Why don't you use the bathroom downstairs?"

"You don't understand. He's been in there for at least

an hour. He can't hog the bathroom like that."

He knocked. "Hey, Ryan, what you doing in there?"

"Nothing," he replied.

"It takes you an hour to do nothing?"

"Just gimme a minute."

He heard the vanity cabinet close and some shuffling of paper. A minute later, Ryan opened the door wearing a blue turtleneck and faded blue jeans.

Jace gave him a slow, appraising glance. "Don't you think it's a little warm for a turtle neck?"

Ryan shrugged and walked past without saying a word.

Ava held her nose and said, "Are you using rubbing alcohol for cologne?"

Jace sniffed, caught off guard by the overpowering scent, as well.

Ava stepped into the bathroom, but Jace grabbed her by the arm. "Wait."

He gently pulled her back into the hallway before stepping into the bathroom. He opened the medicine cabinet and noticed the fairly new bottle of rubbing alcohol was almost depleted. An inch of liquid was all that remained. He focused on the garbage can, filled to the brim with tissues, cotton balls, and several Band-Aid wrappers scattered about.

He exited the bathroom, giving Ava the okay to proceed. Then he immediately walked into Ryan's room where his son sat, hunched over, putting on his sneakers.

"You wanna tell me what's going on?"

"Nothing, just getting ready for school."

"I wasn't born yesterday. What were you doing in the bathroom?"

"I was just taking a shower and getting dressed."

"And what about the alcohol?"

Ryan shrugged. "Just taking care of a few bumps and bruises."

"And how did you get hurt?"

"I don't remember. Happens all the time when I'm playing at school. I'll be fine. Can I eat breakfast now? Don't wanna miss the school bus."

As Ryan walked by, Jace grabbed him by the arm. Ryan winced with pain, although Jace held on with a delicate grip.

"What's the matter with you? I'm barely holding you."

Ryan squirmed in an apparent attempt to withstand some type of pain.

"I'm okay. You just grabbed one of my cuts."

"Don't think you're doing yourself a favor by hiding something from me. The truth will come out sooner or later."

Ryan sighed. "Can I please eat now?"

Jace released his grip, watching as Ryan ran downstairs.

He covered his face with his hand, gently rubbing his forehead. He hadn't even begun his commute to work and stress had inundated his morning routine.

After walking back into the bedroom to grab a few items needed for work, he took a peek at his watch, realizing he didn't have much time left for breakfast.

He hurried downstairs and poured a half-cup of coffee. Ryan and Ava were at the table eating. Several boxes of cereal were stacked in the middle of the table, like the Great Wall of China, blocking off their view of one another.

Jace scanned the kitchen and into the living room. "Where's your mother?"

"I don't know," Ava replied.

He shrugged, thinking maybe it was a good idea he didn't see her until after work. Hopefully, by then, she would be more relaxed, and he could attempt to plead his case once more.

"You two gonna be late for the bus. I can drop you off at the bus stop since I'm already late."

He gulped down the last bit of coffee and grabbed his laptop case. He opened the door to the garage and lurched backward in shock. He ran into the kitchen and looked at the key ring holder hanging on the wall. The spare car key had vanished, along with the Camry.

# Chapter 20

Sarah gripped the steering wheel with a flow of hot lava running through her veins. She sped along with no plan in mind, no course of action, only acting on instinct. She still hung on to a smidgen of hope that Jace was telling the truth, yet even with her insecurities pushed aside, she couldn't help but believe infidelity had intruded upon their marriage.

She was determined to meet the woman who had dared trespass into her family relations and had no inkling of how she would react once face-to-face with this home wrecker.

It hadn't always been this way for her. This jealousy was spawned from her mother's tumultuous marriage. A marriage riddled with infidelity on the part of her father. Her trust in men had become severely impaired ever since she and her mother had fled to St. Louis to escape his cheating ways. And if you threw in her first engagement, which ended in disaster after her so-called fiancé slept with her so-called best friend, then you had a woman who was rightfully on edge and truly believed her actions were well warranted. She did her best to control her jealous rages that tended to pop up from time to time, but in this instant, she was past the point of no return. These jealous demons had surged to the forefront, becoming the driving force for her rash behavior.

She glanced at the clock on the dashboard. Jace would

normally be halfway into his commute, but she wasn't the least bit concerned about how he would get there today. In her eyes, this was only the beginning of his problems, and a small price to pay for shattering her trust.

She peered up the road as the realty office came into view. She didn't recall what time the office opened; she doubted it was this early.

She pulled onto the shoulder of the road, roughly fifty feet from the entrance, and waited. She remained still with her senses heightened, like a lion in the bush, waiting to pounce on its prey. Her anxiety level intensified with each car that sped past, waiting for the first one to pull into the office parking lot. After waiting ten minutes, a truck from the opposite direction slowed and turned in. She squinted and focused on Malcolm's black Silverado, driving along a narrow path to the right of the office and eventually disappearing beyond the side of the building. She remained still, waiting patiently for more employees to arrive, with a special interest in one of the female persuasion.

After several more minutes, she leaned forward, spotting another vehicle entering the lot. A female stepped out and walked into the office.

She reached for the woman's ID kept in the center console and focused on the picture to ensure no problems with mistaken identity. She also had a decent idea of what this woman looked like after she had seen her during their initial tour with Sabrina.

She eased back into the seat, once realizing her intended target had still not arrived.

A half-hour passed with more employees arriving, none matching the woman's description. Her anxiety level had suddenly increased, making it impossible for her to sit still any longer. She shifted in gear and entered the dirt-covered lot. She parked in front of the entrance, a closed sign still posted across the door. She sat, confused, with no idea how to approach the situation.

Minutes later, the door swung open and Malcolm stepped out, flipping the sign for the start of another business day. She stared, waiting for him to notice her sitting in the car. They made eye contact, and he seemed perplexed at her presence. She remained seated with the driver's side window rolled down.

He smiled and said, "What do I owe this pleasure so early in the morning, Mrs. Valentine?" Before she could respond, he continued, "Let me guess. Jace told you about our little spat and you've come to straighten out the mess?"

"Something like that," she said, playing along with his assumption.

Another car rolled up to the far right. She craned her neck toward the vehicle, eyeing a female who exited the car, but this employee also didn't fit the description. She turned her attention back to Malcolm.

He raised both hands, palms facing upward as if to ward off a punch. "Before you jump out to defend your husband, I want you to know I'm just as eager to get to the bottom of what's going on with the issues being experienced in the community. I'll tell you this much, as far as the lake, there were some delays in getting the initial water test results back and additional testing is necessary. You and the rest of the residents in the community will most certainly be notified once the final results are in."

Sarah's attention became distracted once more by another car pulling up in the lot. Malcolm greeted a male employee.

He looked at Sarah with one eyebrow raised. "Are you looking for anyone in particular?"

She reached into the center console, grabbing the work ID. She stretched out her hand. "I was going to return this."

"Where did you get that from?"

"Jace said he found it in the parking lot yesterday when he came to visit you."

Malcolm hesitated. "All I can tell you is she no longer works here. She just up and quit earlier this week."

Sarah's eyes narrowed speculatively. "So, how could Jace have found this yesterday in the parking lot like he claimed?"

"Can't say for certain, but I don't think that's any of my business."

Her anxiety took hold again as a number of scenarios crossed her mind. She pointed to the ID. "Do you know where I can find her?"

"Sorry, couldn't tell ya." He paused. "Even if I did, I don't think I would tell by the look in your eyes. You don't appear to have anything pleasant to say to her."

Sarah gritted her teeth. "You're damn right. And she ain't the only one in trouble."

# Chapter 21

Maria sat on the sofa, in near darkness. Only the soft flickering light from the candle on the coffee table prevented her from being lost in total blackness. The threat had suddenly become real and her electric service had been disconnected.

A soft melody with occasional static emanated from a battery-operated radio on the sofa next to her. She sighed, looking into the dark space before her. Every so often, a car would pass by outside, the headlights filtering through the blinds, reflecting off the walls for a second before submerging her in darkness once more.

Although frustrated with the situation, she was grateful to have a roof over her head. However, even that was in jeopardy unless she came up with extra funds to pay her back rent in two weeks. She offered to do a double shift at the gas mart but had been denied. She had no other choice but to look for a second job, or a better-paying one.

She flicked on the flashlight resting in her lap. With no access to the internet, the job search suddenly became more challenging; her only outlet was the employment section of the newspaper.

She viewed a few ads, placing a star next to a couple of possibilities, yet they were few and far between, especially with no college degree under her belt. She ran her finger down the paper, pointing to an ad for exotic dancers.

Although far from conceited or vain, she figured, with her looks, she could make some fast money. However, she hesitated, unsure if she could handle the humiliation of shaking her God-given assets in front of a room full of men. Then again, if it paid the light bill and kept a roof over her head, it might be worth the humiliation.

With her cell phone out of service, she grabbed the landline, hoping and praying a dial tone still existed. The continuous monotone sound on the other end indicated her wish had been granted.

After a few rings, a deep voice echoed on the other end, saying hello. She hesitated, her mind wanting to respond, but her mouth wouldn't move. She quickly slammed the phone to the receiver.

She sighed, leaning her head back and closing her eyes, which was visually not much different from having them open. She thought of happier times to help ease the stress as an image of her childhood village came to mind. She remembered, as a child, sitting on wooden stools, shucking corn with her mother to prepare for the evening meal, while her father strolled in the fields, picking the daily harvest. Next came a walk to the water pump to fill several buckets for laundry and bathing. She had felt a sense of great accomplishment each day for assisting the family in their daily routines. Her chores had been a heavy burden but rewarding at the same time. As her mother use to say, *su trabajo nunca es hecho hasta que usted piense en una nueva tarea.* Simply translated, *your current job is never done until you think of a new task.*

She reluctantly faded back to reality. She opened her eyes, the dark room acting as a blunt reminder of her situation. She regretted not knowing anyone in the area who could help.

Just as quickly as this thought had crossed her mind, she took heed of her mother's advice and thought of another task. She pointed the flashlight in front of her, using it as a guide, reaching into her tote bag and pulling out a sheet of paper.

# Chapter 22

On weary heels, Sabrina ambled down the aisles at the local supermarket. Another eight-hour day of number crunching and manipulating spreadsheets were enough to make anyone sluggish. Not to mention her enthusiasm for this accounting job had disappeared some years ago, at about the same time she'd realized her paycheck wasn't enough to support her spending habits. She labored through each day, biding her time for a promotion or a new opportunity with another company—whichever came first. In the meantime, her full-time position coupled with the part-time tour guide gig was enough to pay the bills and allow for a night on the town every once in a while.

She walked into the produce section, pushing a squeaky shopping cart. She scanned the mountain of cantaloupes piled on the stand, squeezing each one to determine its ripeness.

Her attention shifted, disrupted by a familiar voice and the overpowering scent of Old Spice after-shave. She looked over, into the next aisle, as a man and woman conversed. With the gentleman's back partially turned, she caught enough of his side profile to determine it was her ex-husband. *That bastard.*

She glanced at the young lady, who displayed a wide smile, apparently enjoying the conversation.

"Don't fall for his tired-ass pickup lines," she

whispered.

She stood in disbelief with several thoughts consuming her.

The prince had turned into a frog. It had been a few years since she had last seen him, but time had been more of an enemy than a friend to him. His once neatly trimmed black hair, with tight hairline edges, had evolved into a barren landscape as if all his hair follicles had quit working. Sabrina could tell this was definitely the result of a botched head shave from the nicks scattered over his exposed scalp. She analyzed further, not realizing how oddly shaped his head truly appeared with no hair to camouflage the deformity.

She glanced down at his midsection, which had developed a small pouch, making him appear three months pregnant. She initially smiled, thankful they were now divorced and she didn't have to be seen with this shell of a man out in public. But her smile eventually leveled off, interrupted by a fire brewing in her gut. *How could this sweet young lady be attracted to this no-frills, no-charm, no-style, no-good-for-nothing man?*

The fire inside grew, thinking about all the nonsense he had put her through during their brief marriage.

On impulse, she placed her hand around the biggest cantaloupe she could find, with the urge to fire it at this sorry excuse for a man, before coming to her senses and suppressing the tempting thought.

Seconds later, her cell phone chimed with a loud melody. Several customers in the area turned their heads, including Mr. Old Spice.

She instinctively ducked behind the fruit stand, having no interest in being seen by him at that moment. She reached for the cell in her bag and shut off the ringer without looking at the caller ID. She refused to answer, for fear he would hear her voice. She pretended to fix her shoe then quickly rose to her feet with her back turned. With stealth-like precision, she darted into another aisle, out of sight, hoping he didn't notice her.

Her list of grocery items suddenly became shorter. She promptly grabbed her necessities and rushed to the checkout counter.

While waiting for the items to be scanned, her eyes darted around the area. She became impatient with the clerk who moved with sloth-like agility.

"Can you please speed it up? I'm kind of in a hurry."

She eventually grabbed the bags and shuffled her way out of the store. She stuffed the groceries in the trunk before sitting in the car and pulling out her cell. An envelope appeared on the minuscule screen, informing her a message had been left.

*"Hi. My name is Maria. Not sure if you remember, but you came by the realty office and left a note with your contact information. When you get a chance, can you please call me? I was wondering if you could help me with something."*

She left a callback number and the voicemail ended.

Sabrina quickly redialed the number and received a

busy signal. "Damn!"

She looked up to see her ex approaching a car on the other side of the lot. Her nostrils flared in anger.

"That fool has been out of my life for a few years and somehow still finds a way to screw up my plans."

She drove off with every intention of calling Maria back once she arrived home.

# **Chapter 23**

Jace's highly anticipated return home to see Sarah had finally arrived, but at this moment, he wasn't there to express his terms of endearment. He had tried reaching her by phone all day, but she wouldn't pick up. He now stood only minutes away from confronting her face-to-face.

The taxi pulled into Granwin Estates, his anxiety increasing as he neared the house. His blood pressure spiked after paying the forty-dollar fare, which could have simply been avoided if Sarah hadn't pulled her disappearing act this morning.

He unloosened his tie and marched up to the door, swinging it open to an unusually quiet house. He walked down the hall, following the light that emanated from the kitchen. His target had been found, sitting on a stool by the kitchen island. She turned with her arms folded and her face contorted into an angry mess.

*The nerve of her to look at me like I did something wrong.*

"Where are the kids?" he asked, not wanting them to hear the inevitable screaming.

"Upstairs."

A brief pause followed. He did his best to harness his anger and not jump down her throat immediately.

"Did you have fun taking the car for a joy ride this morning?"

"I was just listening to your advice and paid a visit to the realty office."

Jace shook his head and let out a massive exhale. "Guess you forgot the fact we only have one car—my only method of transportation to work, by the way. Which meant I needed to call a taxi to and from work and spend some unnecessary money because of your spontaneous joy ride. And I can't begin to tell you how bad it looks for someone to be late for work, especially during their first week on the job." He leaned forward, putting both hands on the edge of the kitchen island. "Also, if you hadn't noticed this morning, I had to play referee to another Ryan and Ava war without any help from you, which completely slowed down our morning routine, and because of your joy ride, I didn't have a car to drop them off at the school bus. This meant they needed to run to the bus stop and barely made it on time."

Jace paused to suck in some air and to also see if any of this was getting through to Sarah.

"Does any of this bother you? Do you feel any hint of remorse?"

Sarah nodded. "Yes, I do feel bad for the kids."

"But not me?" Jace said, pointing to himself.

"Why should I? Don't turn this around like you're the victim in this story. Since when is the cheating spouse the victim?"

Jace gritted his teeth and closed his eyes to harness the anger that threatened to choke out all rational thoughts in his head. Then he turned away from the table and took a few strides to figure out a different angle of attack.

He turned back around. "So, what did you find out during your visit to the office?"

"I find it interesting that you claimed you found this ID in the parking lot yesterday, but Malcolm told me this woman up and quit last week."

"So, what does that have to do with me finding the ID in the parking lot yesterday? It obviously was lost and somehow ended up on the ground."

"Oh, and it was just a coincidence that you found it, forgot to return it before you left the office, and it stayed in your pocket until I found it?"

Jace held in a laugh as Sarah's attempt at sarcasm turned out to be the spot-on truth. "Yes, that's exactly what happened."

"Sorry, Jace, I'm just not buying that story. I can't believe you convinced me to relocate," she said, and then paused before standing. "Uprooted our family all the way out here"—she paused again, tugging at her wedding band—"and have the damn nerve to cheat on me after only one week of moving to this strange city." She wiped the tears from her eyes and launched the wedding band at Jace.

He watched as the wedding band bounced off his chest and fell to the kitchen floor, coming to a rest by his right foot.

He felt like a suspect put on trial and sent to jail for a crime he didn't commit.

With desperation breathing down his neck, Jace had to think outside the box to convince Sarah of his innocence. In the past, he'd always approached this subject with caution, fully aware of her sensitivity, but the caution light had just turned green, and it was time to pull out the ace in the hole, although anger wasn't his weapon of choice.

He sighed, picking up the ring off the floor. "I'll admit to cheating once in my lifetime. It was fourteen years ago, a year before we got married. A day I'll never forget. It was my mother's birthday and, as always, I paid a visit to her gravesite. I remember it was raining that day. And up until that point, I followed a ritual each year I came to visit her. I would kneel in front of her plot, toss a single red rose, and tell her she was the only woman of substance in my life."

He approached the island and gently placed the ring in front of Sarah. "Well, things changed on that day. I kneeled before her with a confession. I told her I found another woman. I told her about this amazing young lady who I was dating for the past year. She was like no other woman I'd met before. And this time, I was holding two red roses.

"I tossed them both on the grave and asked my mother for a sign to let me know if she approved of this new woman in my life." Jace blinked a few times to hold in the moisture accumulating in his eyes. "As God is my witness, the moment I threw the roses on the grave, the rain stopped and the sun peeked through. The next day, I bought a ring," he said while pointing to the ring on the table. "And with this ring, I proposed to the new woman in my life. She accepted, and the rest is history."

Sarah remained quiet, sitting with a sullen look on her face, no doubt touched by the story.

He placed his hand under her chin. "Now, if you think I'm going to cheat on the woman my mother gave my blessings to marry, then you really don't know your husband."

Sarah wiped the tears from her cheeks and ran out of the room without saying a word.

# **Chapter 24**

The next morning, Jace turned on his side, still half-asleep but bothered by a horrible itch that continued to persist around his back. He attempted to bend his arm behind him in an attempt to scratch, but the most irritated part of his back was out of reach.

He forced his eyes open, squinting at the striped rays of sunlight filtering in from the window blinds. He sat up, bending his arm behind him once more to respond to that annoying itch.

He turned to look for Sarah, but the bed was empty. As far as he was concerned, she'd been non-existent since their confrontation last night. She hadn't said a word to him, let alone looked him in the eye since that time. He surmised his story had an impact on her emotionally, and he regretted not telling her sooner, especially if he knew this would be the wake-up call she needed to conquer her jealous demons.

The irresistible itch suddenly returned and interrupted his moment of retrospect. He ran his hands across the bedspread, feeling for any foreign particles. For a moment, he thought about bed bugs, but the mattress was only a month old, and the sheets had just been washed.

He shrugged and walked to the bathroom, intent on taking a hot shower to hopefully ease the irritation. He lathered up and let the hot water spray against his back. His efforts helped momentarily as the itching subsided, yet after stepping out of the shower to dry off, the itching turned into a slight burning sensation.

He stood in front of the vanity mirror, wiping off the fog with a tissue. With his back turned, he craned his neck around to catch a glimpse.

"What the hell?"

With his vision slightly impaired by the condensation, it was clear enough for him to see several red blotches scattered over his back.

He reached for some powder, pouring it generously on his back. The powder offered some relief, which was the best he could do until he figured out how the marks had appeared and what he needed to do to get rid of them. He proceeded to get dressed and made his way into the kitchen for a weekend breakfast.

He entered to see Sarah and the children engulfing pancakes and bacon.

"Good morning," he said.

He received a less-than-enthusiastic greeting from the children and absolutely no response from Sarah.

He ignored her silence, already coming to terms she would speak to him when she was ready. He sat and piled his plate with a stack of pancakes.

"Does anybody have any plans this weekend?" he asked, gently pushing his back against the chair to scratch the itch that persisted.

"It would be great if we could throw some things on the grill, but I don't think any one of us wants to go out back today," Ryan said.

Ava grabbed her nose. "Yeah, that smell is awful."

Jace shook his head in disgust. "I would have figured they'd have the test results from the water samples by now."

"The results are delayed," Sarah mumbled.

"Excuse me?" Jace said, surprised she had actually spoken.

"I said the final test results have been delayed."

"Who told you that?"

"Malcolm. He told me yesterday at the office."

"Oh. Were you planning to tell me?"

"Yeah, but I got a little sidetracked," she said without making eye contact.

Jace shrugged and continued to eat, doing his best to ignore the urge to scratch.

He turned to Ryan. "Can you please pass the syrup?"

Ryan reached over to hand Jace the syrup, his sleeve riding a quarter of the way up his arm, revealing a red blotch, scattered just above his wrist. Jace couldn't tell if it was just a coincidence, or if Ryan had a similar rash outbreak.

Jace kept himself at ease, pretending he didn't notice. He poured the syrup, and all the while realized at once what Ryan must have been doing in the bathroom the other morning.

With his curiosity in full bloom, he pointed to Ryan. "Can I see you in the living room for a moment?"

Ryan followed him out of the kitchen.

"What happened to your wrist?"

"What are you talking 'bout?"

"I saw the marks above your wrist."

"Oh . . . that. I don't know how it got there. It's starting to go away."

"Is that why you were in the bathroom so long the other morning?"

Ryan shrugged. "Yeah. Something like that."

"Do you have these marks anywhere else on your body?"

"Kinda. On my stomach and back."

Jace's heart rate increased. "Let me see."

"Nah. I don't think you need to see."

"Yes, I do because I think I have the same problem."

"You do?" Ryan said in a high-pitched tone.

"Let me see, and I'll tell you."

Ryan peered down the hall to make sure no one was approaching. Then he lifted his shirt with Jace grimacing at the sight.

A sea of red marks were scattered around his stomach, most centered midway, running parallel to his belly button. Jace turned him around, following the patches that snaked around to his back. Ryan quickly pulled down his shirt.

"What the hell is going on? I have the same rash on my back. Do they itch?"

"Just a little. Not as bad as before."

"Did Mom change the laundry detergent?"

"I don't know."

Jace shrugged. "I wonder if Mom and Ava are having any issues with their skin? If so, then we have a bigger problem on our hands."

# Chapter 25

Sabrina looked at her itinerary for the day, with a few hours left before her tour guests arrived at the airport. She wished it were more like six hours, in the hopes of sleeping longer.

She sat up in bed, sluggish, unresponsive, and not her usual upbeat self. These were the days she dreaded the responsibilities of having a second job. Some weekends were meant for sleeping, and this was one of them.

She tugged on the shade, ushering in a sudden rush of sunlight before a soft humming resonated from the nightstand. She rushed over, picking up her cell.

"Hello?"

"Hi . . . Is this Sabrina?" a female said with a hint of an accent.

Sabrina's eyes lit up at the possibility of who this might be on the other end. "Yes, is this Maria?"

"Si . . . I mean, yes."

"I'm so glad to finally get in touch with you. I've been trying to reach you for a bit but kept getting a busy signal."

"Sorry, I've been having problems with my phone service."

An awkward silence followed before they both tried speaking at the same time.

"I'm sorry," Sabrina said. "Go ahead."

"I'm guessing you're surprised I'm calling after what

happened when you visited the realty office."

"Well, I'd always hoped you would call, but I also couldn't blame you if you didn't. I'm sure it's hard getting up the nerve to call a complete stranger in response to a note that made no sense to you."

Maria let out a timid laugh. "Yeah, I guess so."

Another moment of silence followed before anyone spoke.

"So . . . you're probably wondering what that note was all about?" Sabrina asked.

"Uh, yes, but that's not the only reason I'm calling."

"Okay, let's start with you first. What's on your mind?"

"Well . . . I really don't know where to begin. I guess I'll start by saying I don't work at the realty office anymore. I started a new job."

"That's good news . . . I hope?"

"Not really. The new job isn't what I wanted, but I couldn't be too picky since my bills need to get paid."

"I know exactly what you mean. You do what you need to do to keep a roof over your head and food on the table."

"Yes, but this new job is only temporary, and unless I find something better, it's going to be a struggle for me."

"Are you looking for help finding a new job?"

"Yes, I guess so. It's just that I feel so embarrassed to even ask a stranger, but I didn't know what else to do. I don't have any other family or friends in the area who can help."

"First of all, I must say you know how to tug on someone's heartstrings, and second, you can officially consider me your first friend in the area."

Maria laughed. "Okay."

"Now that we got that out the way, what kind of job are you looking for?"

"I can do anything you want me to do. I can be an administrative assistant, maid, or even a cook."

Sabrina laughed. "Slow down. Let me rephrase the question. What do you have the most experience doing?"

"Administrative assistant."

"Do you have an updated resume?"

"It's probably been a year since it was last updated."

"Why don't you start by emailing it to me."

"I don't have access to a computer."

"Then maybe you can mail it. I may have some positions available at my company."

"Do you know how long it will take to possibly find a job there?"

"It depends on how soon we can find an opening that fits your skills. Also, we don't know how soon we can get you an interview."

"Oh."

"Why? You don't sound too happy."

"I kind of need the job as soon as possible."

"I know that feeling," Sabrina said. "If you want to speed things up, maybe you can meet me sometime this weekend and hand me your resume."

"Okay. I like that idea."

Sabrina looked at the time, realizing she needed to get moving in preparation for her tour appointment.

"I have some business to take care of during the day. How does later this afternoon sound?"

"That may be a problem. My shift starts at four."

"Where do you work?"

"At the new Gas-n-Go on Route 66."

"That's not too far. I should be done with my business by then and can meet you there before you start your shift."

Maria cleared her throat. "You don't have to go out your way because of me."

"It's not a problem. We're friends now, and that's what friends are for. I'll meet you there before your shift starts."

# **Chapter 26**

While holding his nose, Malcolm pressed his thumb on the doorbell, waiting patiently for someone to answer. He made a conscious effort not to breathe in too deeply, for fear of getting sick from the foul odor emanating from the lake.

The door swung open as Mr. Aderlee appeared. "I'm so glad you were able to make it. Did you get a sample of the not-so-fresh air?" Mr. Aderlee asked.

"Yes. I didn't realize it was that bad. Hoping we'll have the results of the water samples soon so they can figure out the next steps in getting this lake cleaned up."

Malcolm looked around. "Where's the misses?"

"She's taking a nap. Not one of her better days."

Malcolm entered the living room populated with a montage of pictures; some on tables, others hanging on the walls. The majority were family portraits with some candid shots of special occasions scattered about. He stood wide-eyed, impressed with the display.

"You can open your own exhibit with all these pictures."

"Family is all I have now. Having these pictures keeps me in good spirits. Sometimes I'll sit in the living room and just stare at them. It puts a smile on my face. It also keeps my mind off my wife's failing health." He pointed to a black and white wedding photo. "You know our fifty-year anniversary is coming up in a few weeks."

"That's wonderful. Not too many couples can say the same," Malcolm said as he craned his neck to get a panoramic view of the massive photo display.

"Everyone looks so happy. Must have been fun growing up in a family like that. Are your children still in the area?"

"No. They all moved out of town. They have families of their own and come visit as often as they can."

Malcolm continued to stare at the pictures. After a few moments, he felt a tap on his shoulder.

"Malcolm?" Mr. Aderlee said.

Malcolm blinked, transporting himself out of his childhood horrors of the past, and into the fairy tale living room of the present. He sighed heavily. "I'm sorry. I was off in my own little world. Why don't you show me what I came here to see in the first place?"

Mr. Aderlee led him down the basement stairs and pointed to the walls. Malcolm studied the maze of hairline cracks scattered about the wall. The cracks varied in length, covering a generous portion of the wall from carpet to ceiling. He noticed the other walls showed similar damage.

"When did you first notice these cracks?"

"It happened recently. I would say after the rainstorm we had last week."

"Are you sure they weren't there before that?"

"Yes, I'm almost certain. I know I'm an old man and my eyesight is not all that great, but I'm sure I would have noticed these cracks if they were there before. I don't know if the rain is causing the problem, but thankfully, it hasn't rained since then."

Malcolm pressed his thumb against a few of the cracks as several pieces of paint flaked off and fell to the carpet. He bent down to pick up the paint chips and remained on one knee in deep thought.

"Do you mind if I take pictures?" He reached into a duffle bag strapped around his left shoulder and pulled out a digital camera, snapping several pictures. "How about we also take a look at your backyard?"

Mr. Aderlee led him upstairs, to the patio door in the kitchen. Malcolm stared at the murky sight, getting up close and personal with the offending body of water. A brown tint reflected off the top of the lake, now displaying characteristics more reminiscent of a swamp. The grass surrounding the outer rim had turned brown as if winter had taken hold and drained all the chlorophyll from each blade of grass.

"Do you mind if I step outside?"

Mr. Aderlee's looked on with concern. "You sure you want to do that? That smell can make you wish you didn't have a nose."

Malcolm smiled. "I'll hold my breath."

Mr. Aderlee opened the door. "If you hadn't guessed already, I'm staying behind."

Malcolm stepped onto the deck, taking short, quick breaths to minimize the amount of rancid air entering his lungs. He covered his nose, descended the stairs, and stepped onto the grass. The soil gave away slightly, upon absorbing the full weight of his massive frame.

He walked around the side of the house, focusing on the four-foot cement foundation protruding from the earth. He found several lightning bolt-shaped cracks scattered around. He snapped several pictures before proceeding around the perimeter of the house, looking for further damage. Then he returned to the backyard, looking to the right, at Jace's house, staring without expression.

Was this truly a case of each house settling or did the rain have something to do with it? Two houses out of a community of one hundred weren't enough to convince him a widespread problem was occurring. He needed to spot-check other houses in the area to ease his fears.

His concerns also shifted to the changing weather pattern. The wettest time of the year was upon them, meaning more frequent rainstorms. If the rain was indeed the culprit, he couldn't imagine what might happen.

He returned to the deck, taking off his shoes before entering the house, concerned about tracking in mud.

"What do you think?" Mr. Aderlee asked.

"My first instinct is to say the house is just settling. Definitely a process all new houses go through. I can get you in contact with a handyman who can patch up the cracks for you. I'd also suggest you monitor it to make sure it doesn't get worse. In the meantime, I'll check around the community to see if anyone else is having a similar problem."

Mr. Aderlee looked on with concern. "Is there anything else we should do?"

He placed his hand on Mr. Aderlee's shoulder. "Don't

worry; I'm not going to let anything happen to you or Mrs. Aderlee. I told you I'll take care of you when you first moved in. We'll get this all straightened out and make this the worry-free retirement home you were expecting."

# Chapter 27

"This looks like the place," Sabrina said.

She pulled into the gas mart, parking in front of several vending machines. She perused the area, looking for Maria. After a few minutes of waiting in the car, she exited and approached a Dasani vending machine, fumbling for change to purchase a cold bottle of water. She took a few gulps and leaned on the driver's side door of her car, patiently waiting.

She glanced at her watch, wondering if Maria would ever show up. She peeked around the side of the building and noticed the tail end of a compact blue car sticking out. She crept up to the car with a familiar female sitting in the driver's seat.

"Maria?"

"That's me."

She approached Maria. "I would never have noticed you here if I didn't get out of the car."

Maria exited the car. "I'm sorry. I just didn't want to be out in the open, sitting in the car for everyone to see."

Maria stretched out her hand, giving Sabrina a folder. "Here it is."

Sabrina grabbed the folder and tucked it under her arm.

Maria displayed a playful smile. "Aren't you going to look at it to see if I'm at least qualified?"

Sabrina laughed. "Haven't I heard that line before?" She opened the folder. "I'll take a look, but I don't want you to be late for your shift."

"I still have a few minutes," Maria said then grimaced. "I'm sure it's probably not the best resume you've seen. As you can hear, English isn't my native language. If you have any suggestions to improve it, let me know and I can make changes and give it back to you."

"Don't worry about that. It looks decent enough to me. Besides, I know you need something as soon as possible. I'll get it to my human resources department and see what happens."

Sabrina eyed Maria, thinking of where to go next with the conversation. "How do you like your new job?"

"It's okay, I guess," Maria said, shifting her name tag pinned just beneath her shirt collar.

Sabrina gave a long, searching look, hoping for more information. Her curiosity as to what happened at the realty office proved much too overwhelming to ignore, and she still needed to broach the subject of the note she left for Maria. She really didn't expect Maria to divulge any information, even if she asked. But she wasn't sure unless she tried.

"Hope I'm not being too nosy, but what happened to the job at the realty office?"

Maria shifted her eyes to the ground, rolling her shoe on a pebble. "It just didn't work out. Let's just leave it at that."

Sabrina nodded, respecting her wishes.

"My shift is about to begin. I need to leave."

"Go ahead. Don't wanna make you late."

Maria approached the entrance of the gas mart before turning around with a puzzled look on her face. "I still don't understand."

"Understand what?"

"Why are you gonna help me? You don't even know me."

"I'll put it to you this way. If a stranger wasn't there to help me in my time of need, God knows where I'd be today. I'm just paying it forward, and you happen to be in the right place at the right time."

# **Chapter 28**

"Ouch!" Jace said, wincing as Sarah gently rubbed his back with hydrocortisone lotion.

He lay flat on his stomach, fantasizing about getting a soothing massage, but in reality, it felt like a cactus rolling on his back.

He clamped his teeth. "Not so hard."

"I'm trying to be gentle. I wanna make sure I'm covering all the spots. I had an easier time putting the lotion on Ryan's back."

He squeezed his eyes tight while she dabbed more lotion on the affected areas.

"I still don't understand why you and Ava don't have any problems with your skin."

"Are you mad because you both don't have bulletproof skin like me and Ava? Guess it's just a woman thing."

"All jokes aside, I'm thinking we may have a problem with our water. For the past couple days, I noticed it would come out a little cloudy when you first turned it on and then clear after a while."

"So what? That used to happen to our water sometimes when we were in St. Louis."

"I think this is different. We should all probably stop using the tap water for now."

"I don't think that's gonna work. You're talking about the same water we use to brush our teeth, wash our clothes, and take our showers."

"I know it'll probably be hard, but I think we can make it work."

Sarah frowned. "I'm gonna have to disagree with you. I don't think the water has anything to do with it. Maybe there's something in the food causing you and Ryan to break out. Besides, how would you take a shower? Were you planning to use bottled water to wash up? Or maybe you could just boil the tap water."

"Until I know what's going on, I think that's a good plan, and I highly suggest the rest of the family does the same."

"Maybe I'll take your suggestion and not use the tap water to brush my teeth, but that ain't happening with my showers. I can't function without a hot shower."

Jace shrugged. "Okay, can't make you do it, but I'm making sure Ryan and Ava stop using the water."

Moments later, Sarah applied the last coating of lotion.

"I'm sorry," she said.

"No need to apologize. If you don't want to stop using the tap water, then that's your prerogative."

"I'm not talking about the water. I've moved on from that. I'm sorry about driving you crazy with the jealousy fits these past few days."

Jace remained on his stomach before sitting up and wincing at the shift in body position. He stared at Sarah with eyes wide open. "Call nine . . . one . . . one."

She flinched. "Why? What's the matter?"

"I'm going into shock because you're actually

apologizing to me."

Her face immediately relaxed as she nudged Jace in the stomach. "Don't scare me like that." She exhaled before continuing, "I've been doing a lot of thinking about the story you told me. Was it true?"

"You mean the story with my mother?"

Sarah nodded.

"Of course. I wouldn't make up a story like that if it involved my mother."

"How come you never told me before?"

Jace shrugged. "Guess I just thought of it as a moment between a mother and her son."

"I can respect that." She hesitated for a moment. "I hope you can understand my point of view."

"Yes and no. I can see how your past experiences might cause you not to trust men, but we're married. I've been with you for so long that I don't understand why you think, after all this time, I would decide to cheat on you."

She looked away, focusing her eyes on the floor. "I just think of myself as a plain old housewife. Look at me. I've been reduced to a couch potato. Can't work because of these damn headaches, my home business never panned out, and I've been sitting at home, gaining weight." She grabbed her waist. "Forget about pinching an inch; I can easily pinch four. I'm just a lazy, no good for nothing—"

Jace covered her mouth. "Stop insulting yourself." He moved his hand away. "Now I get the picture. You think of yourself as an unattractive housewife and I'm going to go out to find somebody else." Jace rubbed his chin in deep thought.

Sarah tilted her head. "Uh-oh. I feel another one of Jace's hypothetical scenarios coming."

He snickered. "You know me so well."

"Let's say you had a great idea for a new product. You did a few years of research and testing and realized this was something that can potentially make you rich and happy. You start a business with this product as the main attraction. After ten years, the business was more successful than you ever could imagine. Now, what if a new product came along and you knew if you tried it, it would cause your original product to turn on you and you would lose everything you worked so hard for? Now would you be foolish enough to take a chance on the new product?"

Sarah thought for a moment. "If you put it that way, no."

"I wouldn't either. Now, I'm sure you have no problems figuring out how that story ties into us."

Jace yawned, looking at the time. "I think that's enough for tonight. I'm hoping this lotion will help ease this itching and I can have a good night's sleep."

***

Hours later, Jace stared up at the ceiling during the predawn hours, trying his best to ignore the itching that had subsided somewhat. Sarah lay sound asleep next to him.

Although the quiet, peaceful room made it the perfect environment to sleep, these were dangerous hours for Jace. There was nothing worse for him than not being able to sleep and letting his mind wander through what he called 'the dungeon.' This was the place where fear, worry, anxiousness, and negative energy called home. This was also the place where dreams, peace, solace, and lofty aspirations met their untimely end. Jace did all he could to avoid going into the dungeon, but his efforts were in vain.

He immediately thought about the relocation and all that had happened in the past few weeks. This new place he called home seemed more distant and strange than ever before. The honeymoon was over. The infatuation with the house had disappeared. For the first time since the move, he doubted his decision to relocate. Any preconceived benefits for the family were not working out as expected. The experience had been nothing short of frustrating for Sarah, although a good deal of it was self-inflicted with her jealous insecurities. There hadn't been much interaction with any neighbors, besides Mr. Aderlee. Most neighbors kept to themselves, and Jace realized he was guilty of the same behavior.

Jace's expectations at the new job now appeared to be delusions of grandeur. No corner office with large windows overlooking the mountainous landscapes. Not much comradery with other coworkers, although he understood he hadn't been there long. No challenging job duties. And if you add in Jace's genuine attempt to help Maria by enlisting Sabrina's services, which hadn't turned out like he hoped so far, then all of his grand expectations with the move had fallen completely flat.

He thought about the condo in St. Louis, now looking like Utopia. No mysterious chemicals were polluting the lakes, no unexplained cracks in the building's foundation, no dead fish or geese, and no rash attacking anyone's skin. Everything was normal and, at times, boring. If there ever was a time he didn't mind being bored, it was now.

He also wondered if he'd moved for the right reasons. A part of him believed he did it for the benefit of the family. Another part believed he had acted selfishly and moved to escape his past. His gut instinct leaned toward the latter.

A sudden thrust of guilt overwhelmed him. He reached up to his chest, rubbing the outline of the locket, through his shirt, looking for guidance.

A smile crossed his face, thinking of his late mother, a woman of stone, who never displayed any emotional weaknesses. He was always amazed at her self-control in any situation, good or bad. She personified the saying, *when the going gets tough, the tough get going.* How would she have reacted to all these problems? She most likely would have demanded being moved to another house, somewhere far from the lake. If that wasn't possible, she would have unleashed her wrath to get the lake cleaned up ASAP. He laughed at the vision of Malcolm and city officials sucking up the water in the lake with a straw just to get his almighty mother off their backs. He could only imagine the possibilities. But, however she reacted, he knew she would make it right. She always made it right.

Jace reluctantly peeked at the clock, realizing he only had an hour left before the alarm went off. He forcefully closed his eyes, hoping to take advantage of this last hour for a quick nap.

# Chapter 29

"Fantastic! Thanks for the good news," Sabrina said then hung up the phone.

It paid to be good friends with someone in human resources. There were several new administrative positions available, in which external interviews hadn't begun, but that would change today after Sabrina's recommendation. Although on short notice, she had received word that Maria had the opportunity to come in during the afternoon for an impromptu interview. She had no idea if Maria would even be available, but she'd already accepted the interview appointment, hoping and praying Maria could fit it into her schedule.

She picked up the phone and dialed.

"Guess what? I was able to land you an interview this afternoon."

"What?"

"I'm sorry for the short notice. This was the only time this week the hiring manager was able to squeeze you in. I hope you're available?"

"What time?"

"At two."

"I guess that'll work. I'm not scheduled at the gas mart until five, but I don't know if I'm ready for an interview today. My hair is a mess, and the dress suit I want to wear is dirty. I also haven't been on a real interview in a while."

"I can help you prepare. You just need to know the basic questions. If you can spare some time, why don't you meet me for lunch and we can do a mock interview?"

"What's that?"

"Think of it as a practice interview."

***

They met at a quaint café close to Sabrina's downtown office. They squeezed into a booth, sitting on burgundy leather padded benches. A dimly lit sconce attached to the wall, along with a ceiling fan overhead, gave off a relaxing ambiance.

Maria had her hair pinned up in a tight bun and a slither of hair dangling down the right side of her face. Her look was completed with a white blouse under a navy blue business suit jacket.

Sabrina patted her freshly braided hair that was pulled into a ponytail at the top of her scalp. She wore an olive green skirt, just below the knee, and a white blouse with olive green stitching on the collar. Both women were dressed to impress and attractive enough to get all the male attention they could handle, but Sabrina thought otherwise. She took out a small mirror from her bag, making sure her makeup was up to par.

She laughed. "And you told me you look a mess." She put the mirror back in her bag. "I was just making sure I looked good enough to hang with you."

Maria laughed. "I did my best to look presentable."

"Girl, please. I would need to hire a movie makeup artist to look that presentable."

They both laughed. The waitress eventually took their order, and they waited for lunch to be served.

"I still don't feel good about the interview," Maria said.

"Sorry for the short notice again, but I think you'll have an advantage by going first. My recommendations normally carry a lot of weight."

Over the next twenty minutes, they proceeded through the mock interview. Sabrina also gave Maria a crash course on the company's history.

"I think you'll do fine," Sabrina said, finishing off her lunch.

Both women stopped talking for a moment with only the sound of muffled conversations from other patrons circling their booth.

Maria sat, drumming her fingers on the table. "I still don't know why you're trying to help me. Are you expecting something in return?"

"Like what?"

Maria shrugged. "I don't know. That's how it's always been with my experience."

"So, do you not trust me and think I'm doing this for my own selfish reasons?"

"No, I don't think so. It's just that I never met anyone who offered to help me without asking for something in return."

*Here's my chance.* Sabrina took a sip of her sparkling water. "I am getting something in return." She reached into her bag and pulled out a business card.

Maria squinted at the small print.

*Y.N.A*
*Sabrina Newman – Volunteer Counselor*

"I don't expect you to know what this is, which is why I'm going to tell you. It stands for *You're Never Alone*."

Maria looked on with her face contorted into a confused mess.

"It's an agency I volunteer with to assist women—or men—cope with any type of abuse or harassment situations. I help them find the strength to free themselves from those imaginary chains that bind them from running away from the situation."

Maria locked eyes with Sabrina for a moment before shifting her gaze down to the table.

Sabrina continued, "I'm just following one of the principles I learned being a volunteer counselor. It goes like this. Lend someone a helping hand now and your generosity will be rewarded in future installments. So, that's just a long-winded way for me to say that's what I'm getting in return by helping you."

"Now I get it," Maria said. She took a sip of water and held her mouth open like she was about to speak then quickly closed it.

"Did you have a question?"

"Uh . . . no."

"Come on, Maria. I've only known you for a few days, but you can't fool me. You can ask me anything you want.

Don't be afraid."

Maria focused her eyes down at the table, swirling the straw in her glass of water. "How long have you been volunteering as a counselor?"

"About five years. Right after my divorce."

Maria stared with her mouth partly open. "You were married?"

"Yes. Do you find that hard to believe?"

"A little. It's just . . . you look so young."

"Thank you, but I'm not as young as I look. I probably would have looked even younger if I didn't have to go through the stress of dealing with my ex-husband." Sabrina sighed. "Don't get me started on that fool."

"You don't have to talk about him. I don't want you to bring up any bad memories."

"Don't worry. It's therapeutic to talk about it. Believe it or not, I used to be a victim of abuse."

Maria gawked in disbelief.

"It was more verbal than physical. I was a lot more shy and insecure during those days. I didn't develop my tough skin until after the divorce."

"I don't believe that."

"It's true. Being a counselor taught me how to turn that negative experience into a positive one by helping others get out of abusive relationships."

Sabrina focused on Maria for any change in body language or facial expression, hoping this would open her up to discuss her situation, but Maria remained silent. Sabrina didn't want to give up that easily and continued with the subject.

"I also learned the worst thing any woman can do is remain silent if they're being abused or harassed in any way. It's like trapping yourself in solitary confinement, with each wall representing a negative consequence. In front of you, there's self-doubt. To the right, there's fear. To the left, there's hopelessness, and behind you, there's pain. There's no way out unless you decide to tear down the walls by breaking the silence and getting help."

Maria kept her eyes down on the table, fidgeting with her napkin. She eventually grabbed the napkin off the table and dabbed her eyes.

"Are you okay?" Sabrina asked with concern.

Maria shrugged.

"I didn't mean to upset you. Is it something you care to talk about?"

"Not now." She sniffled. "Maybe another time."

Sabrina bit her bottom lip. She didn't intend to bring Maria to tears. She'd only hoped to coax her into discussing what may have happened with Malcolm. This evidently was a sensitive subject and gave Sabrina all the proof she needed that some form of harassment or abuse had occurred in the past. Now it was a matter of narrowing the details, but this was not the time to continue her quest for answers.

She reached into her bag, grabbed her pocket mirror, and gave it to Maria. Maria stared at her reflection and wiped off the eyeliner smearing the top portion of her cheeks.

Sabrina forced a laugh to try to lighten the mood. "I'm

sure this is just what you needed before an interview."

"I'll be okay." Maria finally made eye contact with Sabrina. "And thanks for the talk. It helped more than you'll ever know."

# Chapter 30

Jace sat across from Sarah in the kitchen after arriving home from work. Throughout the day, he had attempted to regain his focus and adopt a more positive attitude about the relocation experience, yet a good portion of his thoughts took up refuge in the dungeon.

After a quick hello, he took off his blazer and filled a bowl with the beef stew that simmered in a pot on the stove. He sat at the table and ate without saying a word.

"Are you okay?" Sarah asked.

He shrugged and continued to eat.

"That's not too convincing," she replied.

"I'm fine."

"What happened to the happy husband I'm used to seeing after work?"

"I told you I'm okay," he said with an edge of impatience creeping into his voice.

"Did you have a bad day at work?"

"Yeah, I guess you can say that."

"Something you wanna talk about?"

"Not really."

Sarah looked on with concern. "Can I ask you a question? And I need you to be completely honest. Do you regret moving out here?"

"No. Why do you say that?"

She tilted her head to the side. "Come on. You expect

me to believe that?"

"Why not?"

She stared without saying a word.

"Okay . . . okay. Yes, I regret moving out here. Is that what you wanted to hear?"

"It's not about what I wanted to hear. It's about how you truly feel."

He sat back in the chair with his arms folded. "Go ahead and say it."

"Say what?"

"Tell me how I was wrong for convincing the family to move in the first place."

"That's not my point. I'm not trying to embarrass you or say I told you so. I just wanted your honest opinion."

"Look at it through my eyes. I dragged the family here, saying how great this move would be, and it hasn't been what I expected."

"Don't put it all on yourself. No one had a crystal ball. We didn't know what would happen."

"You obviously had a hunch, and I should have listened to you. Now it's on me to make things right. I got us into this mess, and now it's time for me to get us out."

"What is that supposed to mean?"

"Whatever comes to mind."

Sarah studied his face. "Jace, don't do anything stupid."

# Chapter 31

Sabrina frowned after playing the voicemail from her coworker and hung up the phone in dismay. Her day at the office had barely begun, and now she had to be the bearer of bad news and inform Maria she didn't get the job. Her ego suffered some bruising, as well, since this was the first time one of her recommendations had been dismissed so quickly. Then again, she had taken a chance by sending a candidate whom she had just met.

She sipped her tea, contemplating whether to call Maria now and get it over with or meet her for lunch again and relay the bad news face-to-face. She dialed.

"Hi, Maria."

"You caught me rushing out the door. I'm doing the day shift today," Maria said.

"Oh, I don't want to hold you up from getting to work. It can wait till later." She pondered for a second. "If you want, maybe we can meet up at the café for lunch again and talk?"

"Okay. I get a break today at one."

***

Sabrina entered the café, running through her mind how she would tell Maria. In most other situations, she had no problems being blunt and getting right to the point, but this was different. She had to handle this with sensitivity and care.

She approached the hostess, but before she could speak, she felt a tap on her shoulder.

She turned to see Maria, wide-eyed and appearing anxious to hear the news. They proceeded to sit and order lunch.

Maria took a sip of water. "So, what's the big news?"

Sabrina looked on with a less-than-impressive smile. She abruptly straightened her mouth, realizing how foolish she was about to look trying to smile and deliver the bad news. She cleared her throat. "You didn't get the job."

Maria's face immediately shifted, struggling to stay cheerful as she received the solemn news. "Oh. Okay. Guess it wasn't meant to be."

Sabrina reached out, placing her hands on top of Maria's that were resting on the table. "It's not over. We can't give up yet. We'll find you something."

"Guess you're right. Things could be worse. At least I still have a roof over my head."

"That's the spirit. It won't be long before another job falls in your lap."

There was a momentary pause while they both indulged on a chicken Caesar wrap.

"You've been so busy with helping me find a job, we never had a chance to talk about that day you showed up at the realty office," Maria said before wiping some dressing that spilled under her bottom lip. "Why did you write that note?"

Sabrina smirked. "You mean, the bogus job application?"

"Yes," Maria said with a slight chuckle.

"I was just responding to a mysterious note you left for somebody else."

Maria looked on, visibly confused. "Who?"

"Jace. He was the guy you gave your note to at the realty office, asking him not to leave you alone with Malcolm. Don't you remember?"

"Oh. I didn't know you knew him."

"I was his tour guide that weekend. We've stayed in touch ever since."

"Why did he tell you about the note I gave him?"

"He was concerned about you. Anybody would have been after what you wrote." Sabrina took a sip of water. "After he found out I did volunteer work at YNA, he told me what happened. We both assumed something may have been going on between you and Malcolm, so I figured it was only right to investigate."

Maria displayed a gracious smile. "And all this time, I didn't think anybody cared." She placed her right hand over her heart and tapped it three times. "That's a custom in my village when saying thank you to a close friend."

The conversation temporarily stopped as Maria drummed her fingers on the table. "I've been doing some thinking about what you told me at the café a few days ago, and I think I'm ready to talk."

Sabrina did her best to hold in her excitement, feeling proud that she had gained Maria's trust enough to open up. She went along, as if clueless to Maria's prelude to confess.

"About what?"

"About what happened at my last job. I won't go into too much detail, but let's say Malcolm liked me more than just a coworker. It first started with the way he would look at me, and sometimes he would make these sexual jokes that made me very uncomfortable."

Sabrina shook her head in disgust.

"The day that Jace came into the office was the first day I was ever alone with Malcolm, and I was nervous."

"So, that's why you gave Jace the note?"

"Yes. I panicked and didn't want him to leave, so I wrote the note."

"Did Malcolm do anything to you after Jace left the office?"

"Not really, although he came pretty close to me a few times while he was talking, but—"

"But what?"

"Um . . . a few days later, he offered me a raise and was looking for certain favors in exchange."

"What do you mean, favors?"

"He took me out to lunch. Then, on the way back to the office, he drove to the middle of nowhere and asked me to kiss him."

Sabrina's brows wrinkled in annoyance. "That son of a bitch! I knew he was up to no good. Please tell me you didn't kiss him?"

"Thankfully, no. To make a long story short, he let me go after I spit in his face," Maria said with a smirk.

Sabrina stared with her mouth wide open. "You seriously spit in his face? Not a speck of spit that mistakenly flies out someone's mouth when they're speaking, but a full-blown, fill-your-mouth-with-saliva-and-eject-a-wad-on-someone's-face type of spit?"

Maria nodded with a huge grin on her face.

Sabrina held her hands up and proceeded to clap. "That's what I'm talking about. Good for you." She reached up with her hand held in the air and waited for Maria to reciprocate with a high-five. "So, how did he respond to that moment of humiliation?"

"He kicked me out of his truck and drove off."

"What? How did you get back to the office?"

"He came back to get me after he realized he was wrong."

Sabrina shook her head. "Wow, that's some story. Did you at least contact your HR department and report this as sexual harassment?"

"Since it's his business, he is the HR department. It didn't matter anyway because he apologized and offered me an even bigger raise, so I accepted his offer."

Sabrina's head dropped. "That's not the answer I was hoping to hear. You poor soul, he was just using you. That's common behavior for someone like that. They shower you with apologies and gifts to try to regain your trust and then . . . *wham*, they're at it again, most times worse than before. So, what made you decide to leave?"

"He found your fake job application before I did and was expecting me to tell him what it was about."

Sabrina displayed a sheepish grin. "I'm so sorry about that. It's all my fault. I should have taken the application with me when I left."

"That's okay. Because of that, I found the strength to quit and move on with my life."

Maria finished off her wrap. "I could be here all day talking to you, but time for me to go. My lunch hour is almost up, and I have a fifteen-minute drive back to work." She placed a twenty-dollar bill on the table. "This should cover my lunch."

Sabrina grabbed the bill and handed it back. "Keep it. Lunch is on me."

Maria put the twenty back on the table. "Thanks, but I can't do that. I need to pay you something."

Sabrina folded the bill and placed it in Maria's hand. "After setting you up for failure with Malcolm, the least I can do is pay for your lunch."

Maria shrugged. "Okay. You win."

She departed while Sabrina stayed behind to pay the tab. *This was turning out to be the start of a trustworthy friendship*, she thought. She was thrilled that Maria had finally opened up about what had happened but not the least bit happy with what she'd heard. She sighed, feeling relieved that the mystery of the note had been resolved, and she was eager to share the news with Jace.

# Chapter 32

*It has to be pure coincidence*, Malcolm thought. He spread out the pictures he had taken at Mr. Aderlee's house across his office desk, scanning them intently. He attempted to recall the pictures that Jace had shown of the cracks in his basement the previous week, but it was difficult for him to get a visual without seeing the pictures once more. He struggled to convince himself these cracks were part of the settling process, mostly due to the thought of these cracks appearing all in one night, as both Mr. Aderlee and Jace had claimed.

His mind went from one concern to another, upon his anticipation of viewing the latest monthly sales report.

He opened the report and shook his head at what it displayed. He'd had a hunch it would be bad, but not this bad. Sales were down, along with his company profit. He struggled to break even. Not his idea of a successful business. He had always anticipated a small drop-off. As with all new products, enthusiasm waned after a certain period of time, and the grand opening of Granwin Estates was no different. However, this was worse than expected, and the recent issues within the community were no doubt a catalyst to the extreme drop in interest. This wouldn't have been a major problem if he'd successfully sold houses outside the community, but that wasn't the case. Granwin was his bread and butter. Without it, he didn't have a chance.

He turned his attention to a pile of bills, stacked on the corner of the table. Some of them were overdue, including his rent for the business. He closed the report and gently placed his head on the table, adding this to his list of problems.

He reached into his desk, looking for a cigarette to calm his nerves, but there were no more. He checked his pockets, also coming up empty.

He grabbed his truck keys and exited the office, on a quest for cigarettes and a chance to meet up with an old friend once more.

# Chapter 33

The wind-swept rain pounded the glass door, ushered in by a sudden thunderstorm. Maria looked outside, elated she had left her lunch date with Sabrina just in time to avoid getting caught outside in the deluge.

She stood behind the cash register, more at ease about the situation with Malcolm. With Sabrina by her side, she was no longer alone. In addition to having Sabrina's support, she had extra insurance in her handbag, in the form of a can of pepper spray, resting on the side, easily accessible and ready to use. She also kept a pocketknife hidden in a side pocket. Along with these items and a new air of confidence, she felt fully protected, ready to do battle, if necessary.

Except for a young gentleman who approached the register with several items, no other customers could be found throughout the mart. They exchanged pleasantries.

"I'll be right back. I forgot something," he said before walking over to the refrigerated soda section.

She glanced over at the front door as a figure appeared outside. The door chimes sounded and, to her horror, Malcolm stepped inside, shaking off an umbrella. Maria's stress levels spiked, caught off guard by his sudden presence.

He strolled toward the refrigerated soda section without looking in her direction.

The young man returned to the register with a sixteen-ounce bottle of Sprite. She remained silent, staring at Malcolm's every move. The young man waved his hand to get her attention.

"I'm sorry." She began ringing up the items.

Before she could finish, Malcolm stepped in line directly behind the gentleman, waiting his turn. She made a concerted effort not to make eye contact with him. She glanced at the items on the counter, unable to remember if she scanned everything.

"I'm sorry, sir, I've got to scan your purchases one more time."

Although she wasn't looking directly at him, she could feel Malcolm staring, with her comfort level decreasing by the second. Her hands trembled while raising them to type on the register. For a split-second, she forgot what buttons to press.

"Are you okay?" the young gentleman inquired.

"Uh . . . sure."

"If it's going to cause too many problems, don't worry about the soda."

"No. Just give me a second."

She focused her attention on the entrance, hoping to find a new customer walking through the doors, but no such luck. She tried desperately to think of a way to get the young man to stay until Malcolm left.

She swallowed the large lump in her throat and met eyes with the young gentleman. "Do you mind if I help the customer behind you first? It'll take a few minutes to ring up your order again, and he only has one item."

Before the gentleman could say anything, Malcolm responded, "That's okay. Let the young man go first. This soda isn't the only item I'm interested in."

She realized it was up to her to deal with him one-on-one, not knowing what to expect.

She let out a sigh, ringing up the young man's purchases once more. He then paid and exited the store.

Malcolm stepped forward.

She looked down, positioning her left hand under the counter, a few inches away from the can of pepper spray sitting in her bag.

"You should be ashamed of yourself for trying to rush me out of the store."

She continued to look away without saying a word.

"I need a pack of Marlboro Lights."

With the cigarette shelf located behind her, she feared turning her back completely away from him. She positioned herself at an angle, enough to grab the cigarettes and keep an eye on him at the same time.

"Have you enjoyed working here for the past week?"

She remained quiet. *How the heck did he know that?* She placed the cigarette carton on the counter, along with a book of matches.

"I saw your car parked in the employee space earlier this week, and I figured I'd pay you a visit. I was disappointed when I didn't see you, so I figured I'd try again today, and lucky me, I found you."

She stayed silent, not the least bit amused.

He stretched out his hand, holding a few bills to pay for the cigarettes and soda. She carefully grabbed the money, being extra careful not to touch his fingers.

"I see you developed manners now. No more snatching things out of people's hands."

Maria offered no response.

"Oh, by the way, how's your friend?"

Her eyebrows furrowed momentarily, confused at his question.

"How soon we forget. Remember she paid a visit to the realty office? The same friend who you swore you didn't know?"

Her heart fluttered in a panic. She continued to avoid eye contact.

"It's too late to play dumb now. I've already seen you two together."

She shuffled her hands through the register, fumbling to get the correct change. She pulled out a couple of worn singles and a quarter, placing them on the counter. She positioned her left hand under the counter, grasping the can of pepper spray once more.

"I already warned you not to lie to me, and now I have to think of a fitting punishment." His eyes roamed from her face, down to her breasts.

Although fully clothed, she felt violated in the worst way, as if he could see her bare chest. Her eyes were drawn to the middle of his white shirt, the same one he'd worn during her day from hell, as a faded ketchup stain remained visible. *Cheap detergent.*

She flashed back to the incident in his truck, with him trying to take advantage of her and expecting her to kiss his discolored, moisture-challenged lips. For a hot second, she fantasized about grabbing a few tubes of Chapstick and throwing them on the counter, to be of service to his lips, which were still crying out for help.

She took a deep breath, thinking there was no telling how far he would have gone if she had followed through with that nightmare-inducing kiss. *The nerve of him.* Sabrina was right; this man didn't deserve any respect. But he did deserve every ounce of spit that had slammed against his cheek that day.

She finally looked up, meeting his eyes with a cold stare, the pendulum once again swinging from fear to anger. He was no longer her boss. He couldn't tell her what to do anymore. Her index finger rested firmly on the trigger, waiting to unload the burning mix of ingredients onto his face.

She cleared her throat. "Get outta my store!"

His wry smile dissipated in seconds.

The door chimes sounded as another customer entered.

He snatched his change off the counter and looked at the clock on the wall behind her. "I'll see you when your shift ends." He turned and exited the store.

Maria froze, her bold attitude deflating with each passing second. She lunged for the phone under the counter, her hand shaking while pressing each button.

"Sabrina, it's Maria. I need a big favor. Can you meet me at the gas mart around five?"

"What's the matter?"

"I'll explain when you get here, but promise me you'll be here."

"Okay, I should be able to leave work a few minutes early."

"My car is parked out back; you can meet me there."

***

Maria glanced at the time as it approached five o'clock, with the rain continuing to fall off and on. She gathered her belongings, waiting for Sabina as her shift relief arrived. Shortly after, a knock could be heard at the back door entrance of the store.

Maria's coworker turned and said, "Expecting anybody?"

Maria nodded. Just beyond the refrigerated soda section, a twenty-foot-long, narrow hallway led to the back door. A bathroom and a closet containing store supplies were located within the hallway.

She grabbed her bag and walked through the hallway. A flickering fluorescent light bulb barely illuminated the area. An unpleasant odor of mildew and stale urine penetrated Maria's nose upon passing the bathroom. She stepped within a few feet of the door, listening for movement outside. The deluge of rain pounding the pavement made it difficult for her to focus on any movement. The metal door didn't have a peephole, which would have been ideal at this particular moment.

She pressed her ear against the door, listening more intently. Three loud knocks pierced her ears.

She jumped back from the door and caught her breath before speaking. "Sabrina? Is that you?" She stood quiet for a second. "Sabrina?"

Still no response.

She crept closer to the door while pulling out her pepper spray. She quietly turned the latch to unlock it. She grabbed the doorknob with one hand and firmly gripped the pepper spray with the other. She cracked open the door, peering through the small opening. She opened the door a little further, with rain spraying her face, but no one was present. She shut the door, not wanting to risk going out any further. She turned around, spotting a figure standing a few feet from her in the hallway, and screamed.

"Maria! It's me, Sabrina."

Maria clutched her chest. "Don't ever do that again."

Maria's coworker came running into the hallway. "Are you okay?"

"Yes," Maria responded.

Sabrina patted her on the shoulder. "I'm sorry I scared you like that. I knocked on the back door a few times, but I wasn't sure if you could hear me, so I went through the front."

Maria laughed. "You should feel lucky. I was about to empty this can of pepper spray in your face."

Sabrina's eyes narrowed speculatively. "What's going on? Is everything okay?"

"N-no," Maria stuttered. "Malcolm came into the store earlier. To make a long story short, I kicked him out of the store, and he wasn't too happy."

"Good for you."

"Not really. He said he was coming back after my shift ends."

"For what?"

"I don't know, and I don't think I want to find out."

Sabrina folded her arms. "Don't let that fool intimidate you." She grabbed Maria by the arm. "Come on; I'll follow you home."

# Chapter 34

Squinting through the rain in close pursuit, Sabrina followed Maria's taillights onto a narrow two-way road, her car shaking each time a vehicle zoomed by in the opposite direction. The windshield wipers were set to the highest speed but still struggled to keep up with the deluge of rain that drowned the car.

She squinted through the window, Maria's red taillights blurred by the rain. Her vision became further impaired by the condensation forming on the front windshield. She eased her foot off the accelerator, glancing at the console. She switched on the defroster and then focused her eyes on the road once more. There were now about six car lengths between her and Maria as she approached an intersection with a steady green light. Maria's car cleared the intersection at about the same time the light turned yellow and eventually red. Sabrina jammed her foot on the brakes, stopping a few feet shy of the red traffic light, not wanting to run the risk of racing through the light in these poor weather conditions.

She peered up ahead, expecting Maria to stop, but there was no shoulder for her to pull alongside and wait. Maria's brake lights did flash before two tractor-trailers from the intersecting road made a right turn, following behind her.

"Damn!" Sabrina shouted.

Maria was now completely out of view and forced to

keep moving because of the traffic behind her.

Sabrina peered up at the light, waiting for it to change.

"Come on light," she said, tapping her fingers on the steering wheel.

She glanced over to the intersecting road and noticed another truck about to make a right turn in front of her, but the traffic light remained a steady red. She looked to the left, making sure no traffic was approaching from that direction, before promptly pressing her foot on the accelerator. The tires skidded on the rain-slick road, her car bolting into the intersection and swerving around the truck halfway into its turn. Her BMW vibrated from the deep bass of the truck's horn blaring in her direction.

"Sorry," she said.

She focused her attention up the road and saw the taillights of the first truck about a quarter mile away. She knew it wouldn't be a problem catching the trucks, but passing them presented a challenge. Swerving into the oncoming traffic lane and passing two tractor-trailers was no easy feat, especially in these weather conditions. She moved within a car's length of the first truck and said a quick prayer, veering to the left to get a view of the northbound traffic lane. No oncoming headlights appeared, although she hesitated to make her move.

She swerved to the right, directly behind the truck. The truck tires kicked up a misty tidal wave that crashed against her windshield, reducing her visibility down to nothing. She eased her foot off the accelerator to create some distance between her and the truck. This gave her a better view of the northbound traffic lane. She edged over to the left again, no headlights in sight.

Gripping the steering wheel even tighter, she slammed her foot on the gas and swerved into the oncoming traffic lane. The speedometer increased an additional twenty-five miles per hour while driving midway past the first truck. As she cleared it, the taillights of the lead truck came into view. About three car lengths separated each truck, more than enough for her to squeeze between, but with no oncoming headlights in view, she kept her foot on the accelerator in an effort to pass the lead truck. She battled with the steering wheel to keep the car straight on the wet pavement.

Only a short distance remained before she could accomplish her task of passing the massive vehicles, but her adrenaline immediately spiked upon noticing Maria's brake lights flash up ahead. She couldn't determine the reason for the slowdown until she watched the taillights of Maria's car disappear. She recoiled, realizing a sharp turn most likely awaited her up ahead.

She snatched her foot off the accelerator and gently pressed the brake, pulling alongside the midway point of the lead truck's trailer. The curve was upon her, giving her no time to either fall back or pass the truck before the sharp bend. The curve also created a blind spot for any oncoming traffic. She had no choice but to round the curve in the northbound lane, praying no cars were barreling toward her around the bend.

She applied more pressure to the brake, slowing enough to handle the curve. The speedometer dipped upon approaching the bend. She leaned to the right, turning the steering wheel in the curve's direction. The back end of the car swerved slightly as the tires fought to maintain a grip on the road. She regained full control after rounding the bend and thankfully didn't see any oncoming lights. She immediately pressed the accelerator, bypassing the truck and swerving into the southbound lane, behind Maria's car.

Sabrina received an earful from the truck's horn, obviously annoyed at her death-defying maneuvers. She flashed her headlights to notify Maria that she was trailing her once again.

A short time later, she continued following and made a right onto Atrisco Drive, traveling another mile before parking in front of Maria's apartment. She ran into the lobby of the building, behind Maria, to escape the rain.

"Are you okay?" Maria asked.

"Yeah. Just thankful I was able to maneuver around those trucks without a head-on collision."

"I'm so sorry. It was my fault. I should have stopped when the light turned yellow," Maria said.

"Don't blame yourself. You couldn't stop anyway with the two trucks behind you. You did the right thing. If we want to blame somebody, blame me for not following you closer." Sabrina paused to catch her breath. "It doesn't matter now. The bottom line is that you made it home safely without any signs of you know who."

Sabrina let out a sigh of relief. "Why don't you go upstairs and dry off? I need to get moving. I have another stop to make before going home."

Maria placed her hand on Sabrina's shoulder. "I don't think that's a good idea in this weather."

"I know, but I promised Jace and his family I would swing by to give him some information I found out about Granwin that I doubt they know about. I would show you, but the documents are in my car."

Maria shrugged. "Maybe some other time. Just make sure you call me when you get to Jace's house."

Sabrina looked down at her cell phone. "My battery is running pretty low now, and I don't have my car charger. I'm hoping I can get through the rest of the evening without it dying completely." Sabrina motioned her hand as if she was writing. "Do you have a pen and some paper? I'll write down Jace's number so you can still reach me in case my phone dies. Although, I'm sure he wouldn't mind if I used his phone. I'll give you the number, anyway." Sabrina laughed. "Besides, you probably need to call him anyway and thank him for showing concern for your situation."

Maria laughed. "You're probably right."

Sabrina scribbled the number on a slip of paper and waved goodbye.

She drove east on Route 66 as the rain continued to fall. Up ahead, she saw a hint of light illuminating the dark road as she approached the gas mart. She slowed, focusing her attention on one of the self-service islands, spotting a dark-colored pickup truck. She had no plans to stop, but the familiar vehicle piqued her interest.

She pulled onto the shoulder of the road, stopping twenty feet short of the neon, Gas-n-Go sign. She rolled down her passenger window to get a better view, her eyes transfixed on a large gentleman leaving the mart, walking to the pickup.

"I knew it was him. That bastard is probably looking for Maria," she whispered.

She doused the headlights to camouflage the car in the darkness. She slouched in the seat, her eyes barely able to see over the dashboard. She peeked as he pulled out of the service area and made a left onto Route 66, heading west. She slumped further, completely out of view while hearing the roaring engine of the Silverado pass by. She sat up, looking in the rearview mirror, watching the vehicle's taillights disappear into the night.

*Where is he going? Does he live in that direction? Is he driving toward Downtown Albuquerque to do business? Or is he planning to pay Maria a visit?*

Her breath quickened, focusing on that last question. He undoubtedly had Maria's personal information, including her address from her time as an employee. It was no problem these days to map out an address online and get directions.

Maybe she was too paranoid. He wouldn't be foolish enough to try to find her apartment. Then again, she would never forgive herself if he did attempt to find her and something unthinkable happened.

She flashed on the headlights and pulled into the Gas-n-Go lot to make a U-turn onto the westbound lane. The rain continued to cascade from the heavens while she raced along the highway, in pursuit of Malcolm.

She approached the crest of a slight incline in the highway. As she cleared the hill, she spotted the taillights of the truck, about a quarter mile ahead. With her adrenaline pumping, she sped along, closing to within roughly one hundred feet of the pickup truck, before realizing she was approaching too fast. She applied pressure to the brake, slowing to match his speed.

For the next few miles, she stayed a comfortable distance away, cruising at fifty miles per hour. They were a few miles from approaching the Atrisco Drive intersection.

She mustered a forced laugh, thinking how foolish she would feel if he bypassed the intersection and was indeed traveling somewhere else. But she couldn't assume that scenario and had to proceed with the pursuit.

After snapping out of her daydream, she peered up ahead and realized his taillights were closer than before. She eased her foot off the accelerator, matching his speed once again. Her speedometer slowed, yet she still continued to inch closer. She focused her attention beyond the truck, attempting to determine the reason for the slowdown, but there were no other taillights, nothing to warrant his slow pace.

She couldn't understand the reason for the slowdown unless he was onto her game. If she continued slowing down and didn't attempt to pass him for going well below the speed limit, he would almost certainly know he was being followed.

Seconds later, she noticed his taillights shrinking in the distance. Her eyes widened with surprise, realizing his sudden acceleration in speed.

"Oh no, you don't!" she shouted.

She pressed her foot on the pedal to keep pace, nearing a slight turn as her speedometer inched close to sixty. The rain slowed, but the roads were still extremely wet.

His taillights disappeared around the bend as she swerved around the curve to keep pace. Her speed increased, zipping down a straight stretch of road. She continued pressing the accelerator, the speedometer now pushing seventy.

His brake lights flashed up ahead, nearing what appeared to be another curve. She approached before realizing in a horrifying instant she had picked up too much speed on the straightaway. She applied pressure to the brake, slowing upon nearing the curve. The rear tires screeched, spinning along the pavement, losing their grip on the road. She fought with all her might to regain control of the car, but the rear of her BMW fishtailed to the right. She took her foot off the brake, wrestling with the steering wheel to straighten out the car, but her efforts were in vain.

"Oh, God!"

The car twisted into a deadly spin, the tires losing contact with the ground, flipping the vehicle. Sparks flew from all directions as the car skidded on its roof, careening off the road, and toppled into an embankment, turning it into a heap of twisted metal.

# Chapter 35

Malcolm glanced in the rearview mirror, expecting to see the headlights appear from around the bend. Nothing, only complete darkness followed. The mysterious vehicle had suddenly disappeared.

He eased his foot off the pedal, assuming the person following had decided to end the chase.

*Who could that have been? A disgruntled homeowner at Granwin?* He wouldn't have been surprised, especially with the increased scrutiny concerning the lake and other happenings within the community. The complaints continued to mount, and he knew it was only a matter of time before residents took matters into their own hands.

He nodded ever so slightly, realizing that if he was in their position, he would probably do the same. Maybe he should have heeded his first instinct and refrained from throwing his hat in the ring to sell houses at Granwin. He assumed a slight risk came along with his decision to sell, dismissing the possible future ramifications, as he focused more on the potential profit that had been substantial at one point. However, the tide seemed to be turning and his good fortune running out.

But, of greater concern, these scattered thunderstorms paled in comparison to the nasty forecast of high winds and rain in the next few days. If the forecast did come to fruition, he could have a potential disaster on his hands.

He placed his hand on his stomach, the pain leading him from one concern to another. His stomach still ached, and the antacid pills he'd purchased from the Gas-n-Go did nothing to help. He prayed this trip to the doctor would offer a plan of action to help finally resolve this chronic condition.

He bypassed the Atrisco Drive intersection and continued along Route 66.

***

He arrived in front of the receptionist's desk, breathing heavily from his quickened pace in an attempt to arrive on time. He signed in and sat in the quaint waiting area, furnished with an oak brown, upholstered sofa, and a rectangular coffee table, stacked with health and fitness magazines. Before he could get too comfortable, the doctor called him into the office.

He immediately placed a brown medicine bottle on the doctor's desk. "I can't take these pills anymore, Dr. Watts. The side effects are killing me, and it hasn't made my stomach any better."

The doctor grabbed the bottle and shook it. "Sounds like most of the pills are still in there."

"I've taken one a day for the past three weeks, and I can't handle it anymore. There's got to be something else I can take."

The doctor stared at him for a moment, stroking his fingers against his Charlie Chaplin-style mustache. "Have you seen any change in your eating habits or bowel movements?"

"Nothing worth mentioning."

"I did warn you not to expect miracles from these pills, especially since we still haven't been able to figure out exactly what's causing these stomach pains." The doctor studied Malcolm's medical chart. "We've performed all kinds of tests on you and can't find anything wrong. I'm beginning to believe your problem is stress-induced. Stress could be a major contributor to several unexplained ailments, including stomach issues. And, as you described to me, you've had these stomach issues off and on for as long as you can remember. They just have been getting progressively worse."

"I didn't think about that."

"It may be all mental. Maybe a visit to a psychiatrist might be a good idea."

Malcolm folded his arms. "Do you think I'm crazy?"

"Relax. I don't want you to take it that way. It's just that I've done all that I can. All your tests have come back fine. There is absolutely nothing physically wrong with you." The doctor closed his medical folder. "Just do me a favor and think about it."

# Chapter 36

"She's almost two hours late," Sarah said.

Jace gave Sarah a questioning glance. "Are you sure she said she was coming tonight?"

"Yes, positive. She was in a rush when she called. Just told me she wanted to swing by this evening and give us some information she found out about Granwin."

"Did she say where she found this information?"

Sarah sighed. "No. I just told you she was in a rush. I just spoke to her for literally fifteen seconds this morning."

Jace did his best to keep his anxiety under control, not only concerned with Sabrina's whereabouts but extremely curious as to what she could have found that may shed some light on the nonsense that was occurring within the development.

***

An hour later, Jace's body slipped in and out of consciousness, nodding off on the sofa. His eyes shot open upon hearing the phone ring. He picked up to hear a woman's voice with a familiar accent.

"Hi, is this Jace?"

Jace rubbed his eyes, still trying to gather his senses. "Yes."

"This is Maria," she paused. "You know . . . from the realty office. Sorry to disturb you so late, but Sabrina was on her way to your house, and I just wanted to know if she made it there yet."

Jace looked around the room to make sure Sabrina didn't slip in during his nap. "Uh . . . no, she's not here yet."

"Oh." Maria paused. "She left my apartment over an hour ago, and I thought she would have made it there by now. She was supposed to call me when she got to your house, but her phone was dying. Hope you don't mind she gave me your number in case I needed to call."

"No, not at all. I tried calling her cell a few times earlier but only got voice mail," he said.

"Me, too. I also tried her at home, and there was no answer," Maria said.

Jace pondered for a second. "I'll try her a couple more times on her cell. If I don't get her, I might try dropping by her apartment to make sure everything is okay."

"Okay. Please keep me updated if you hear anything."

Jace tried the cell and landline phones but received voicemails on each. With his patience worn thin, he grabbed his car keys and rushed out the door in search of Sabrina's apartment.

***

After a half-hour drive, he neared his destination, according to the directions. He rounded a corner and came upon a street lined with garden apartments on both sides. Although the darkness made it difficult to see, the streetlamps gave off just enough light to reveal well-manicured landscapes with trimmed hedges, trees surrounded by red cedar mulch, and brick pathways leading to each building entrance. He proceeded up the street until he came upon an empty parking space. He closed his eyes, breathing in deeply, attempting to collar his anxiety, while hoping Sabrina would be home, safe and sound.

As he entered the building and made his ascent up the stairs, he could hear a couple of voices not too far off in the distance above him. After clearing the last step, he turned his head to the right and focused on two police officers standing by a door. Upon approaching and looking at the address he jotted down, he realized they were standing in front of Sabrina's apartment.

"Excuse me, sir, do you live here?" one of the officers asked.

"Uh, no, but my friend does. I was just going to visit her."

"What's your friend's name?"

"Sabrina Newman," Jace said with his heart rate quickening.

The officers eyed one another before one of them turned to Jace. "We regret to inform you, your friend was in a serious car accident this evening. We came upon her car in a ditch and had an ambulance take her to Presbyterian Hospital in critical condition."

Jace stared in stunned silence.

"The address on her car registration led us here. We were looking for next of kin, but no one's home. Do you know if she lives by herself?"

Jace shrugged, only able to communicate in gestures.

"Do you know of any family members we can

contact?"

Jace shook his head. He wanted to know further details, but he couldn't think straight, let alone put together words that made meaningful sentences.

The officer passed Jace the number to the local police station. "If you have any questions or find any way to contact a family member, please don't hesitate to call. We're praying for your friend to pull through."

The police officers departed, leaving Jace reeling from this horrifying news.

***

With his heart pumping at a furious pace, Jace pushed his hands against the revolving glass doors of the hospital, in an attempt to make them turn faster. Sarah followed closely behind, just as eager to get an update on Sabrina's condition.

The clock approached the midnight hour, with Jace struggling to stay awake. He would normally be asleep at this time on a work night, but his adrenaline wouldn't allow that to happen.

He approached the welcome center. A middle-aged woman, with her hair pulled into a bun, sat behind the desk.

"I'm looking for Sabrina Newman," Jace blurted out before the woman could speak.

She tugged on her glasses, resting them farther down her nose. "Is she a patient or an employee?"

"Patient."

The woman typed a few keystrokes on the computer. "Sorry, sir. I don't see that name listed anywhere on the patient list."

"Please check again," Sarah said before proceeding to spell out Sabrina's last name.

The woman checked one more time. "I'm sorry, but she's not on the list. When was she admitted?"

"Sometime tonight. She was in a car accident."

The woman nodded. "That might explain it. I'm guessing she came through the emergency room. If that's the case, I'm sure all her admission paperwork hasn't been completed yet."

Jace frantically looked around. "Which way is the emergency room?"

"Are you a family member?"

"Yes," Jace said at about the same time Sarah said no.

The woman sat with her arms folded, visibly annoyed. "Well, either you are or aren't."

Jace looked at Sarah, agitated at her choice not to stretch the truth, especially if it would help gain them access to the emergency room.

"Hold on a minute," the woman said. She picked up the receiver and dialed a number. After a quick conversation, she disconnected. "They did confirm a Sabrina Newman was admitted a short while ago, but as we speak, she's having emergency surgery. Unfortunately, I can't tell you any more than that." She pointed to the sofas in the waiting area. "I'd suggest you have a seat and wait. I'll find the doctor performing the surgery and have him update you with anything new."

With no further resistance, Jace and Sarah followed the

woman's suggestion and walked toward a sofa. He planted himself on the plush piece of furniture with Sarah sitting directly beside him.

Laughter emanated from a sitcom playing on a TV mounted on the corner wall. A fifty-gallon, rectangular fish tank occupied most of the space on the adjacent wall. A large school of fish, displaying an array of colors, swam back and forth through the blue-tinted water. A coffee table stood in the middle of the U-shaped connecting sofas, with various medical magazines spread along the top. The calming atmosphere assisted in lowering Jace's anxiety somewhat, although he wouldn't be completely free of any angst until an update on Sabrina's condition could be provided. He had a slew of questions that required immediate answers, and all he could do was wait.

***

An hour passed with no news on Sabrina's condition. Jace glanced over at Sarah, her head nodding periodically as she struggled to keep her eyes open. He thought of Ryan and Ava, who were fast asleep at home. He hated leaving them alone but didn't want to disturb them, especially with another school day approaching. He had left a note on each of their bedroom doors just in case they woke up during the night and wondered where they were.

His attention suddenly shifted to a familiar figure spinning through the revolving doors. She walked to the front desk and conversed with the receptionist.

Jace approached. "Hi. Maria?"

She turned. "Jace?"

He nodded. "I'm glad you got my message."

"Any news on Sabrina?" she asked.

"Last thing I heard she was in surgery. I've been here for over an hour waiting for an update."

Maria's eyes glistened with moisture. "I pray she'll be okay."

The woman behind the desk said, "You might as well join them in the waiting area. I'm sure a doctor will be down soon to give you an update."

Jace approached the waiting area with Maria following. Sarah's eyes were closed, and a part of him hoped they remained that way. He had no idea how she would react if she woke up to see Maria sitting beside him. As he neared, however, Sarah's eyes opened.

Jace flinched, displaying a shameless grin. *How ironic.* He introduced Sarah to the woman who had unknowingly been a thorn in his marital bliss. Sarah flashed an unimpressive smile as both women proceeded to participate in a cordial shake.

Jace shifted his eyes in Sarah's direction, praying she would behave and not cause a ruckus. Although, he did have some hope that Sarah's jealous insecurities with Maria had been tempered somewhat after his mother's gravesite story.

Jace offered Maria a meek smile. "Have a seat. Hopefully, the doctor will be here soon with some good news."

Both women sat, allowing just enough room for him to squeeze in the middle.

He let out a forceful sigh. Waiting for an update on Sabrina's condition was enough to worry about, but he now had the added pressure of being sandwiched between his wife and the mistress that never was. He sat with beads of sweat trickling from under his armpits and down his side. He made a conscious effort to lean closer to Sarah.

"Do you know what caused the accident?" Maria asked.

"No. I don't have any details," he said, looking straight ahead, purposely not making eye contact with Maria.

He took a deep breath, upset with himself for letting this interaction with Maria and Sarah consume his thoughts while his main focus should clearly be on Sabrina's health. He sat, tapping his right heel on the floor as Sarah remained quiet.

He tilted his head in Sarah's direction. "You okay?"

She nodded unconvincingly.

Jace was unsure if her quiet behavior was due to the stress of waiting to hear news about Sabrina or being uncomfortable sitting by Maria, or a combination of the two. Instead of subsiding, Jace's anxiety intensified. His heart rate quickened, with sweat forming on his brow. He swallowed, attempting to wet his parched throat, but it didn't help.

"Sorry, ladies. You'll have to excuse me. I'm a little thirsty."

He followed a sign posted on the wall, pointing to the vending machines. He also figured it wouldn't be a bad idea for the women to get to know each other. Maybe that would convince Sarah even more that nothing had happened.

He rounded the corner, leaving Sarah all alone with the phantom mistress.

# Chapter 37

Sarah watched Jace disappear down the hall. Her comfort level went from bad to worse. With Jace no longer acting as a buffer, she was now exposed and didn't like it one bit. She never imagined she would feel intimidated by this beauty queen sitting an arm's length away from her.

Looking at Maria's stunning appearance in person made her feel severely inadequate on a physical level. She hated to think this way, but if Jace had cheated on her, at least he'd picked a swan instead of an ugly duckling.

She quickly batted her eyelids, drawing herself away from those superficial thoughts and on to the real reason they were at the hospital.

She turned to Maria. "I pray Sabrina will be okay."

Maria puffed out her cheeks before exhaling. "I feel like I've known her forever. She's such a sweet person." Maria dabbed her eyes with the back of her hands, wiping the tears that rolled down her cheek. "She's helped me out so much, and she barely even knew me."

Sarah reached into her bag, handing her a tissue. "I have a good feeling that she'll make it through this. She's a strong person on the inside and out."

Silence followed as Sarah contemplated what to say. *Here they come again.* She did her best to ignore the jealous demons inside her, relentless in their pursuit to be pushed to the forefront of her mind, no matter the circumstances.

With these unwelcomed demons temporarily in control, she had the sudden urge to pry and see if she could gather any clue as to whether Jace had been telling the truth about his relationship with Maria. But, even if something had gone on, she realized there was no way in hell that Maria would admit it to her face. Not to mention how stupid Sarah began to feel by entertaining these ridiculous thoughts while Maria sat next to her, feeling heartbroken for their mutual friend.

Sarah closed her eyes in an attempt to immediately banish these demons from her mind. She took a deep breath and figured she would carry on with some small talk to lighten the mood and keep her jealous insecurities in check.

"Leave it to my husband to go find something to drink and not even ask if we wanted anything. You have to excuse his manners. I know I taught him better than that."

"That's okay. I don't know if you know the story. I guess you can say he's the one who introduced me to Sabrina. Without him, I would have never had her friendship."

Maria's eyes continued to water. "I still can't believe what happened to her." She dabbed her eyes once more. "I just feel so guilty because I'm the one who asked her to meet me after work. If it wasn't for me, none of this probably would have happened."

Maria continued to sob with her head down as Sarah patted her on the back in an attempt to provide some level of comfort.

At that instant, it all became clear to Sarah as she

pushed the green-eyed monster deeper into the recesses of her mind. Maria wasn't the least bit interested in Jace at this moment. She wasn't there to flirt with him, spend more time with him, or make her jealous in any way. She was there to support Sabrina, hoping and praying she would make it through this ordeal.

A sudden wave of emotion flooded Sarah's body, prompting her to shed some tears. On the one hand, she felt a sense of accomplishment for temporarily taming her jealous demons. However, she didn't know if, within the next hour, Sabrina would even still be alive.

# Chapter 38

Jace's head snapped forward, nodding on the couch, before feeling a tap on his leg. He opened his eyes to see a tall figure with a white smock standing in front of him.

"Are you all here for Sabrina Newman?"

"Yes," Jace said, quickly sitting up at attention.

"Is she okay?" Maria asked.

The doctor grimaced. "To be honest, it's too early to tell. She sustained some major injuries with a good deal of internal bleeding. We have her heavily sedated. The next twenty-four hours will be crucial to see how she responds to the surgery."

Jace put his head down, Maria covered her mouth with tears welling up in her eyes, while Sarah sat with a blank stare.

The doctor looked at his watch. "Unfortunately, there isn't much you all can do here at this time. It's well past midnight. I'd suggest you all go home and try to get some rest. You can come back tomorrow, and we will have a better idea of how she's doing."

Jace stared straight ahead with no discernable expression. He was numb, unable to react to the news that ignited the somber mood amongst everyone. He complied with the doctor's suggestion and shuffled through the revolving doors, following Sarah and Maria.

He walked into the parking lot and turned to Maria.

"Where did you park?"

She pointed to the other side of the lot.

Before he could say anything further, Sarah responded, "It's too dark out here to walk by yourself. The least we can do is walk you to your car."

Jace attempted to smile but found it difficult under the circumstances. His tactic of leaving them alone in the waiting area seemed to have paid off. He wasn't sure what was discussed, but Sarah's kind-hearted gesture toward Maria at least indicated they connected on some level.

When they arrived at Maria's car, she turned to Sarah and Jace. "Thanks for the company." She leaned in Sarah's direction, giving her a hug. Then she turned to Jace and did the same.

She sat in her car and rolled down the window. "If you find out anything before I do, no matter what time it is, please let me know."

She drove away, disappearing into the night.

# Chapter 39

Later that morning, Sarah sat up in bed with a crippling migraine. She took a swig of bottled water to chase down the prescription medication she had just consumed. This was the same type of headache that had eventually ended her career. Considering all that had happened in the past few weeks, she wasn't surprised by it. In fact, she had expected it. It was just a matter of when it would occur, and it was no surprise it happened at this moment.

She only had three hours of sleep, after getting home from the hospital at four in the morning. She didn't understand how Jace made it to work. The kids were in school, leaving her to suffer alone, awaiting the news from the hospital on Sabrina's condition.

After resting for a half-hour, the intense headache subsided somewhat, enough for her to rotate her feet off the bed and plant them on the carpet. She took a deep breath and tilted her head up, thinking of a hot bubble bath, usually the last step in her effort to get rid of these debilitating migraine symptoms.

She gathered the strength and stood, making sure her balance was on point before taking a step. On tired legs, she ambled her way to the bathroom and opened the cabinet under the sink, pulling out a bottle of her special aromatherapy-infused bubble bath.

She immediately stopped moving, getting a whiff of an

unpleasant odor.

She approached the toilet and lifted the lid, grimacing at the contents inside. It appeared the toilet had backed up. She flushed, praying the water would go down and not overflow onto the floor. Her prayers were answered as the water twirled around the commode and eventually out of sight.

She slammed the lid, intent on cleaning the bowl, but not before a relaxing bath.

She turned on the hot water valve in the tub and immediately heard a muffled knocking sound coming from the pipes as the water hesitated to flow. She turned the knob further to increase the pressure. The water initially poured out with a cloudy tint before the clarity became crystal clear.

After adjusting the knobs for the optimum temperature, she plugged the drain, and then poured in the bubble bath. A mound of bubbles erupted from the water and a sweet coconut scent permeated the bathroom, overtaking the nefarious odor that had dwelled in the air moments ago. She took a deep breath, invigorated by the sauna-type atmosphere.

She exited the bathroom, closing the door behind her to keep any steam from escaping. She entered the bedroom before undressing and wrapping a robe around her exposed skin, waiting for the water to fill the tub.

She returned to the bathroom, wearing her pink, knitted robe. Upon entering the fog-filled room, she immediately smelled the coconut-scented bath, along with the odor from the toilet that still lingered. She ran over and shut off the water after noticing the bubbles cascading over the bathtub faucet as well as the brim of the tub. She proceeded to disrobe and stepped into the inviting water with her body disappearing under the mountain of transparent orbs.

She sat still for a minute, letting her muscles soak in the heat. She closed her eyes, relaxing further, but struggled to maintain her moment of Zen after the nasty odor suddenly become more intense.

She lifted her right forearm from beneath the bubbles and raised it to her nose. Her relaxed heart rhythm received a sudden jolt as she realized that wicked scent was no longer just coming from the toilet but was now wafting from the tub. She cupped her hands together, lifted them out of the tub, and screamed.

With a sudden burst of anxiety-induced energy, she jumped out of the bathtub, shaking her body as if it were covered with an army of ants. She immediately grabbed the toilet brush and cleared away the bubbles in the tub, revealing a mass of water, no longer crystal clear, but mocha brown.

She lunged for her towel, attempting to soak up the beads of water that remained on her skin. Running the towel across her back, she experienced a tingling sensation on the surface of her skin. She wasn't sure if it was caused by the sudden friction of the towel or a reaction to the brown-tinted water.

As she continued to frantically dry her body, the tingling intensified into a burning sensation across her skin.

She dropped to her knees as the pain quickly became unbearable. She had to get to her cell phone but realized it was sitting on the nightstand in the bedroom, which would be a difficult journey in her weakened state.

With every ounce of determination, she crawled out of the bathroom and into the hallway. Her raw hands and knees ached with pain each time she made contact with the floor. She screamed after noticing an expansive area of red blotches forming on her skin. On shaky arms and legs, she crawled into the bedroom and approached the phone.

# Chapter 40

Jace sat quietly in the boardroom, listening to several members of upper management give their speech on company earnings. He'd only been in the meeting for ten minutes, and his eyes struggled to stay open.

After spending half the night at the hospital, his weary body longed for a nap, although this was not the time nor place for it. He sat around an oval table, in plain view of at least fifteen coworkers and five members of management. Nodding off at this time would not be recommended.

He felt a vibrating sensation on his hip. He peeked down at his cell to see Sarah's name appear on the caller ID. He grimaced, knowing he was unable to answer the phone in the meeting.

The off-and-on vibration continued while he contemplated what to do. He could let her leave a message and check it after the meeting, but if this was a true emergency, he couldn't wait that long. He immediately raised his hand and excused himself from the meeting. He scurried into the hallway and answered, but Sarah had already hung up. He redialed.

"Sarah? Are you okay?"

After a few seconds of silence, she whispered, "H-help me, Jace."

"What's wrong?"

Before she could answer, the phone abruptly

disconnected.

He immediately tried calling back but received no answer.

With a sudden wave of terror enveloping his body, Jace ran to the stairwell and glided down three flights of stairs. He bolted across the parking lot with his shirttail escaping the tucked-in confines of his pants as he twisted and turned from the all-out sprint. His hands hit the car with a thud as he proceeded to yank open the door.

It would normally take him thirty minutes to drive home from the office, but this drive would be far from normal. *I can do this in fifteen minutes*, he thought. Cutting the drive time in half would be next to impossible, but if he was ever going to get close to the impossible, this was the moment to do it. He shifted the car in gear and slammed on the gas, tires skidding momentarily from the sudden acceleration.

As he exited the office parking lot, he contemplated which route to take as the highway allowed him the opportunity to drive faster, but this would also add another mile or so to his journey. Or he could take the local streets, offering a shorter route, though he would have to contend with traffic lights and a more tamed speed limit. Jace shook his head, thinking that tamed would not be part of the game plan at this juncture.

He entered onto the main road, putting him a couple of miles away from the highway on-ramp.

"Please be good to me," he muttered, like a gambler hoping for that lucky dice roll. Though, in this case, the pawns in this game were the traffic lights. He didn't want to think too hard about what would happen if he came upon a red light, but with his desperate attempt to get to Sarah, he could only imagine the traffic light colors would all be three shades of green in his eyes.

With his senses heightened, he weaved in and out of some light traffic as he approached the first light. He sped along through the intersection with the light remaining a steady green. *One light down, two more to go.* The second light up ahead followed suit, displaying a green signal as he cleared the second intersection. Although the third and final light up ahead remained green, he found himself behind a dilapidated van coasting at an abnormally slow speed in the left lane and a city bus in the right lane, matching the van's lethargic pace. He honked his horn, pleading with the van to move to the right lane to clear the path for him. The traffic gods were looking down on Jace as the city bus suddenly stopped to pick up passengers. *Thank you!*

He quickly shifted into the now open right lane, breezing by the van as if it were standing still. With the path now clear ahead of him, he approached the next intersection, but in a matter of seconds, the light switched from yellow to red. The color change didn't matter to Jace as he continued through the intersection, blowing the steady red light and getting a horn full from two cars that barely missed hitting him.

He picked up speed as he approached the highway on-ramp. Suddenly, Jace's Indy 500 impersonation was rudely interrupted by something that normally came with the territory of being a speed demon. The traffic gods giveth, and the traffic gods taketh away, as a swirl of lights presented themselves in his rearview mirror. With his adrenaline still in overdrive, he thought for an instant to keep going, pushing the accelerator harder, to try to outrun the patrol car behind him. He quickly doused that notion as his common sense awoke from its slumber and took the reins. He eased off the gas and edged onto the shoulder of the on-ramp with the patrol car pulling up behind him.

Jace took a deep breath, doing his best to tame the crippling anxiety rattling his inner space. In most other circumstances, he deserved to be pulled over for speeding and running a red light; however, on this occasion, his reason was completely valid. He knew that, but convincing this officer would be another story.

"This should hopefully be an easy one," Jace muttered under his breath. "All I need to do is tell the truth."

Jace reached into his wallet, pulling out the normal documentation requested during a traffic stop, and waited.

He drummed his fingers on the steering wheel and glimpsed in the rearview mirror, impatiently waiting for the patrol car door to swing open.

"Oh, come on!" Jace said, gritting his teeth.

His few seconds of waiting turned into well over a minute. Jace sat seconds away from opening the car door and waving the officer over before there was finally movement. A pair of shoes dropped to the ground from the patrol car and revealed a sight far from what Jace had expected as the officer stood. Jace was used to being the short one in comparison to most groups of men, but the statuesque officer that approached Jace's window would put most men to shame in the height department.

"Are you practicing to be a stunt driver, sir?" the officer said with a voice that appeared to be coming from the heavens.

Jace tilted his head up and focused on the name tag. *Officer Johnson.* "No, Officer. I was just in a rush because my wife is having some type of medical emergency."

The officer bent down, folding his long torso to get a glimpse inside the car. "It appears to me that you're alone."

"I meant to say, my wife is at home, and I was rushing to get to her because of a medical emergency."

The officer nodded slightly. "License and registration, please."

Jace handed over the items. The officer stood with the top half of his frame no longer in view. After a few seconds, he leaned in once more.

"Do you realize you could have caused a serious accident back at that intersection?"

"Yes, Officer. I wasn't thinking straight with the stress of worrying about my wife."

Jace hoped the second mention of Sarah would prompt the officer's sympathetic side to make an appearance.

"I need you to do me a big favor and wait right here while I go back to the patrol car. Don't get out of the car, don't make any sudden movements, and most importantly, do not—and I repeat—do not try to drive off."

"With all due respect, Officer, my wife is in trouble

and I really need to get to her now."

"You should have thought about that before you blew through the red light and endangered your life as well as the lives of the passengers in the other two cars you almost hit."

Jace knew the officer was absolutely right. However, at this moment, he didn't care. He could only think about getting to Sarah as quickly as possible. He refrained from speaking further and figured he would give the officer no more than a few minutes to handle his business in the patrol car.

As the officer departed and walked back to the patrol car, Jace dialed Sarah's cell phone again and received no answer.

Jace peeked in the rearview mirror as the towering officer folded his body back into the patrol car. Jace tilted his head back against the seat, saying a quick prayer, not only for Sarah, but also for his patience, currently being tested beyond belief.

Moments later, Jace focused his eyes on the time as those few minutes he allotted the officer expired, and the officer had not budged from the patrol car. *Now what? Do I dare get out of the car and wave the police officer over? Should I just blow my horn?* Either one of those scenarios most likely wouldn't bode well for Jace, but desperation was at an all-time high for him to continue his journey to reach Sarah.

Acting on blind instinct, Jace rolled down the window and began waving his arm to get the patrol officer's attention. It took a moment before the officer noticed Jace's frantic hand gestures. With his abnormally long strides, the officer approached Jace's window, visibly annoyed.

"I see you have a problem listening, sir. You're already in hot water with the stunt you just pulled at the intersection and now you have the nerve to want to rush me through my procedures? Do me a favor and put both your hands on the steering wheel and don't move a muscle."

Jace complied and started to open his mouth to speak but immediately stopped upon hearing the muffled buzz of his vibrating phone resting in the cup holder. He darted his eyes in the direction of the phone and saw Sarah's name appear on the caller ID.

His heart rate spiked at the sight. His arms flinched to go for the phone before remembering the officer had imprisoned his hands to the steering wheel. He continued to hold on to the steering wheel.

"Officer, this is my wife calling, and I can't even begin to tell you how badly I need to answer this."

The officer folded his arms. "What part of keeping your hands on the steering wheel do you not understand?"

Jace put his head down and closed his eyes. There were moments in every man's life where their pride and ego must be thrown out the window to make room for the ultimate act of vulnerability—succumbing to the act of begging.

He opened his moisture-filled eyes and turned to the officer, not knowing how much longer he had to pick up the phone before it disconnected. "Officer, I'm begging you, can I please answer this phone? I'll put the call on speaker so you can talk to my wife and see that I'm not lying."

It took longer than expected, but some semblance of sympathy finally surged forward as the officer's face softened at Jace's heartfelt plea. He offered a slight nod to give Jace permission to answer.

Jace grabbed the phone and put it on speaker. "Sarah, are you okay?"

A few seconds elapsed before Sarah responded in a trembling voice, "No."

"What's wrong? What happened?"

Jace waited for a response but only heard the sound of labored breathing before the call promptly disconnected.

Before Jace could say anything, the officer said, "Give me your home address. Follow me, and I'll escort you to your house."

Jace followed closely behind the patrol car as it sped along, clearing the path for a much quicker commute. Within fifteen minutes, they arrived in front of the house. Jace unlocked the front door with the officer following behind.

"Sarah, where are you?" Jace shouted.

No response.

He ran into the kitchen and around through the living room with Sarah nowhere in sight. He raced up to the second level, concerned with a foul scent coming from somewhere upstairs. As he approached the top of the steps, the odor became stronger. He followed the scent into the bathroom before noticing the tub filled with coffee-colored water and bubbles surrounding the edges, but Sarah was nowhere to be found.

The officer walked steps behind Jace with his hand resting on his hip, near his service revolver.

Upon exiting the bathroom, Jace slipped on an apparent wet spot. He tilted his head down and saw a trail of water droplets leading from the bathroom into the bedroom. He swallowed hard, following the trail, and stopped just short of the bedroom.

"Sarah? Are you in there?"

He closed his eyes, saying a silent prayer before entering. He stepped in.

"Oh my God!"

Before the officer could enter the room, Jace held up his hand to prevent him from entering. He ran to Sarah, who had collapsed on the floor and was curled up in the fetal position by the foot of the bed. He kneeled beside her and gasped at her nude body, covered in a sea of red blotches as she remained motionless. He focused on her midsection, relieved to see the rise and fall around her rib cage, indicating air filtering in and out of her lungs. He ran to the closet and grabbed one of her summer dresses, draping it over her body before motioning the officer to approach.

"Sarah? Can you hear me?"

She didn't respond.

Before Jace could say anything further, the officer called dispatch, requesting an ambulance.

# Chapter 41

Jace sat in the waiting room at Presbyterian Hospital, almost in the same place he had sat the previous night. Although, this time, he sat alone. Ryan and Ava were still in school and had a few hours to go before it ended.

It had been at least three hours since Sarah had been admitted to the emergency room with no word as of yet on her condition. He also hadn't heard any updates on Sabrina. He tilted his head to the ceiling. His eyes were swollen and red from crying, along with a serious case of sleep deprivation. *What did I do to deserve this*? What were the chances of him being at the same hospital, two days in a row, for two separate, mind-numbing incidents?

He closed his eyes, trying with all his might to see the light at the end of the tunnel, but in his mind, it was an oncoming train. The only light he could see was not at the end, but at the beginning, back in St. Louis. Before the decision to move, before the weekend trip to Albuquerque, before Mr. Kincade had called him into the office to discuss the relocation offer. It became clear to him now. Home is where the heart is, and his was still in St. Louis.

"Hello, Mr. Valentine?" a male voice echoed in the background.

Jace focused on a tall figure standing in front of him, wearing a white coat. He quickly came to his senses, realizing the doctor had some information to share.

He quickly stood. "Is she okay?"

"She's heavily sedated to help ease the pain, but she's going to be okay," the doctor said with a grin, delivering the good news. "She's suffering from first and some second-degree corrosive burns. The water she came in contact with contained some type of unknown substance that led to her burns."

"How?" Jace inquired.

"I'd suggest having someone from the water company come out immediately to test your water. In the meantime, I'm sure I don't have to tell you to stop using the water." The doctor put his hand on Jace's shoulder. "It's probably a good idea for you to go home and get some rest while your wife sleeps. She should be in better condition tomorrow to talk."

***

The next day, Jace left work early to visit Sarah at the hospital. He ascended the stairs with a bouquet of flowers, following signs for the burn unit. He arrived at the room and cautiously entered, not knowing what condition he would find Sarah in.

An immediate temperature change was evident upon entering the well air-conditioned room. The smell of lemon-scented disinfectant tickled his nose.

He paused for a moment, gaping in stunned silence at the first sight of Sarah.

Strips of gauze bandages smothered her body from shoulder to waist with a thin bed sheet covering her legs, the bed propped slightly with Sarah's head leaning to the side as she slept. An IV bag was attached to a stand beside the bed, with a tube running to her right forearm. A beeping sound emanated from a machine on the other side of the bed, keeping track of her vital signs. A bowl of soup rested on a tray beside the bed, along with a plastic cup filled halfway with water.

He placed the flowers at the foot of the bed, staring for a moment with misty eyes. He grabbed the bouquet, gently resting them on a nearby desk, trying his best to muffle the crinkling sound of the plastic wrap surrounding the flowers. He studied Sarah, her eyes fluttering and eventually opening, followed by the hint of a smile. Jace reciprocated with a smile of his own.

"Hi, sweetheart," he whispered, giving her a gentle kiss on the forehead.

"Hi," she replied, her voice cracking slightly.

"How do you feel?"

She cleared her throat before answering, "A little numb." She sat up slightly, wincing in pain. "How's Sabrina?"

Jace mustered a chuckle. "Don't you want to know how you're doing first?"

She grimaced. "From the pain, not too well."

"To answer your question about Sabrina, last thing I heard she was still unconscious, but the internal bleeding had stopped. I'll try to get another update before I leave the hospital." He paused. "Now, are you ready to hear about your injuries?"

"I guess that's probably a good idea."

"The doctor said you have first and second-degree corrosive burns."

"Burns?"

"Yeah. The bath water was tainted with some chemical substance." Jace's eyebrows suddenly scrunched together. "How come you didn't listen to me? I told you not to use the water."

She kept quiet for a moment. "I know, dumb move on my part, and now I must face the consequences. But I'm so glad you stopped the kids from using the water." She looked down at her wrapped torso and grimaced. "I feel like a well-done turkey."

Jace pondered for a second, Sarah's bird reference jarring a concerning thought. "Just like the geese," he whispered.

"What did you say?"

"Just like the geese. I hope the water from the lake isn't contaminating our water supply. Or worse, the community."

She winced in pain once more, attempting to shift her arm. "How can we prove that?"

"Your accident might be all the proof we need."

She yawned. "Whatever they have in this IV makes me drowsy."

She put her head down. "Is this what they call around here the Jeffries Jinx?"

"I don't know. I'm just tired of all this nonsense. Someone is keeping a big secret from us about this place, and I'm going to find out what it is if it's the last thing I do."

He received no response from Sarah.

He looked over at her tilted head and realized she had fallen asleep. He sat for a few minutes, staring at her ravaged body. He hated to think how her skin looked under the bandages. He kissed her on the forehead and sat down on the chair in the corner of the room and eventually nodded off.

# Chapter 42

Jace left the hospital, heading back home. With no plans of returning to work that afternoon, he had some time to unwind before school ended for Ryan and Ava.

Twenty minutes later, he entered the development and immediately noticed a *"For Sale"* sign on the lawn of the first house on the left. He traveled farther and noticed another. He continued down the road, approaching his house, and stared at it with suspicious eyes. He applied pressure to the brake and stopped in front of the curb, his body hit with an unexpected shiver.

He felt a strange sensation, as if the house had eyes, staring back at him. Any other person would view the house as well-kempt with an inviting curb appeal, but it was what was on the inside that mattered the most, and as far as Jace was concerned, the exterior walls were hiding something. Something that might not just be isolated to his house, but all homes in the community. He shut off the engine and sat quietly, in no rush to enter the house.

The neighborhood remained eerily still, showing no sign of life. Every now and then, a stiff wind blew, rustling the leaves on the trees surrounding the area. Minutes later, a car engine purred in the distance.

He peered up the road as a blue Crown Victoria slowed and came to a stop beside him.

"Mr. Aderlee. How are you?"

"Just taking it day by day. At my age, I'm just happy to be able to get out of bed."

Before Jace could respond, Mr. Aderlee said, "Can I ask you a question? Have you been having any problems with your house lately?"

"What kind of problems?"

"Mostly these weird cracks showing up on our walls."

Jace's eyes lit up. "As a matter of fact, yes."

"We were just a little concerned. I had Malcolm come out and take a look. He seems to think the house is just settling."

"Yes, he told me the exact same thing."

Mr. Aderlee's face grew pensive. "Do you believe him?"

"I want to, but I truly don't know what to think." Jace pondered for a second. "Speaking of problems, have you had any with your tap water?"

"No, not that I can think of." He paused for a moment. "Well, now that you mention it, I turned the water on this morning and it came out a little cloudy, but it cleared up after a minute. Why do you ask?"

Jace contemplated for a moment, tempted to tell him about Sarah's accident. Though he didn't want to alarm him any further, he already seemed on edge with the other problems. The last thing he wanted to do was add more stress and anxiety to someone thirty years his senior.

"My water was coming out cloudy, also. Just wanted to know if you had the same problem."

Mr. Aderlee shrugged. "I guess cloudy water should be

the least of our concerns." He looked at his watch. "Sorry, I have to cut you short. I was on my way to the store to get something to settle my wife's stomach."

"Did she eat something bad?"

"I doubt it. She took some pills about an hour ago, and I don't think it agreed with her."

Jace thought for a second. "Is she supposed to take it with food?"

"No. Just a glass of water."

"Was that bottled water?"

"No, from the faucet."

Jace's heart fluttered and he hesitated to speak.

"Is something wrong?" Mr. Aderlee asked.

Jace paused to gather himself, his senses rattled from this terrifying revelation that suddenly consumed him.

"Uh . . . no." He inhaled deeply, attempting to tame his anxiety. He didn't want to speculate as to the cause of Mrs. Aderlee's stomach problems.

Mr. Aderlee stared at him for a moment. "If there's something wrong, I hope you would tell me?"

Jace nodded and displayed a halfhearted smile. "Of course, I would."

Mr. Aderlee shifted the car in gear. "Ok, I trust you. See you around, neighbor." He lurched forward and proceeded down the road.

A slew of thoughts careened back and forth in Jace's head. A part of him wanted to chase down Mr. Aderlee and tell him his theory, although that would waste time, and time was of the essence, especially if Mrs. Aderlee drank any contaminated water. He focused his attention next door, at Mr. Aderlee's house, a sudden sense of dread consuming him.

With sweaty palms, he exited the car and ran to the house. He stood in front of the door and extended his arm to ring the doorbell, receiving no response. He pressed again, holding it down for a few more seconds. Still nothing. He opened the screen to knock on the entry door and noticed it was partly open. He immediately stopped, not wanting to trespass.

He put his ear closer to the crack in the door, listening out for any sounds. He knocked, inadvertently pushing the door open further.

"Hello," he said, loud enough for anyone to hear within a short distance.

He took a few steps into the foyer. The thought of entering someone's home unannounced didn't sit well with him. He was trespassing and, at any moment, fair game to a weapon-wielding homeowner looking to protect their property. Though, under the circumstances, he didn't mind taking a chance.

He surveyed the area, the living and dining rooms positioned identically to his house. He peered down the hallway and into the kitchen.

"Hello? Mrs. Aderlee?

Nothing. Still no answer. He stepped in further, with the living room coming into full view. The furniture was neatly positioned with a mass of family portraits hanging on the walls. Several picture frames and glass figurines adorned the tops of the coffee tables.

He proceeded down the hallway, toward the kitchen, focused on the island in the middle of the room. A head of lettuce and sliced tomatoes rested on the island countertop next to a cutting board, indicating meal preparations were in progress, though there were no signs of anyone in the kitchen. He turned his attention to the floor, spotting what appeared to be the sole of a shoe sticking out from behind the island.

Jace recoiled, taking a deep breath and shuffling his feet to the right to get a better angle. To his horror, the shoes were still attached to their owner. Jace could clearly see, from the waist down, a female sprawled out on the floor, wearing a flower-printed dress. Shards of glass were scattered around the perimeter of the woman.

Jace hesitated for a moment before approaching the fallen female. He knelt, focusing on the woman's back, looking for any rise and fall around the rib cage, but there was none. Jace stood inches away from a lifeless body, facedown on the cold tiles of the floor with a head full of gray hair, no doubt convinced this was Mrs. Aderlee.

He rose to his feet in disarray. His eyes darted around the room and stopped at the phone hanging on the wall. He approached the phone but stopped immediately.

"No," he whispered, realizing anything he touched would have his fingerprints. Although completely innocent, he didn't want any forensic evidence traced back to him. He reached for his pocket, feeling for his cell phone, coming up empty. He ran out of the kitchen, through the hallway, and back outside, racing to grab his cell from the car. Upon dialing 911, he listened intently. However, the call didn't go through.

He sprinted into his house and used the landline to call for help. He knew it would take some time before an ambulance arrived and figured warning others in the neighborhood of this potential water issue would be the right thing to do.

He started the car, driving down the road, looking to alert as many people as he could. He stopped short in front of the next house he came upon and ran to the front door, knocking.

"Hey. Anybody home?"

He knocked with greater urgency, peering into the window to the right. The curtains had parted for a second before closing.

"Please, don't use the water," he screamed.

Still no response.

He ran back to the car, mashing his foot on the pedal, driving farther down the road as another house came into view. He spotted three young girls playing in a sprinkler on the front lawn and he immediately skidded to a halt.

"Stop!" he shouted, exiting the car.

He ran by them, waving his arms frantically. "Please, step away from the water."

The children backpedaled away from Jace.

"Excuse me. What's your problem?" a male voice shouted from the porch.

Jace focused his attention on the porch and spotted a

pot-bellied gentleman in a white tank top, standing with his fist in the air.

"I'm sorry if I scared the girls, but I think there's a problem with the community water."

The young girls huddled around the gentleman on the porch.

"I'm not doing anything," the man said in a stern voice. "You come running onto my property, screaming like a maniac, scaring my daughters. I have no clue who you are."

"I'm sorry, sir. I apologize for trespassing. My name is Jace Valentine. I live down the road, by the lake. To make a long story short, my wife is in the hospital due to some problems with our tap water, and I just came from a neighbor's house who was passed out on the floor. I think she fell sick after drinking the water."

The man's face softened a bit. He walked over to the water valve on the side of the house, shutting it off.

Jace continued, "I'm not sure if all houses are affected but didn't want to take any chances. I suggest you stay away from the water for now."

The man hesitated before nodding his head. "Don't let me find out this is some sort of sick joke."

"Believe me; I wouldn't joke around with something like this."

He hopped in the car, speeding off to warn others.

# Chapter 43

Maria picked up the phone and dialed.

"Gas-n-Go. How may I help you?" the voice on the other end asked.

"This is Maria. I won't be able to make it in today."

"Again?"

"No, I'm still not feeling well."

"This is the second time in one week."

"Sorry, I promise I'll be in tomorrow."

She sat at the kitchen table, her face lifeless, along with her hair pulled into a ponytail, several renegade strands sticking out, matching her underwhelming mood. She rubbed her forehead, attempting to get rid of the pounding headache, which had been rattling her senses for the past few days. There had been no change in Sabrina's condition; still heavily sedated and unresponsive.

Maria continued to shoulder the heavy burden of believing Sabrina's accident never would have happened if she hadn't asked her for help that day.

She sighed, standing to grab a bottle of water from the refrigerator, with the intention of taking some aspirin to assist with her throbbing headache. She consumed the capsule and closed her eyes, imagining herself back in Mexico, amongst her family.

Her home had always bustled with activity as family and neighbors streamed in and out to talk with her father, the self-proclaimed village socialite. He thrived on speaking in front of an audience, giving his advice, making people laugh, and sharing his childhood stories. Many people in the village treated him like a celebrity when they saw him out and about. As a child, Maria could never understand why he was such a big deal, especially knowing what went on behind closed doors in their household with her mother cracking the whip to make sure he pulled his weight when it came to completing any chores.

As she had grown up, she'd realized how much of a blessing it was to be raised by such a selfless father, who rarely thought about his own concerns. She admired his humble nature, never complaining when things were tough, always looking to cheer folks up with a funny story, and doing whatever was necessary to take care of his family. She would give anything now to be sitting with her legs crossed on the floor, listening to him speak, hearing his raspy voice, and laughing out loud at the animated way he delivered his stories.

Her trip down memory lane abruptly ended when she realized the bottle of aspirin had tipped onto the counter, prompting the oblong green and white capsules to roll around in a multitude of directions by her hand, with a few crashing to the floor.

She reluctantly faded back to reality, feeling even more despondent as that pleasant trip back to her childhood only temporarily soothed her depressive state.

She rubbed her bloodshot eyes and tilted the bottle upright before gathering the capsules that had escaped. She grabbed a handful of capsules and moved her hand by the bottle but suddenly stopped.

She slowly turned her fist with palms facing up and opened her fingers, revealing a handful of capsules, her eyes transfixed on the contents in her hand. Her senses grew numb, unable to hear, smell, or feel—completely distorting her version of reality. With her peripheral vision fading, the only thing she could see were those pills in her hand.

She calmly raised her hand to her face, her mouth watering and her mind playing a cruel joke, as if she were about to take part in a sumptuous meal. She tilted her head back and placed her hand on top of her mouth, opening wide. Then she relaxed her grip, letting several of the capsules fill her mouth. She grabbed the water bottle, took a sip and, in one fell swoop, swallowed some of the pills. She repeated the process once again, swallowing a few more. She closed her eyes, her senses still numb.

After a few seconds, her eyes shot open, her senses jolted out of their short trip through suspended animation. She tilted her head down at the table, eyeing the remaining capsules on the counter, and focused her attention on her hand balled into a tight fist. She opened it, revealing several more capsules. In a frightening instant, she realized what she had done.

"Oh Dios," she shouted.

She bolted to the bathroom, slamming the door behind her. She fell to the floor, leaning over the toilet bowl. Her heart pounded uncontrollably, not sure if due to her fear or the effect of the capsules she had just consumed. She thrust her index and middle fingers down the back of her throat, gagging in desperation. Tears flowed from her eyes, along with mucus from her nose, while she forced her fingers as far as she could down her throat. After several gut-wrenching gags, her stomach cramped for an instant before heaving the contents of her stomach into the toilet. She wiped her eyes to try to clear her blurred vision before counting ten capsules floating in the water.

She hugged the toilet bowl, breathing heavily, attempting to gain the strength to stand. After a moment, she flushed the toilet and rose on shaky legs. She wobbled into the living room, collapsing on the sofa from exhaustion and with the horrific realization that she could have possibly ended her life from this sudden short-circuit of consciousness and wicked lapse of judgment.

# Chapter 44

An hour had passed since Jace found Mrs. Aderlee sprawled out on the kitchen floor. A swirl of flashing lights had descended upon the area, an ambulance parked in the driveway, along with several police cars on the street. A small group of neighbors had gathered.

His initial attempt to warn other residents in the community about the water hadn't produced the results he wanted. His mission had only resulted in interacting with a handful of residents and most, if not all, thought he'd lost his mind.

Moments later, two men exited the house, rolling out a stretcher with a white sheet draped over it. He heard the soft sob of a gentleman standing in the driveway, and his heart sank upon noticing Mr. Aderlee crying with his hands covering his face.

A sudden wave of guilt stormed his conscience. *Would the outcome have changed if I told Mr. Aderlee my theory when we met a short time ago? Even if I had told, it wouldn't have changed the fact that Mrs. Aderlee had already drank the water. Besides, it wasn't proven yet that the water was the cause of death.*

He did his best to rationalize and help ease the guilt that consumed him as he remained standing on the sidewalk with the other inquisitive neighbors, nervously glancing around, wondering if anyone would believe his theory. He did take comfort in knowing Officer Johnson had witnessed the injuries from Sarah's bathtub incident. This gave him at least one member of law enforcement who could back up his story if needed. This was also the same member of law enforcement who he owed a great deal of thanks for escorting him home and refraining from giving him a ticket due to Sarah's unfortunate accident.

He swiveled his head from left to right, wondering if Officer Johnson had been called to the scene, though he would be easy to spot, standing head and shoulders above the crowd. He looked by the driveway and focused on an officer standing alone. He approached.

"Excuse me, Officer, do you know Officer Johnson?" Jace asked, raising his voice to talk over all the commotion surrounding the scene.

"I don't know him personally, but I do know he works at my station. Why do you ask?"

"Have you seen him around here?"

"I haven't. Is there something I can help you with?"

Jace thought of just leaving things alone and walking away then figured it wouldn't hurt to notify this officer of his theory. Having two officers aware of the potential water situation was better than one.

"Officer Johnson was at my house next-door a couple days ago, responding to an accident my wife had in the bathtub. There was something in our water that caused burns to her skin."

"Sorry to hear that. I'm hoping she makes a speedy recovery."

"Thanks. I was just worried there may be something in the community water that could have had something to do with my neighbor's passing."

"Sir, we don't know what happened to this victim until an autopsy is performed," the officer said as he trained his eye off to the right of Jace's shoulder.

Jace suddenly felt a tap on his back. He turned to see Mr. Aderlee standing there, his eyes red and swollen from crying. "Did I hear you correctly? You mean to tell me you had an idea my wife was in danger, and you couldn't even warn me when we talked earlier?"

Jace blinked a few times as his face tightened, ashamed to look Mr. Aderlee in the eye. "I . . . I wasn't sure, and I didn't want to scare you," he said, feeling like a witness on the stand being cross-examined in the worst way.

Mr. Aderlee's lips trembled. "How could you do this?" He turned around, looking at the ambulance. "Look at what happened," he said, sniffling. "Now my wife is gone, and you didn't do a damn thing to warn me."

Jace remained motionless, staring at the ground.

Mr. Aderlee placed his hand under Jace's chin, forcefully lifting it until their eyes met. "Don't you hear me talking to you, young man?"

Jace made eye contact briefly before closing his eyes due to a crushing wave of shame and guilt.

"Do you know next week would have been our fifty-year anniversary? And now look. She's gone." Mr. Aderlee's voice trailed off, sobbing. He raised his right arm, opening his hand.

The officer lunged and grabbed his wrist as it started toward Jace's face.

"That's not necessary," the officer said.

The officer motioned for Jace to leave the area before he led Mr. Aderlee away.

Jace walked away in total disarray. He sat on the curb, feeling like a piece of trash just thrown on the street. His energy had been drained instantly, sitting with his head between his legs. A part of him wished the officer hadn't stopped Mr. Aderlee and allowed him to proceed with a hard smack to the face. He deserved it, along with every ounce of pain that would have accompanied the smack.

He had thought he hit rock bottom already, but this moment just proved there were depths of despair that he had yet to navigate through. Here he was again, with his mind and body taking up refuge in the dungeon. The negative thoughts were coming fast and furious, leading to an immediate headache. He squeezed his eyes tight, saying a quick prayer to help him get through the moment.

After hearing a car door slam shut, he looked up to see a Silverado parked across the street. Out stepped Malcolm, walking by the driveway. It was as if his prayers had come in the form of Malcolm acting as a distraction.

Jace stared intently, his head aching from emotional overload. He flashed back to the last time he had seen Malcolm during their brief confrontation at the realty office. What if he was holding back information about the community? Why would he not tell anyone if people's lives were in danger? He needed answers, and he needed them now.

With renewed vigor, he stood and maneuvered his way by the driveway in hot pursuit. He squeezed through the small crowd that had gathered and broke out into the open, standing behind Malcolm.

Malcolm turned around. "Jace, I don't have time to discuss anything with you now."

Jace agreed this wouldn't be the best moment to talk about his concerns. "When the time is right, will you be ready to tell me and the rest of the community what's going on?"

He stared at Jace. "I don't know what's going on and that's what I'm trying to find out." He surveyed the scene. "Do you know what happened?"

"I'd like to say no."

"Well . . . do you or don't you?"

"I was hoping you could shed a little light on that."

Malcolm sighed heavily. "Look, I have no time to play guessing games. If you want to talk about this further, you can call me at my office in a couple of hours." He pointed to the ambulance. "Now, if you'll excuse me, I have to continue on to the real reason I came here." He turned his back on Jace and walked to the front entrance of the house.

A scowl developed on Jace's face, and then he shouted, "Since you're so concerned about the welfare of the people in the community, maybe when you're done, you can visit my wife in the burn unit of Presbyterian Hospital."

Malcolm turned around. "I'm sorry to hear that."

"Me, too. Who would have thought soaking in a

bathtub could be dangerous to your health."

Several groans escaped from the group that had gathered.

"Yes. You heard me correctly. My wife received burns over half her body because the bath water was tainted with some foreign chemical."

"What are you talking about?" Malcolm asked.

"That's one of the many questions I have for you. And until I find out what's going on, I shut off the water valve to my house." Jace craned his neck, eyeing the congregation around him. "I'd suggest you all do the same."

"How do you know it's not just a problem with your house?" a voice said amongst the masses.

Jace shrugged. "We don't know, and until we do, I think you all need to follow suit."

"Wait a minute!" Malcolm interrupted. "You can't make everybody shut off their water because of an isolated incident."

"You're right. I can't make them do anything. They can run their water at their own risk."

A man behind Jace said, "Do you think this is related to the contaminated lake that killed the fish and geese?"

Malcolm threw his hands up. "Wait a minute. Did we all forget why we're here now? I'm just responding to a call I received concerning a neighbor who had a serious accident, and you all are fixated on the water?" He surveyed his small audience. "I agree this all needs to be addressed, but this is not the time nor place. If you all want to discuss this further, you can meet me at my office in a couple of hours."

****

Jace arrived at the realty office. There were several other cars in the parking lot, though no sign of Malcolm's pickup. A crowd of about fifteen people had gathered, roaming the parking lot and engaging in small conversations.

Jace exited the car as a woman approached. "He hasn't shown up yet," she said.

"Did someone check to see if the door was open?"

"I don't know," she responded.

Jace approached the front door and tried to open it, but it wouldn't budge.

"I tried it already," a man said. "Guess we'll just have to wait until he shows up."

Jace focused on some tire tracks engraved in the soft soil, along the side of the building. He walked around and followed the tracks to the back of the building. He rounded the corner and spotted Malcolm's Silverado parked, nestled up against the rear wall of the building. He approached a metal door and raised his hand to knock, but no one answered. He surveyed the area and noticed a basement window, ground level to the right.

He approached, kneeling while pressing his nose against the window and cupping his hands around both sides of his face to shield the sun's glare. Although the dust-covered window made it difficult to see, he could make out what appeared to be stacks of boxes piled in the basement. He brushed his hand back and forth over the outside of the window to clear some of the dust before hearing the back door swing open.

"Can I help you?" a familiar voice echoed from not too far away.

Jace fell on the seat of his pants, looking up to the left to see Malcolm standing at the back door entrance. He sprang to his feet, dusting the dirt from the back of his pants.

"No. I'm okay," he replied, feeling somewhat embarrassed. He gathered himself. "Me and the other neighbors were up front waiting for you. I didn't know if you were here, so I came around back to see."

"Interesting place to look for me. Go around to the front. I'll be there in a minute to open the door."

Jace complied and walked back up front.

Malcolm eventually opened the door. "Wow! Didn't expect this large of a group." He shook his head. "Not enough room in my office. Guess we'll just stay out here."

He remained on the porch. "Since this is an informal meeting and we have such a large crowd, we need to keep things civilized. Whenever you have a question, if you could be so kind as to raise your hand, I'll choose each person to speak one at a time."

Jace immediately raised his hand, along with most of the residents who had gathered. Malcolm pointed to an elderly woman in the front.

"What happened to that poor woman today?" she asked.

"It's too early to tell. Her husband said she had a heart

condition, but we won't know anything until an autopsy is complete."

Jace raised his hand once more, yet Malcolm pointed to another man.

"What about the lake? What's being done about that horrible smell?"

"Once we have the results back from the water samples, a determination can be made on the next course of action to clean up the lake."

Another lady yelled, "I've seen enough already; my house is on the market now. Only been living there for five months and had nothing but trouble."

Jace raised his hand once more, doing his best to respect Malcolm's wishes and not yell out his question without being called upon, but his patience was running short.

Malcolm looked in Jace's direction, pointing to the gentleman directly beside him.

"And what about the cracks in our walls?"

"That's all part of the aging process of new houses. It needs time to settle, which can lead to cracks. As part of the building warranty, if you call the contractor's number, they can have someone come out and patch up the cracks."

"The same gentleman said, "It's not just the walls, I see cracks in people's driveways, sidewalks—they're all over the place."

Jace looked around as more hands went up. His frustration brewed, knowing Malcolm purposely avoided his hand, looking to tick him off, and it was working. He cleared his throat and asked, "What are you going to do about the water situation?"

Malcolm put his hands on his hips, shaking his head. "I knew one of you would mess up the flow." He turned to Jace. "Do you mind waiting until I call on you?"

Jace's face flushed with heat. His face hardened as he looked at Malcolm with seething eyes. "Oh, come on. You gotta be kidding me. We're not in school. This is serious business. My wife is suffering in the hospital from something that shouldn't have happened, and I need to find out what the hell is wrong with the water!"

"Yeah. What about the water?" someone else yelled. "If there's something wrong with it, I think we all need to know."

"Right now, we can only treat it as an isolated incident," Malcolm said.

"Isolated my ass!" Jace shouted. "So, you're telling me no one else should be concerned?"

Malcolm glanced around the congregation of neighbors. "It depends on the answer to the following question. Has anyone else experienced anything wrong with their water?"

The crowd grumbled, yet no one offered an affirmative response.

He focused on Jace. "This is why I say it's an isolated incident."

"I find it too much of a coincidence the water in my house was contaminated less than a couple weeks after the fish and geese came up dead in the lake." Jace moved his head from right to left, scanning the group. "Am I the only one who feels this way?"

"He has a good point," a woman said in the back.

"We don't know if it's the same problem," Malcolm said. "Besides, don't you think, if this was a widespread problem with the water, we would have gotten more complaints or injuries in the past few days?"

Jace bit his lip, tempted to mention his theory about Mrs. Aderlee, but remained silent.

Malcolm continued, "If anyone is still worried about it, feel free to shut off your water valve, but I don't think it's necessary."

"What if it's not an isolated incident?" a man standing in the front asked. "Don't you think someone from the public water company should come check things out to be on the safe side?"

"In case you all didn't know, any homeowner with a private well system is responsible for maintaining it, and that means all of you," Malcolm said, waving his hand across the parking lot.

"Private well system?" a few people yelled in unison.

"Yes. Each house in Granwin is connected to its own private well."

"Nobody told me this!" a woman shouted.

Someone else shouted, "I knew about it."

"I'm sorry if you all didn't know. You were all given this information at one time or another before you purchased the house."

Jace yelled out, "I find it hard to believe that not all of

us knew this."

"Each of you should have looked through your contract papers more carefully," Malcolm said.

"This is bull!" someone yelled.

Malcolm took a few steps by the edge of the porch. "Hold on a damn minute! You need to give me credit for meeting with you all in the first place. Truthfully, my obligation to each of you could have ended after you signed the papers and closed on the house." The crowd's noise simmered. "I could have taken my commission and run, but that's not my style. I wanted to make sure each of you was comfortable in your new homes, and that doesn't seem to be working out. Now, as a courtesy, I can give you a number to a company that can take a look at each of your well systems to make sure they're up to par." He twisted his head from left to right, surveying the concerned residents. "Remember, I'm not doing any of this because I have to, but because I want to. Now, if anyone still has a problem with that, you can schedule an appointment and meet me on an individual basis. This meeting is over as far as I'm concerned."

He walked inside, slamming the door behind him.

# Chapter 45

Malcolm remained by the door for a moment, anticipating a knock, or possibly even a rock through the window. Neither occurred. Varied conversations were taking place outside, but none of them appeared to be pleasant. The situation was unraveling quickly, along with his sanity.

The talking eventually subsided, followed by a chorus of car doors slamming and engines roaring. Malcolm peeked out the window and watched the last few cars leave the premises. In an instant, a sense of quietness settled in, all commotion outside ceasing.

He sat down on his office chair and took a deep breath while closing his eyes. His energy levels were completely depleted after having to deal with the past couple hours of drama. The residents were getting restless, and he had no tangible solutions to calm their fears. Who could blame them after his promises of a safe and comfortable living environment were not coming to fruition? Not only were the residents unhappy but the commercial property owner had concerns about him paying the business rent on time, since he had failed to do so the previous month. In addition to the rent being late, he had withdrawn money from his savings to help pay it in full, and he wasn't in any position to do that a second time.

This was not his idea of a successful business, and it

had put him in an unenviable position of needing to sell some assets to keep things afloat. He thought about parting ways with his precious classic 1965 Thunderbird, which could fetch him a pretty penny. Selling the car, in addition to some of the old family business artifacts, could result in enough money to assist with paying his expenses over the next few months. But he realized this might prove to be a risky proposition, especially if the downturn in business continued.

Although he had never thought it would come to this, he started to entertain a second and absolute last resort option of selling his house and relocating to start his business fresh, somewhere else in New Mexico. He understood a decision like this would not only impact him but the rest of the Winchester Realty team. This would mean alerting all his staff agents and having them search for another place to make a living. He would also need to consider the current state of the market. Being a seasoned real estate professional in a buyer's market, he knew he couldn't put the house on the market without shelling out money to pay for the much-needed home repairs.

He stood and put his hands on his hips with his thoughts drifting from the worries of the future to the more immediate concerns of the present. The day's events were most certainly memorable, culminating with the horrible news of Mrs. Aderlee's death. His heart ached from her loss and for the now widowed Mr. Aderlee. After convincing them to move in, he had done everything he could to ensure them a peaceful retirement home, and now the guilt from what had happened was unrelenting.

It would probably be a few days before he could find out the cause of death, but he hoped and prayed it had nothing to do with the water. He hoped the mystery of the polluted lake could be resolved and cleaned up quickly. He hoped the housing foundation cracks were indeed caused by settling. He hoped for a great deal, but his window of hope was getting smaller with each passing day and each unexplained phenomenon. His prior research of the land had pointed out many areas of concern, most of them labeled as highly unlikely.

He sighed, realizing these recent events, along with the impending storms, could mean the highly unlikely was upon him . . . and there was nothing he could do to stop it.

# Chapter 46

Clearing the last flight of stairs, Jace entered the second floor east wing. This time, he wasn't alone. Ryan and Ava followed closely behind, each with a bouquet of pink roses.

He entered Sarah's room, holding his index finger against his lip to make sure there was silence, unsure if she was sleeping. He rounded the corner, surprised to see her sitting up in bed, watching the TV hanging from the corner wall. She smiled while Ryan and Ava rushed to give her the flowers and a gentle hug. Jace followed with a light kiss on the forehead.

"What a difference a day makes," he said.

She grimaced. "Don't let this fool you. They gave me some medicine to take the edge off the pain, but I will say I'm feeling high as a kite right now."

Ryan and Ava sat quietly, undoubtedly saddened at Sarah's physical appearance.

She looked at them. "I know it's not easy for you guys to see me bandaged up like this, but I'll be okay."

They both nodded as Ava wiped a tear from her cheek.

Sarah focused on Jace. "Did they finally get the test results from the lake back?"

"As far as I know, they're still testing. I have a hunch the water in our bathtub was polluted with the same substance from the lake."

Sarah bit her bottom lip. "I hope you're wrong."

"Me, too. But after what happened yesterday, I don't think I am."

"What happened?"

"Unfortunately, I found our neighbor, Mrs. Aderlee, laid out on the floor. And I wouldn't be surprised if the water had something to do with it."

"Is she okay?"

Jace shook his head. "No, she was dead at the scene, and I, unfortunately, was the lucky one who found her. And when I'm ready, I'll need to tell you about what happened between me and Mr. Aderlee."

Sarah stared with a confused look on her face. "So sorry to hear about Mrs. Aderlee. And what happened between you and Mr. Aderlee?"

"As I said, I'm not ready to talk about that now. Not that I'll probably ever find out but, for my sake, I hope the autopsy reveals she didn't die from drinking contaminated water."

"Okay, we can talk about it another time." She paused for a moment. "So, what if your assumptions are right about the water? Don't you think you need to warn people about what's going on?"

"Already did. Me and some other residents in the community had a meeting with Malcolm at the realty office. Other neighbors are having issues, but not with their water. At least, not yet."

"Are they going to wait until someone else ends up like me?"

Jace shrugged. "They better not. I also found out something else about our water. It's not connected to the public water system."

"It's not?"

"Nope. It comes from a private well."

"Nobody told us that."

"According to Malcolm, this was all included in our paperwork when we purchased the house. I guess, with all the forms we had to look at, we could have just missed it."

Sarah put her head down. "This is just getting worse by the minute." She quickly looked up, her eyes suddenly widening. "How could I forget? How's Sabrina? Please tell me you have good news?"

"Not really. Last I heard, she was still in a coma."

"Did you at least get a chance to see her?"

"No. She's still in intensive care."

"I hope she makes it through this," Sarah said with a wounded look in her eye.

Silence overtook the room. Ryan and Ava continued to sit quietly, apparently not interested in joining the conversation.

"What about the information Sabrina was going to give us?" Sarah asked.

"What about it?"

"Do you think they were able to save some of her stuff from the accident?"

"I don't know. Why?"

"I assume, if she was coming to our house to give us whatever information she found out about the community, she may have had something in the car with her."

"I never really thought about it." His eyes narrowed with suspicion. "Who knows? She might have found something that may help give us a clue as to what's going on in the community."

"Even if they do have some of her belongings, where do you think they would be?" Sarah asked.

He scratched his chin. "Some place close to her. Maybe even in her hospital room, locked away somewhere."

"And how do you suppose we get to it?"

Jace thought for a moment. "I'll find a way."

Sarah raised one eyebrow in a questioning slant. "Don't do anything stupid, Jace."

***

Jace watched Sarah's eyelids struggle to stay open. She'd been awake for the entire two-hour duration of their visit, but her battered body needed the rest, as her eyelids eventually closed. Jace looked over at Ryan, who had fallen asleep, as well. Ava remained awake, staring at the TV.

He whispered, "I'll be back soon. If your mother wakes up, tell her I went to run an errand."

He exited the room and into the hallway, approaching the nurses station. He stopped in front of the U-shaped work area, with several computers, phones, and miscellaneous medical folders scattered on the desk. There were a few office chairs, but only one was occupied. He cleared his throat to get the attention of the lone nurse who sat with her back turned, typing on a computer keyboard. She swiveled in Jace's direction.

"How can I help you?"

"I was visiting my wife in the room down the hall and wondered if I can visit another patient?"

"I don't see why not. Do you know what room?"

"No, but I believe she's still in intensive care."

"Oh." The nurse glanced at the time. "Unfortunately, there's only limited visitation hours in that ward, and that ended about an hour ago. Maybe you can try tomorrow."

Jace grimaced. "Do you think I can just sneak in for a few minutes today?"

"No, I'm sorry, can't let you do that."

Jace shifted his eyes around the nurse station and came upon a white doctor smock, draped over one of the vacant chairs sitting out in the open.

"Guess I have no choice. I'll work something out tomorrow." He focused his attention at the computer on the opposite side of the desk. "Can you at least give me a room number so I know where I'm going tomorrow?"

"Hold on." The nurse turned back to the computer. "What's her name?"

"Sabrina Newman," Jace said while inching up to the vacant chair, now within reach.

She typed vigorously on the keyboard before a search yielded results. She turned and said, "Room 425. Visiting hours start at noon tomorrow."

"Thanks. One more question. Where's the nearest bathroom?"

She pointed to the left, down the hall. He quickly

walked to the door and entered. He scurried to the stall at the far end and closed the door. He reached under his untucked, burgundy Polo shirt and pulled out the white smock. He put his arms through the openings and adjusted the garment around his shoulders. It engulfed most of his minuscule frame, but it had to do.

He looked down, below his knee, which was the only part of his cream-colored khaki pants that were exposed. He looked the part of a two-year resident and hoped everyone else in the hospital thought the same.

He placed his hand on the stall door to open it before immediately stopping. He flashed back to what Sarah had said. *Don't do anything stupid.* This most certainly fell under the category of stupid, but it no longer mattered. He was fed up with being an innocent bystander, blindsided by these mysterious events. Proactive instead of reactive was his new motto.

He took a deep breath and then exited the stall. He stood in front of the mirror, taking one last glimpse before stepping into his world of deception. He peeked out of the bathroom and toward the nurses station down the hall. The same nurse sat in the chair, still occupied by the computer. He quickly walked in the opposite direction, approaching the stairwell.

He ascended the steps until he reached the fourth floor. He positioned his head up against the narrow rectangular window, up above the door handle. Several doctors and nurses roamed the floor, disappearing in and out of various rooms. The floor layout was similar to the one he had just left with the nurses station midway down the hall to the left. A couple of wheelchairs and rolling beds were scattered up alongside the walls, along with other medical apparatuses not familiar to Jace. He looked on the wall at the room closest to him, attempting to locate room 425.

"Four hundred," he mumbled.

He focused down the hallway, convinced Sabrina's room was most likely somewhere past the nurses station. He squinted to the opposite end, at the illuminated exit sign above the stairwell door. He surmised it might be much easier to gain access to Sabrina's room from that stairwell instead of walking down the hall in the midst of all the commotion. Although it could provide the camouflage he needed to get through unnoticed, he didn't want to take a chance.

He turned and descended the stairs until he came upon the third floor. He peeked through the glass, which in total contrast to the fourth floor showed no sign of activity, except for a lone nurse standing down the corridor. He waited a few minutes until she disappeared into a room, then stepped into the hallway and focused his eyes on the nurses station, where one nurse sat, but was consumed by paperwork. This was his chance.

He spotted a wheelchair positioned against the wall and grabbed the handles. He pushed it down the corridor, approaching the nurses station, and prayed she would stay busy enough not to notice him.

He came within a few steps before her head jerked up. He waved, not knowing what else to do.

She followed with a wave of her own. "You must be new around here," she said in a raspy voice.

"Uh . . . yeah."

"What unit are you covering?"

"Um . . . the burn unit. I needed a wheelchair and couldn't find one on my floor. Is it okay if I borrow this one?"

"Sure. She gazed at his borrowed doctor robe. "In case you weren't aware, you need to have your work badge displayed at all times. Where is it?"

Jace looked down and felt around the left pocket covering his chest before frantically searching the floor around him. He hadn't thought about a work ID, and this stolen doctor's robe didn't have one attached. "I must have lost my ID. I knew this would happen again. The metal clip on my ID is defective and keeps coming loose. Do you know where I can get another?"

She stared for a moment. "Human resources."

"Thanks. Nice chatting with you, but I need to go." He continued beyond the nurses station.

"Excuse me," the nurse said.

He immediately stopped, almost tripping over the wheelchair.

She pointed in front of her. "Wouldn't it be easier to take the elevator?"

Jace took a deep breath before focusing on the elevator bank. He was temporarily crippled, not only physically but also mentally. If there wasn't enough weight on his shoulders pretending to be a doctor, now he was asked to perform a simple task to most but a gut-wrenching phobia in his world. At that moment, he wished his claustrophobia from the accident had manifested itself in the form of something else, other than an elevator ride.

From his past experiences, there was never an easy way out when dealing with this phobia, and this time was no different. He had to say something—anything. Pausing too long could certainly blow his cover. He sighed heavily as if attempting to exhale away the fear and nervousness.

"For some reason, we're having trouble with the elevator doors on our floor. That's why I took the stairs. We already called maintenance. I'm sure they're on it now."

She hesitated for a moment before nodding. "Please be careful going down the stairs with that wheelchair. And don't forget to go to human resources to replace your lost badge."

Jace exhaled with relief before finally proceeding past the nurses station and near his stairwell of choice. He approached the last room before the stairwell entrance and turned back to make sure he wasn't being watched. He rolled the wheelchair into the last room and quickly ducked into the stairwell door. He raced up the stairs, back up to the fourth floor. He once again peered through the glass and up against the wall, now much closer to his goal, eyeing room number 428.

He focused on the activity throughout the floor before working up the nerve to enter the hallway and bypass several nurses who were too busy to notice his presence. Like a wolf in sheep's clothing, he stealthily meandered through the flock until he reached his destination.

# Chapter 47

The room seemed empty from Jace's point of view, though the L-shaped layout limited his vision. His current vantage point only allowed him to see a visitor's chair and a cabinet mounted to the wall. The remaining area was out of sight unless he walked in further and cleared the short hallway leading into the room. There was no turning back. He had to enter and pray no nurses were inside.

He took a few steps in, clearing the wall, and suddenly stopped, his eyes attempting to adjust to the first sight of Sabrina. She'd become host to a network of tubes flowing from her body to several machines that beeped intermittently. He bit his bottom lip and winced at the once vibrant young woman, now unrecognizable, reduced to a vegetable, and kept alive by medical machines that Jace had never seen before.

The top portion of her head was covered with a gauze wrap, down to the top of her ears. A white patch covered her right eye, while the left one remained closed with several scrapes and cuts surrounding her eyelid. Tubes filled each nostril, along with what appeared to be a tube implanted in her throat, covered by bandages. Both arms lay still beside her with palms facing upward, an IV implanted in her left arm while the right arm was exposed from the elbow down, showing off a myriad of bruises.

He closed his eyes, overwhelmed at her condition. He

wished he'd kept his mouth shut and not told Sabrina about Maria. He could have dealt with it on his own and never involved her, and this could have all been avoided.

The world, as he knew it, was collapsing on his shoulders all at once, riddled with concerns and worry from Sarah's accident, to Mrs. Aderlee's death, and culminating with this horrific sight before him. He felt severely punished by some form of bad karma that had boomeranged his way. Whatever the reason for his misfortune, he had to find the strength to continue.

He focused his eyes once more, looking at Sabrina. Although her body lay ravaged with life-threatening injuries, she was still technically alive. She hadn't given up. She could still pull through. He gathered the strength to approach closer.

He leaned over the bed and whispered, "Sabrina?"

No response.

"Sabrina, can you hear me?"

Still no response.

He looked over at the machinery flashing with various lights, giving off beeping sounds on occasion, and noticed a change. There was one machine in particular that he had become familiar with while visiting Sarah. Both women were hooked up to a heart monitor, displaying the number of beats per minute. He thought for an instant he was hallucinating, but to his amazement, Sabrina's heart rate had increased slightly after calling her name.

"Sabrina?" he called again, overjoyed at the subtle signs of life.

She didn't respond physically, but her heart did all the talking he needed to hear. He smiled. This one, unlike many others, this one oozed with relief, lifting a portion of the burden weighing so heavily on his shoulders. She was fighting back, and now it was his turn.

He placed his hand on the bedrail, closed his eyes, and said a silent prayer. He batted his eyelids, mindful that, at any moment, someone could come walking into the room.

He scanned the room, searching for a locker or closet that could possibly contain her personal belongings. He focused on a closet door to the right of the bed. He approached and twisted the knob, but it didn't turn. He gripped the knob tighter and attempted to turn once more, hoping the knob was just stiff, but that wasn't the case. A keyhole was engraved in the knob.

He darted his eyes around the area, looking for any item that could potentially pick the lock. He fumbled around a desk located next to Sabrina's bed, pushing aside various items. In his haste, he accidentally knocked over a tray containing fresh gauze bandages. The tray crashed to the floor, making a sound loud enough to be heard outside the room. He cringed, hoping no one heard, but his hopes were dashed upon hearing squeaking footsteps outside in the hall.

He frantically searched the room for a place to hide. He turned around to see the bathroom door partly open. He ran inside and closed the door gently.

"Hello. Anyone in here?" he heard from just beyond the door.

He remained silent, with his back against the wall,

unable to see in the dark enclosed space. The only smidgen of light came from under the door crack on the floor. He remained motionless, homing in on any sound outside. The silence was broken by the rattling of a tray and the irritating squeak of metal rubbing against the tiled floor, most likely the desk being shifted.

After a few seconds of silence, he shifted his head down by the crack of the door and spotted the shadow of two objects, possibly shoes, standing just outside the door. In a terrifying instant, he realized he hadn't locked the door. He reached for it, gently feeling for the position of the knob. Upon finding it, he pressed gently to secure the lock, praying it wasn't loud enough for someone to hear. As he pulled his hand away, the doorknob rattled.

"Anyone in there?" a female voice asked.

The knob rattled again. After a few seconds, the rattling stopped. Common sense told him to stay put for a few minutes, but his instinct told him to get the hell out before someone returned with a key.

He pressed his ear against the door, attempting to figure out if the nurse had left the room. The silence was encouraging, though not enough proof for him to exit. He kneeled on the ground and bent over, positioning his head sideways, against the floor, allowing him to see just beneath the crack and scan the entire floor. His senses confirmed the room was empty. He turned the knob, which released the spring, and popped the lock out. He cracked open the door and exited. He looked over at Sabrina's lifeless body once more, still encouraged by the positive signs he'd received from her vitals, but this was no time for rejoicing.

With his back against the wall, he peeked around the corner and down the short hallway, leading to the room entrance. Several doctors whisked by the room, busy with their daily job duties. He took several deep breaths and marched into the hallway, blending into the sea of white clothing worn by the various medical staff maneuvering through the halls. He calmly walked to the stairwell entrance and exited the floor.

As he ran down the stairs, he shed the doctor's smock and folded it flat enough to fit under his shirt once more. He entered the second floor and ran back into the bathroom where his act of deception had all started. He stuffed the smock in the garbage then exited, returning to Sarah's room. She remained asleep with Ryan now awake and Ava staring out the window.

"Where were you?" Ryan asked. "We're hungry."

"I'm sorry. Guess we can grab something to eat now while your mother sleeps."

Ava stared at Jace. "What's wrong, Dad? You look like you seen a ghost."

"I'm fine," he said, nodding unconvincingly. He grabbed the baseball cap sitting on top of Ryan's head. "Do you mind if I borrow this?"

"Hey. What are you doing? You never ask to wear my baseball caps."

"Sorry, but I need it now."

He adjusted the cap and pulled it as far down as he could over his face.

Jace exited the hospital, relieved and unscathed by his recent escapade. He left with mixed emotions—encouraged by Sarah's progress and Sabrina's subtle signs of recovery, but discouraged by his unsuccessful attempt to find Sabrina's belongings, if they still even existed. This was only a minor setback in his mind. It was time to raise the stakes and continue his pursuit for answers, and what he had in mind next, may just top the list on Sarah's category of stupidity.

# Chapter 48

"Dr. Wesley, Mr. Winchester is here to see you," the receptionist shouted into the intercom.

Malcolm sat on a worn microfiber sofa in the waiting room. He took a deep breath before standing and approaching a white door. He placed his hand on the knob, paused, and turned toward the receptionist who gave him an encouraging nod. He twisted the knob and proceeded inside.

He adjusted his eyes to the sparsely lit room. Several pine bookcases lined the corners of the room. The doctor sat in the middle, behind a chestnut office desk. An abstract throw rug with various designs laid flat in the middle of the room.

"Come in and have a seat."

Malcolm sat in front of the desk, gripping the arms of the chair. He tugged on his collar that had bunched up around his neck upon sitting.

The doctor sat upright in his chair. Peppered gray hair rested on top of his head and thick, horned-rim glasses sat on the bridge of his nose.

"Welcome," the doctor said.

Malcolm returned a forced smile.

"I want this to be as painless as possible for you. I want you to relax your nerves, forget your worries, and be as open as you possibly can," the doctor said. He leaned forward, looking at a chart in front of him. He took the glasses off the bridge of his nose, resting them on top of his head. "Tell me why you're here today?"

"To be honest, my primary doctor suggested I come here. Been having some health issues, but they can't find anything physically wrong with me. My doctor thinks it may be all mental or stress-related."

"Do you have reasons to be stressed?"

"Plenty."

"Care to elaborate further?"

"Most of it from my job. I'm a real estate broker with my own business, but things ain't been going too well lately."

"Besides the job, are there any other issues worrying you?"

"None that I can really think of."

The doctor continued to stare, as if looking for more. "Let's go back to what you said a moment ago. You used the word *plenty*. That means there are other things bothering you. Am I correct?"

He glanced away for a moment before locking eyes with the doctor once more. "I guess."

The doctor leaned back. "I'm sure this is uncomfortable for you, and I'm not expecting you to blurt out your darkest, lifelong secrets. Without honest input from you, I can't do my job and can't help you. It's like a baker without dough or a carpenter without wood."

"I get the picture, but it's not every day you tell a stranger what's really on your mind."

"That's true. But I'm a stranger who's going to offer

you what will hopefully be a resolution to your problem." The doctor grinned. "I'm also a stranger who will be charging for this session, so you might as well get your money's worth."

Malcolm let off a nervous laugh. "Good point." He hesitated, looking away from the doctor for a moment. "But I just don't think this is going to work. I'm sorry. I have to go." He turned and started walking to the door.

"I'm sure you thought long and hard about setting up this appointment, Mr. Winchester," the doctor said. "Now I can't force you to tell me anything. Only you know when you're ready to talk. Though, my guess is you're ready to talk now since you took time out of your busy day to meet with me."

Malcolm put his hand on the doorknob and stopped. He sighed. The doctor was right. This hadn't been an easy decision to come here. He initially had to deal with his insecurities of being labeled crazy for going to the psychiatrist. But deep down, he had known he had to overcome this and muster the courage to make an appointment. Maybe opening up would ease the stress and get rid of the nagging stomach issues. This would also give him a chance to share a childhood secret that had plagued him for the past thirty years. A secret he theorized had been a catalyst to these stomach issues. A secret that he had never told . . . until now.

He turned and faced the doctor. He walked back to the chair and sat.

The doctor nodded to give some encouragement.

"Let's rewind to a few minutes ago, and I'll ask again: are there any other issues worrying you?"

"Yes. It's a rather old story. Goes back to my teenage years. But I . . . I don't know where to begin."

"That's all up to you," the doctor said while folding his arms. "I'm in no rush. Take your time."

Malcolm closed his eyes. He focused on one day in particular that he would never forget. "Might as well sit back. This is going to be a long story." He cleared his throat. "I had just come home from my part-time job, feeling good because it was my eighteenth birthday and it was payday. I also had a glimmer of hope, since it was my birthday maybe things would be quiet for a day at home. As usual, I was greeted by my cat, Oscar. Most times, this was the highlight of my day. I had opened the front door, hoping to maybe see a birthday cake on the table or presents, but"—he hesitated—"there was no cake, presents, or dinner. Instead, there were empty wine and beer cans, which I knew meant trouble.

"I could hear the yelling in the back bedroom. I walked to my younger brother's bedroom and opened it. I found him shivering and crying in the corner. I guess that was some kind of comfort spot for him. I closed the door, hoping we couldn't hear anything. I was always taught by my father to never enter the room when the door was closed, but I was a man now—eighteen years old and no longer a kid.

"I rushed to the door and pushed it open to see my father hovering over my mother on the bed. He had his hand in the air, ready to swing. From the bruises on my mother's face, I could see she had been hit several times already. Unfortunately, I was used to her face looking like that whenever she was abused, but I finally felt I was old enough to help her."

Malcolm shifted in the chair and continued, "My father said, '*What the hell are you doing in this room, boy?*' Normally, I would just shake at the sound of his voice, but I didn't this time. I tried to stand up to him. I said, '*Get off my mother.*' He looked at me with his bloodshot eyes and said, '*Come over here and make me.*' Without hesitating, I walked toward him and, in the blink of an eye, he jumped off the bed and pushed me against the wall so hard that I blacked out for a second.

"I finally woke up and saw him standing over me. He said, '*You think you're a man now because you turned eighteen?*' I was surprised he remembered my birthday and my age. He said, '*Real men don't challenge their fathers; they accept what they do and learn from it.*' He looked me in the eye and said, '*I want to teach you a lesson about being a man. Being a man means taking risks.*' He helped me off the floor. He looked at my mother who was crying with her face buried in the pillows. He told me to wait outside the room for a minute.

"A few minutes later, he came out with one hand behind his back and led me to the front porch. He opened the door and told me to grab my cat and place him on the ground in the front yard. He took his hand from around his back, holding a silver handgun. I took a few steps back, scared out of my mind. He told me to put my hand out, but I couldn't do it. He turned to me and said, '*What did I tell you? Put your damn hand out.*' I was so scared at this point I couldn't do anything else but listen to him.

"He placed the gun in my hand and said, '*Here is your first test to becoming a man. Ever heard of Russian roulette? There are six chambers in this gun, and one of them contains a real bullet. I want you to aim the gun at that sorry cat of yours and pull the trigger.*' I was so scared I couldn't talk. He said, '*I'm only going to tell you this one more time, and if you don't do it, I swear I'll run back in that house and beat your mother like she's never been beaten before.*' I remember my eyes tearing up. I couldn't get up the nerve to reach for the gun. He said, '*I warned you,*' and started walking back to the house.

"I was finally able to get a word out and agreed to his crazy game. He turned and gave me the gun. I looked at my cat, who was sitting on the grass without a clue as to what I was about to do. I stared at my cat, almost trying to will him to run, but he didn't. I looked back at my father, who seemed to be enjoying the moment. I raised the gun with my arms shaking. The gun felt as heavy as a bowling ball. My index finger was shaking when I put it on the trigger. My cat just sat there and purred. I looked back at my father, hoping this was a sick joke and he would tell me to stop, but he didn't. I turned back to my cat, and aimed the gun in his direction, and closed my eyes before pulling the trigger. *Bam!* The sound made me jump. I opened my eyes and, by some miracle, my cat was still alive. I thought, *Maybe I missed*, although I did purposely aim slightly off target.

"I turned back to my father, who was laughing. '*Bam!*' he yelled. '*Fooled ya. I've been practicing my gunshot sounds, and what do you know . . . it worked.*' I was so nervous. I didn't realize my father was the one who made the sound. He said, '*You passed the test.*' He started laughing again and walked back toward the house.

"All the anger I held in all those years came to a head at that moment. As my father walked onto the front porch, I raised the gun and aimed it square in the middle of his back. Without hesitating, I pulled the trigger and heard a soft click, but there was no gunshot. I tried again and again until I knew it bypassed all six chambers, but the gun never went off. My father walked into the house not knowing what happened. I opened the chamber to the gun, and they were all empty. I remember dropping the gun and grabbing my cat before running off."

He opened his eyes, looking back at the doctor. "That was all she wrote. I knew I couldn't stay in that house any longer. I realized I still wasn't strong enough to protect my mother, and I also knew I was capable of trying to murder my father."

The doctor jotted notes on a sheet of paper before he eventually stopped. "Where did you go?"

"I had a good friend that I stayed with."

"Did you ever come back to the house to check on your mother and brother?"

"I came back from time to time, only when I knew he wasn't around. I also did call them whenever I got the chance, but if my father picked up, I would hang up and try again another time."

The doctor shifted the glasses on his face. "Why do you think your mother stayed in that abusive relationship?"

Malcolm shrugged. "I wish I knew."

The doctor continued writing in his notepad. "And what about now? Are your parents still living?"

"I don't know about my father. I haven't talked to him since I left home thirty years ago. I kept in contact with my mother up until the time she passed about ten years ago."

"And what about your brother?"

"I've been trying to contact him recently, but the only number I have is not in service." Malcolm winced in embarrassment. "I can't believe I'm telling you all this."

"It's perfectly fine. It's good to get this out of your system."

The doctor squinted, looking at his notes. "I'm sorry to hear about all you went through. It seems to me you have no closure. Not sure why your mother stayed, not sure why your father did what he did, no contact with your brother. This is an ongoing chapter in your life that's not going to end until you decide to end it."

Malcolm interrupted. "I don't understand. That chapter of my life has ended as far as I'm concerned." He pointed to himself. "Look at me. I worked my way out of that mess to become a successful adult. I didn't allow the past to dictate my future. I could easily be strung out on drugs or alcohol, but I'm not. I could be in jail, but I'm not. I blocked it all out and concentrated on being the successful person that I am today. Shouldn't I get applauded for that?"

The doctor gave a soft clap. "I agree. But blocking it completely out is also a problem. From the story you just described to me, you remember it all in vivid detail. That means it's still fresh in your mind. I can see now why you have health issues. These memories are still bottled up, causing havoc to your mental and physical state."

"So, what do I do?"

"You already started the healing process by opening up to me." The doctor took a sip of water. "Bottom line, Mr. Winchester, is you have to make a choice. You've come to a crossroads. Going to the right means acknowledging what happened in the past, realizing you can't change it, learning from those negative experiences, and moving on with your life." The doctor leaned forward before continuing. "There's a saying that describes this perfectly. Accept what is, let go of what was, and have faith in what will be."

Malcolm nodded. "I like that. Need to keep that one in mind."

The doctor gestured with a thumbs-up. "On the opposite end of the spectrum, going to the left means blocking the past out entirely, keeping it bottled up, letting it spread like an infection until it ultimately brings you down." He glared at Malcolm. "It's your choice for which way you decide to go."

# Chapter 49

The car shuttered upon Jace pulling the steering wheel slightly to the right and onto the grass embankment. Then he doused the lights and shut off the engine. With his visibility reduced to near zero in the darkness, he grabbed a flashlight resting on the passenger seat. He flicked the switch, pointing the cone-shaped beam onto the passenger seat, revealing a couple of items—a pair of latex gloves and a crowbar. He tore open the package of gloves, placing them on each hand, and then grabbed the crowbar.

He peered through the rearview mirror, looking for any headlights in the distance. He could barely make out the path of the road but didn't see any oncoming traffic. He opened the door and stepped outside. The quietness of the car cabin was replaced by a chorus of chirping crickets.

He walked alongside the road, doing his best to tune out the nighttime orchestra and listen for any oncoming traffic. He pointed the flashlight a few feet in front of him, making sure he stepped on solid ground. He proceeded farther until he came upon the dirt-covered parking lot of the realty office. As expected, the area was empty, with no vehicles in sight.

He edged his way across the parking lot, with the crunching sound of dirt pebbles rattling under his feet. He approached the front of the building before he heard the faint roar of an engine in the distance. He ran to the side of the building and shut off the flashlight, waiting for the vehicle to speed by. Then he switched the flashlight back on, walked around the building, and approached the rear. He peeked around the corner, shining the flashlight in the open area.

He arrived at the back entrance door and attempted to wedge the crowbar between the doorjamb, near the lock. He pushed with all his might, yet the crowbar tip barely pierced the opening.

Holding the crowbar with his right hand, he stepped back and lifted his foot, hitting the back end of the crowbar with a solid kick, but the door didn't budge.

"Dammit!"

He looked down to the right, at the window he'd found the other day. He approached, kneeling to get a better look. He pushed the flashlight against the glass, struggling to see inside, the glass caked with dust and some sort of brown residue. He tapped on the glass with his knuckles. The glass gave away slightly with each knock.

He grabbed the crowbar and turned his head, covering his eyes. He rammed the crowbar into the middle of the pane with shards of glass flying through the window and into the basement. He listened out for an alarm, but none sounded. He pressed a button on his watch, illuminating the time.

"Ten minutes," he whispered. He figured he had about that much time to waste if a silent alarm did trigger before the police swarmed the building.

He proceeded to clear the glass that remained on the

outer edges of the window with the crowbar. He pointed the flashlight directly below the window, spotting some boxes piled up not too far from the window opening. He slid feet first through the window, slowly tapping his foot, feeling for the top of the box. While still holding onto the windowsill, he eased his way further, applying more of his weight onto the box, hoping the stack was sturdy enough to support his weight. The boxes began to wobble when he attempted to apply his full body weight. They tilted ever so slightly, prompting him to grab the windowsill before the boxes tumbled to the floor.

He hung onto the windowsill with his fingertips, his body dangling precariously above ground. His fingers began to cramp. Realizing he couldn't hold on much longer, he glanced down, straining to see the mess of boxes on the floor. He had no choice but to let go and hope the boxes would be enough cushion to lessen the impact of his fall.

"One . . . two . . . three," he counted, releasing his grip.

He crashed on top of the boxes with a *thud*.

He lay in shock for a second, coughing and rubbing his eyes from the dust shrouding the air. Besides his aching right elbow, he had taken the fall better than expected.

He rolled off the boxes until his feet touched solid ground. He swayed his arm back and forth with the flashlight, perusing the area. He noticed a multitude of boxes stacked on top of each other, surrounding the room. A chipped wooden table sat in the middle of the floor, covered with dust. The air was stagnant, with the stench of mold and mildew. Jace covered his nose with the crook of his elbow, not wanting to breathe in too much of the unhealthy air.

He pointed the flashlight to the opposite end of the wall, displaying a six-foot-high metal shelf, occupied by various books lined in perfect rows.

"What the hell am I looking for?"

He focused the flashlight on the mess of boxes that had broken his fall. Several boxes were split open. He reached in, grabbing a handful of paper and glancing at several of them.

"Nothing but real estate mumbo jumbo."

He tossed the papers on the floor, realizing he was running short on time. He shined the light on the door leading to the entrance of the room, secured with a deadbolt. He figured something important had to be down here.

He lurked over to the metal bookshelf and read some of the titles. He swiped his gloved fingers over the book covers to clear away some of the dust that had settled. Most were real estate related, along with several encyclopedias. Nothing important.

He looked at his watch once more. *Few minutes left.* He kicked a stack of papers onto the floor in frustration, realizing this was a complete mistake. He had no idea what he was looking for, and there was no time to continue looking through the mound of boxes and miscellaneous papers scattered about the room. *Time to go.*

He focused his attention up at the window he'd originally entered, but it was too high for him to reach without anything to stand on. He surveyed the room, looking for a few sturdy boxes to stack up below the window. He spotted a few resting in the corner and walked over, grabbing the top box and dragging it over by the window. He grabbed the second box and stacked it on top of the first one below the window, but when he neared the third box, he noticed a metal shelf positioned in the far corner. There were four shelves, each of them containing several cardboard boxes of the same size, but there was one item that stood out from the rest.

Sitting on the middle shelf was an antique wooden crate with a padlock attached. He trained his flashlight on the faded letters imprinted on the crate reading, "*Property of RJ C&M.*" He darted his eyes around, searching for the crowbar, before realizing he must have lost it during the fall, and there wasn't enough time for him to search for it. He glanced around to see if there was anything else that could be used to break the lock but came up empty.

He grabbed the lock and tugged on it, hoping by some wild chance the lock would be open, to no avail.

He looked at his watch. It was now beyond the ten-minute window he had allotted himself. There was no time to contemplate further. He finally grabbed the third box and stacked it on top of the previous two. He climbed on the stacked boxes and slowly stood with the boxes wobbling slightly. He couldn't afford another tumble to the ground and did his best impersonation of a high-wire balancing act in a circus. The boxes eventually steadied as he reached his arms up toward the windowsill. With both elbows resting on the sill, he dragged his body back up through the window, mindful of the broken glass surrounding the area.

He dusted the dirt and other debris from his shirt and pants before walking to the front of the building.

Minutes later, he arrived back at the car and drove off, no longer a law-abiding citizen, but a wanted criminal.

# Chapter 50

The phone rang, waking Malcolm out of his slumber. The police informed him of a break-in at the office.

He threw on a pair of wrinkled jeans and a T-shirt, rushing out the door.

***

He drove into the parking lot, amidst a swirl of flashing lights.

An officer approached. "Appears to be a break-in from the basement window in the back. Follow me."

They walked around back, approaching the shattered window.

"The basement is a mess," the officer said, pointing a flashlight through the window opening.

Malcolm peered at the officer. "What about upstairs, in the main office?"

"Seems to be untouched. But you might want to double-check."

Malcolm raced to the front and entered. He was relieved to see the floor just as he had left it. He ran into his corner office and flicked on the light. This room also appeared to be untouched.

He returned to the basement, where the officers continued to search for clues. He turned on a light switch in the corner, a dull blue light flickering, eventually radiating a steady beam, giving off a better visual of the ransacked room.

Another officer entered, surveying the scene. The officer turned to Malcolm. "Do you have any idea what they were looking for?"

He shrugged. "Just a bunch of business and real estate related items down here." He laughed. "Maybe I have some new competition moving into the area, trying to uncover my secret to success."

"Glad to see you have a sense of humor about this."

The officer continued to peruse the area. "It's going to take some time before we can search and try to gather some clues. We'll dust for fingerprints and look for any footprints. There may even be some traces of blood around the broken window. I'll need you to hang around a little while so we can file a report."

"No problem," Malcolm said. He glanced up at the broken window and mumbled, "I may already know who did it."

# Chapter 51

Jace quickly pulled his mouth away from the coffee mug as the hot liquid scorched his top lip after being startled by the doorbell.

"Who could that be this early in the morning?" Jace knew whoever it was, there wouldn't be much time for chitchatting as he was moments from beginning his commute to work.

He walked to the foyer and opened the door, doing his best to mask his surprise upon seeing Malcolm standing in the doorway.

He regained his composure. "What do I owe this pleasure so early in the morning?"

"First, it would be thoughtless of me to not ask how Mrs. Valentine is doing. Is she still recovering in the hospital?"

"She's doing much better but still in the hospital. Thanks for asking."

A few seconds of awkward silence followed.

"Is there anything else I can help you with?" Jace asked.

"Yeah, there is."

Jace interrupted, "Don't mean to be rude, but please make it quick. I need to get to work."

"This will only take a moment of your time, and I'll get straight to the point. Someone broke into the realty office."

Jace stared with his eyes wide open, attempting to put on an Oscar-winning performance. "I'm sorry to hear."

"I've already filed a police report, and they've been looking over the crime scene."

A few drops of sweat rolled from under Jace's armpits and down his side.

"So, what can I do for you?"

"I had a few witnesses tell me they saw a beige Camry parked near the office."

Jace shrugged.

"Is it just a coincidence you have a beige Camry?" Malcolm asked.

Jace swallowed the lump in his throat. "Am I the only one with a beige Camry in Albuquerque?"

"No, but if you know something I don't, I would appreciate it if you can be honest and let me know."

"Sorry, I can't help you. It's also time for me to go."

Malcolm winced. "This is what I don't understand. Whenever you have a problem, I must drop everything I'm doing and answer all your questions, and now that I need some assistance, you're trying to run out on me."

"Well, seven thirty in the morning on a Monday is not a great time to talk, especially for a man who needs to go to work."

"Do you think this is a convenient time for me? I'm normally hard at work by now, but I'm taking time out of my busy work schedule to discuss something I think is very important."

"What's there to discuss? I told you I don't know anything about what happened last night."

Malcolm laughed. "How did you know this happened last night?"

"Well . . . why would you be coming to my house this early in the morning? I just assumed it happened last night."

"Come on, Jace. Can you just be honest with me?"

Jace gritted his teeth, adrenaline racing through his veins. He knew this was going to be a battle, one worth being late for work.

He stepped out onto the porch, closing the door behind him. He stood no more than a few feet away, his head tilted up, doing his best to look Malcolm straight in the eye. "You're asking me to be honest. I don't think you've been honest since the day I met you."

"How so?"

"Let me count the ways. For one thing, the love of my life is in the hospital, still recovering from this contaminated water that mysteriously appeared in my house."

"What does that have to do with me being dishonest?"

"Oh, come on! I'm sure you have an idea of how this happened and you just refuse to tell anyone."

"Wait a minute. I thought we took care of this during the community meeting at the office. I told you I'll have someone test your water and—"

"Excuse me, but testing the water is not taking care of the problem. I need to know how it got contaminated in the first place and what's being done to resolve the problem."

"You think, if I knew how it got contaminated, I

wouldn't tell you?" Malcolm pointed his finger at Jace, nearly touching his chest. "Let me tell you something. I'm concerned about you and everyone else in this community because, without you, I wouldn't be where I am today. You're the customer, the consumer. You purchase the homes, which in turn gives me more business. Now, why would I put you in jeopardy and possibly ruin my reputation and lose business?"

Jace gritted his teeth and fired back, "Don't give me this sob story about caring for the people in the community. Fact is, my wife received burns all over her body for simply taking a bath, you have an elderly woman who suddenly died for reasons unknown, you have mysterious cracks in people's houses and driveways, a contaminated lake with dead fish and geese, people in the community selling their houses like hot cakes, and all you've done so far is promise to have someone test the damn water!" He paused to catch his breath. "You must have a clue as to what's going on, and don't stand here and lie to my face like you don't!"

Malcolm smirked. "Just like you're lying to me about what happened last night."

Jace glared at Malcolm. "Okay, so what if I tell you I broke into the office? Does that mean you'll tell me what's going on in the community?"

"No, because I don't know."

"Now we're back at square one. This conversation is pointless. We're just going in circles."

"On the contrary, this conversation was extremely helpful. At least you admitted breaking into the office."

"I didn't admit to a damn thing."

Malcolm squinted at Jace with suspicious eyes. "What were you looking for?"

Jace did his best to maintain eye contact and avoid looking away, which would be a dead giveaway for anyone with a guilty conscience.

"Better yet, why did you do it?"

Jace sighed. "All I can say is when a man's family is threatened, he'll go to drastic measures to protect them. Since you weren't giving me any answers as to what was going on, I had to try to find out for myself."

"So, what did you find?"

"Okay, so you want to play this game. Answer this question for me. What can you tell me about RJ C&M?"

"Why is that important for you to know?"

"Just curious."

Malcolm stared for a moment and did not offer an immediate reply.

"Come on. I'm being truthful to you. The least you can do is return the favor," Jace said.

"It's just part of an old family business."

"What kind of business?"

"It's a business my father owned."

"Do you mind helping me out here and giving a little more information?"

"You need to be lucky I gave you this much information."

"What's stopping you from giving me more? You owe me, my family, and the rest of the people in the community a damn good explanation as to what the hell is going on."

Malcolm stared at the ground. "Do you think this is easy for me? Do you think I enjoy seeing people unhappy, hurt, or even killed, for that matter? This community was going to be the key to my business getting back on track. In case you didn't know, I was on the verge of closing the business down a few years ago before the plans for Granwin Estates came into the picture. I figured this was my chance to sell some houses and have a profitable business again. I struggled along until the community was built and, for a while, it worked. I sold some houses, thanks to you and a few of your neighbors, and that kept me afloat for a while longer. But now, with all that's happened, I'm worse off than before. I'm losing business, and people don't want to deal with me anymore. It's over for me. I probably shouldn't even be telling you this, but I'm packing things up and shutting down the business. It's just best I move and start fresh somewhere else."

"Sorry to hear about your failing business, but do you think running away from your problems is going to solve them?"

Malcolm shook his head. "What other choice do I have?"

"How about being a man and telling the truth about what you know? I can only imagine the guilt you'll have to deal with if you choose not to admit what's going on and just ran away, leaving us all wondering what dirty little secret you've been hiding and what the hell happened to this promising community."

Malcolm looked down at the ground and remained silent.

Jace eyed him intently, noticing Malcolm's bold persona quickly fading. He seemed vulnerable, and Jace figured this was his chance to dig deeper while his guard was down.

Malcolm sighed. "You're really pushing it, Jace."

"Hey, you pushed me, so I'm only pushing back. So, I'll ask again, what does RJ C&M stand for?"

"RJ stands for Robert Jeffries."

Jace stood perplexed for a second. "Wait, are you trying to tell me he was your father?"

Malcolm nodded.

"Well, I'll be damned. So, you're blood to a living legend around here."

Malcolm shrugged. "If that's what you want to call him."

"But, why do you have a different last name?"

"Winchester is my mother's maiden name. I took her name back for good reason."

"Wow," Jace said, no doubt intrigued by this startling news. "So, now that I know what RJ stands for, how about C&M?"

Malcolm shook his head. "No more, Jace. That's about all you're going to get out of me now."

Before Jace could utter another word, his cell phone rang.

"I'm sorry, that's someone from my office calling. I really need to get to work."

Jace suddenly stopped, forgetting he had admitted to breaking into the realty office, and realized, at any moment, Malcolm could move forward with pressing charges against him.

"Now what?" Jace asked. "You gonna have me arrested?"

"That would normally be the next logical step, but I think you and your family have been through enough. Let's just call it even for now."

# Chapter 52

Malcolm walked back to his truck, feeling oddly relieved at the conversation. He had received confirmation that Jace had indeed broken into the office, which he had always suspected. He also couldn't believe he had just admitted to Jace that Robert Jeffries was his father. This was something he held closely under wraps and hadn't mentioned to anyone until now. Under normal circumstances, he would have never thought about moving forward with that confession, but he felt he owed Jace something for having the balls to admit he broke into the office.

He started the truck and pulled out of the driveway. A part of him did want to press charges against Jace for the crime he had committed against his property, but the remorse he felt for not only Jace but his other clients in the community was becoming too much to bear. This was the least he could do for Jace, to make up for the horrible experience he and his family were suffering through since they'd moved into the community. He also felt he owed Jace even further after getting his poor wife into a frenzy when she had come to the office that day, looking to throttle Maria. He could have easily told Sarah the truth about Maria's ID dropping in the parking lot, which would have validated Jace's story, but being vindictive came easy for him. He figured his little spat with Jace at the office about the pictures had given him the green light to practice his vengeful ways. He could only imagine the havoc that had transpired in the Valentine household that day when Sarah had confronted Jace.

Despite the ominous storm clouds surrounding the events over the last few weeks, Malcolm held on to some form of optimism he would get through this, that the sun would come shining through sooner than later. A part of that optimism was due to his decision to move forward with selling some assets and preparing to put his house on the market, and the proceeds from one of his biggest assets were confined in a briefcase sitting on the passenger seat next to him.

He completed a cash transaction for the Thunderbird and received more than he'd expected for the sale. Cash was king, whether it was selling a house, or in this case a car. He was planning to use a portion of the money to help pay for the upcoming office rent due and another portion to pay for the home repairs needed in anticipation of selling the house. And from his calculations, he would still have a decent amount of money left over.

His optimism was also a byproduct of the visit to the psychiatrist. Admitting to that awful experience on his eighteenth birthday had been refreshingly therapeutic. He'd never thought holding those bitter moments inside could do so much damage to his physical, mental, and spiritual well-being.

He produced a smile with the anticipation of turning over a new leaf, forgetting about the past, and having faith in what would come in the future. It was time to forge ahead and mend fences, attempt to reconstruct any bridges that might have been burned in the past, and ultimately make things right with the people he'd mistreated. He wasn't sure how things would work out with the first attempt on his apology tour, but he was about to find out.

# Chapter 53

Maria's anxiety level intensified as the clock read 3:55 p.m., and she was still at least fifteen minutes away. She smashed her foot on the accelerator, approaching the intersection. The light was a steady yellow and turned red while she zipped through the intersection, doing her best to make up for lost time due to some unexpected traffic. To make matters worse, the falling rain had slowed her commute, making it virtually impossible for her to arrive at work on time. The storm that had been forecasted to hit was upon the city, and she dreaded having to go to work, but there was no way she could miss another day.

Fifteen minutes later, she swerved into the Gas-n-Go parking lot. She jumped out, trying to pin her name tag on her shirt, racing toward the entrance, attempting to avoid the puddles of rain scattered about the parking lot.

She rushed in through the doors with the familiar chimes going off. She took a few steps inside, stopping immediately and looking over at the cash register. An unfamiliar female stood behind the counter, looking at Maria's name tag.

"Glad you can join us," the woman said.

"Sorry I'm late," Maria said. "Are you a new employee?"

"No," the stout woman replied, shaking her head as the folds of skin sagging from her neck jiggled.

Maria shuffled to the counter. "What happened to the other girl?"

"She left when her shift ended at four. But I wouldn't even bother coming behind the counter to join me," the woman said with a stern look on her face.

"What do you mean?"

The woman pointed to her tag adorned with several gold stars. "I'm the regional supervisor for Gas-n-Go. I've been here most of the day, welcoming customers to our newest location."

"Oh," Maria said, grimacing.

"I've heard some things about you and, to be honest, they weren't all pleasant. Calling out twice in one week during your second week of employment was bad enough, and now being fifteen minutes late for your shift on top of that is unacceptable."

"I—"

"No need to explain. Sorry, dear, but three strikes and you're out."

Maria stood, visibly confused.

"Let me put this in words you'll understand. You're fired."

"No. You can't do this to me. I just started. I promise I'll never be late again. I . . . I've just been going through some tough times."

"Sorry, hon. I don't know where you're from, but in this world, you can't unexpectedly call out two days in your first couple weeks of employment, along with being late today, and expect to still have a job."

"But who's going to cover my shift now?"

"Someone is already on the way to take your shift. I'll be covering until they arrive. You'll be receiving your release paperwork in the mail from headquarters."

Maria's eyes welled up with tears. "Please give me another chance. I'll work extra hours to make up for it."

The woman raised her finger and pointed to the door.

Maria wiped the tears rolling down her cheek and turned, nearing the door. She grabbed the handle and was about to step outside.

"Hold on a minute," the woman said from the counter.

Maria turned with a glimmer of hope.

"Some large man with a goatee came in ten minutes before you did. He wanted me to give you this slip of paper."

Maria unfolded the paper, wiping her eyes to clear her blurred vision.

*Please call me at the office. I tried calling you a few times, but the call didn't go through. Even if it did go through, I doubt you would have taken my call anyway, which is the reason why I wrote this note. I would like to make a truce and offer you your job back, but it's only temporary. I'll explain further if you call. I'll be at the office for the next few hours.*

*P.S. I swear no funny business.*

*Malcolm*

Maria crumbled the paper, shoved it in her bag, and raced out of the store.

A short time later, she pulled alongside the road, with the realty office coming into view on the right. She tilted her head up at the sky and closed her eyes, looking for guidance from up above.

Here she was, suddenly back at square one, with no job and a relentless influx of bills that kept coming.

She straightened out the crumbled note, feeling like a detective in the thick of an investigation, with her second attempt at deciphering a mysterious note that had come her way. She unexpectedly mustered a nervous laugh. It was the type of laugh only experienced by those individuals going through a sudden crisis that left them deliriously panicked and unsure of how to cope with the wicked circumstances that had come their way.

She sighed, cupping her hands around her face. *What the hell am I doing here?*

Her last interaction with Malcolm at the Gas-n-Go had been far from pleasant, and this was the absolute last person she should be volunteering to meet with. She could have easily reached out and called him, as he'd suggested in the note, but her judgment was severely impaired at the moment. She was frustrated, desperate, overwhelmed, and angry all at the same time—a lethal combination as she tried to maintain her sanity, which was only hanging on by a thread. And, for some crazy reason, she didn't mind if the thread broke.

The old Maria would have avoided any further confrontation with Malcolm at all costs, but her previous interactions with Sabrina were bringing about a noticeable change. With a shot of Sabrina's fiery personality injected into her veins, she was no doubt ready for battle. There was only one way for her to know if Malcolm was sincere about giving her job back, and if this was a trap, she was ready to unleash her fury on the man who had started her descent into this black hole of despair.

She reached into her handbag, pulling out a can of pepper spray, along with a pocketknife. She proceeded with placing the pepper spray in her right coat pocket and the knife in the left before driving into the parking lot and shutting off the engine.

She motioned the sign of the cross before exiting the car and running to the entrance, attempting to dodge the raindrops. A closed sign was plastered to the front door. She glanced at her watch. It was still well within business hours.

She shrugged and tried to turn the doorknob, but it was locked. Maybe this is a mistake. She pondered for a second before backing away from the door and marching back toward the car. She pulled out her key ring, looked for her car keys, and immediately stopped. She focused her eyes on a silver-plated key and swiveled her head around to the front door, realizing she had never relinquished the office key when she'd quit. She contemplated whether to proceed with her original plan. It was all or nothing.

She returned to the front door and inserted the key,

turning the knob. The door creaked open. She peeked inside before stepping into an office devoid of life. She perused the area, noticing open drawers to several file cabinets. A few brown boxes rested at the base of each cabinet.

*Thud!* She heard something hit the floor and focused on a door partially opened, near the back of the office. She shuffled her way across the floor, and as she approached, a motorized noise resonated on and off from within the room.

She tilted her head between the door and doorframe to find Malcolm hovering over a box with various papers in his hands. Next to him was a paper shredder. He carefully dipped each sheet through the slot as the shredder devoured each piece. The room was cluttered with several boxes scattered about. Piles of paper rested on his desk, along with a black briefcase. This was obviously not the norm.

He shredded the papers at a frenetic pace. She thought about knocking to alert her presence, but she didn't want to startle him. She was intrigued by his actions and decided to observe further.

He grabbed the briefcase on his desk, carefully opening it with the top tilted upward, blocking the contents from her view. He reached for a cream-colored business envelope alongside the desk, stuffing it with an article from the briefcase. He sealed the envelope with his tongue and placed it on his desk.

He quickly looked up without warning, and Maria leaned back out of view, hoping he hadn't seen her.

"Who's there?" he asked.

Her first instinct was to run out the front door, but she

knew he would probably hear her. She turned toward a five-foot-high metal cabinet, resting against the wall, and tiptoed toward the cabinet, kneeling behind it, out of view. She heard the creak of the office door as it opened wider.

"Anyone there?"

Although frightened, she smirked at the irony. There she was again, hiding from him as she had done at the Gas-n-Go a week ago. She sat on the floor with her head between her legs, eyes closed, like a child cowering in a corner.

"Hello?" he said once more.

At that moment, her body responded to a rallying cry, which suddenly surged forward. She shook her head in defiance, her forehead wrinkling and her eyebrows turning in anger. *Enough!* She was tired of the running, tired of the fear, tired of the emotional stress that this man had put her through.

She turned her head to the side and envisioned Sabrina sitting beside her, helping her to her feet, giving her the strength and courage needed to get up and kick this man's ass.

With a clenched jaw, she placed her hand in her left pocket, grabbing the pocketknife. She inhaled deeply before rising to her feet with the knife hidden behind her back.

Malcolm took a step backward, apparently startled at the surprising company.

"Oh. It's you. You could have knocked on the door instead of scaring me half to death." He paused, pondering for a second. "I'm guessing you still have the office key."

She nodded ever so slightly.

He motioned his hand around the office. "Come on in. I'm glad you accepted my invitation."

Malcolm walked into his office, out of view, but she didn't follow. Her feet were rooted to the floor. She gripped the handle of the knife with such force that her fingers started to lose feeling.

He backpedaled into view. "Are you coming? I think I have something you'd like to hear."

She stared, her eyes wide open, still not budging.

"Okay. I guess we can just talk out here."

He motioned his hand across the office. "As you can see from the mess, a big change is coming. Business is not what it used to be and, for that reason, I've decided to close up shop."

She swallowed in an attempt to clear the lump in her throat with her grip on the knife relaxing ever so slightly. Her left shoulder tingled with her arm still crossed behind her back.

"This is also the reason I'm asking for your help." He offered a sincere gaze. "I apologize from the bottom of my heart for what happened between us. It was stupid, unprofessional, and just flat-out against the morals of any real man. I was going through some issues at the time and didn't know how to deal with them. I'm not trying to use that as an excuse for my actions, but I honestly don't know what else to tell you besides I'm sorry and it will never happen again."

She stared coldly, not saying a word.

"Since then, I've been receiving professional help and made up my mind to move on with my life, and this is where you come in. I must say things have been different since you left. I've gone through two assistants, and if you ask me, you did more in one hour than they both did in a day. I didn't realize how good I had it while you were here and, for that reason, I would like to offer you your old job back, but there's a catch."

Maria's heart rate spiked as she whipped the knife from around her back, pointing it in his direction with bad intentions.

"Hold on, wait a minute," he said, taking a step back. "I'm sorry if you took that comment the wrong way. Just wanted to inform you that the job is only temporary. I'm hoping to have everything packed up within a few weeks."

She continued to point the knife, breathing heavily.

He stared for a moment at her threatening stance. "I really don't think the knife is necessary. I'm trying to have a civilized conversation and would appreciate it if we can do this without a knife involved."

Maria shook her head without saying a word.

Malcolm shrugged and continued, "Okay, guess we'll do it your way, if it makes you feel more comfortable." He pointed to one of the boxes on the floor containing stacks of paper. "I've been struggling to try to sort through all this paperwork during the transition, and there's no way I can do it by myself."

He extended both hands. "I'm willing to give you money upfront if you agree to help me." He pointed into his office. "There's an envelope on my desk with some money I was going to use for something else, but you can have it instead. Now, we can do this in a couple of ways. I can go in and get it and bring it out to you . . ." He paused.

Her eyes narrowed with suspicious intent while a flash of lightning illuminated the room. She shook her head ever so slightly, looking for option two.

"Or you can follow behind me, into my office, and get the envelope yourself."

She contemplated option two while a rolling boom of thunder rattled the office.

"If it makes you more comfortable, I'll walk with my hands up in the air while you follow behind me."

She displayed a slight hint of a grin, pleased at his latest offer.

He turned toward the office, raising his hands in the air. "Whenever you're ready."

She wanted to take a step, but her legs were firmly planted on the floor as if covered in cement. She managed to take one step away from the wall, and he nodded to give her encouragement to continue.

The palms of her hands were peppered with sweat, with the handle of the knife sliding from her grip. She took another step, approaching him while he continued to stand with his hands up and back toward her. She came within a few feet and stopped, motioning her head for him to start walking.

Each time he took a step, she followed with one of her own. Her heart jumped at the periodic crackle of thunder.

They continued taking one step at a time, into the office, his desk coming into view. She stared at his massive back. *Easy target.* One plunge of the knife into his neck could end everything, but whatever little bit of sanity she held onto prevented her from following through with that barbaric thought.

They neared the desk, where the briefcase lay open, facing the wall, the contents temporarily out of Maria's view. As she closed in, the corner interior of the briefcase became visible. Her eyes widened upon seeing what appeared to be at least four stacks of one-hundred dollar bills, wrapped with rubber bands.

"Do you mind if I close the briefcase? There are some personal items inside."

He proceeded to shut the briefcase, the top engraved with large chromed initials, *M.W.* He raised his hands back in the air. "As you can see, there is an envelope on the desk. Go ahead and take it."

She motioned for him to take a step back before grabbing the envelope. She felt the envelope which, from its feathery weight, didn't appear to contain anything of substance. She hoped this wasn't a ploy to get her in the office.

She raised the knife to the envelope, sliding it across the top, and peeked inside. Five crisp one-hundred dollar bills rested in the fold.

"That can be yours right now if you accept my temporary job offer."

She tapped her foot in a fit of nervousness. A flash of

lightning illuminated the room once more. She looked in the envelope again. This was more than she had made at the Gas-n-Go in one week. Not to mention tax-free. But, at what cost? Working for him again meant seeing him almost every day, although temporarily. Spending more time with him meant more opportunities for him to try to go on another fishing expedition, and she had since retired from her unpleasant role of playing the bait.

"If that's not enough, I'm willing to pay you two hundred dollars a day, tax-free, until the move is complete. That is my offer. Take it or leave it." He stretched out his hand, waiting for a handshake. "Do we have a deal?"

# Chapter 54

The storm was upon them and not expected to slow anytime soon.

Jace peered out the bedroom window while the wind-driven rain pounded the pavement. It had only been raining for a few hours, but the streets were already flooded. A flash of lightning illuminated the sky, followed by a crackle of thunder that echoed around the house. Jace stared, oddly relaxed at the fury of Mother Nature. It gave him a moment to take his mind off the drama that had inundated his life these past few weeks.

He closed his eyes, relaxing further, almost to the point of sleepiness. Then his eyes shot open at the sound of a siren. A fire engine and a police car raced down the street and eventually out of sight. Jace couldn't imagine a fire raging anywhere in this deluge of rain.

Moments later, more sirens sounded as another fire engine and several other emergency vehicles zipped by. This was indeed out of the ordinary. Something was happening—something big.

"Hey, Dad."

He turned to see Ryan and Ava standing in the doorway.

"Are you watching the news?" Ava asked.

Jace turned on the TV. To his surprise, the news was broadcasting live from a helicopter, hovering over Granwin

Estates, showing aerial footage of a house that had partially collapsed. Jace's stress and tension returned in an instant.

He jumped at the sound of his phone ringing.

"I'm so glad to hear your voice," Sarah said when he answered. "I've been trying to get through for the past ten minutes, but I kept getting a busy signal."

Before Jace could say a word, Sarah asked, "Are you all still in the house?"

"Yes, why wouldn't we be?"

"Don't you know what's going on? Get the kids and get the hell out!"

"What are you talking about? We're fine."

"Haven't you been watching the news?"

"Yeah, I just turned it on. Our house is still standing."

"But for how much longer? There are sinkholes opening everywhere."

"Sinkholes?"

"There's no time to explain. Just get the hell out of the house and come to the hospital."

Without further delay, Jace disconnected.

He turned to Ryan and Ava. "Grab your sneakers and jackets. We need to go."

Ryan immediately ran out of the room while Ava remained standing.

"You're scaring me, Dad. What's the matter?"

"No time to explain now. Just grab your things."

He raced over to the closet, tripping over the carpet and crashing to the floor. He sprang up, ignoring his aching knee, and proceeded to grab a pair of sneakers. He swiped a yellow parka hanging in the closet before running into the hallway.

He heard an unsettling creaking noise, similar to the sounds from a while ago when he had first noticed the cracks in the basement walls. He was unsure if it was due to the wind and rain pounding the house or something worse.

"Come on, kids; we gotta go."

He ran into the kitchen and grabbed the car keys from the key holder. He opened the garage, with the windswept rain blowing in from the outside, dousing the front end of the car.

With Ryan and Ava strapped in, he shifted into drive, the car lurching forward into the smothering rain. There were several other cars on the streets, attempting to escape the chaos. He immediately thought of Mr. Aderlee, hoping and praying he'd already left.

Just as the thought crossed his mind, he looked to the right, squinting through the rain, and spotted Mr. Aderlee's car leaving the driveway and pulling into the street. He waited for his car to pass then followed behind him.

The windshield wipers swayed back and forth at a furious pace but were no match for the relentless rain. Several more emergency vehicles passed in the opposite direction. Jace could only imagine the scene he was leaving behind.

He zigzagged through the streets, following Mr. Aderlee's lead, attempting to avoid any floods, or worse, any collapsed road.

He eventually approached the front of the

development. Several police cars were lined up, guarding the entrance, only allowing emergency personnel to enter. A few officers in lime-green parkas directed traffic in and out of the community.

Mr. Aderlee made a right turn, and his taillights eventually disappeared into the unforgiving weather. Jace proceeded to make a left, heading to the hospital.

He looked in the rearview mirror. "You kids all right?"

"Yeah. But what happened back there?" Ryan asked.

"I don't think we want to know."

"Where are we going?" Ava asked.

"To the hospital to see Mom. We should be safe there."

He continued north on Interstate 25, the rain showing no signs of letting up. Jace couldn't comprehend the thought of them escaping a battleground full of sinkholes in the middle of a community that they called home. He wondered if the house would even survive the night. He also prayed everyone escaped unharmed, but after seeing the collapsed house on the news, he would have been shocked if there were no casualties.

He took a deep breath, placing his left hand in the middle of his chest and rubbing it in circles, but something was different—horribly different. There was no knot protruding from the center of his chest where the pendant usually rested. He felt farther up, closer to his neck. Still nothing. He slowed and pulled along the shoulder of the road.

"Why are you stopping?" Ryan asked.

Jace turned on the overhead light. "Does anyone see

my chain in the car? Maybe on the floor somewhere?"

Ryan and Ava gave a quick look around.

Ava shrugged and said, "No."

Jace glanced down at his lap, and then on the driver's side floor. He brushed his feet in circles, hoping to hear the jangle of the chain. He turned his attention to the passenger seat and floor before rummaging his hands through the center console. He placed both hands on the back of his neck, patting it up and down, not wanting to believe the chain was missing.

A sudden rush of heat flushed his face. Not a day had gone by in the past thirty years where that chain wasn't around his neck or at least somewhere in his possession. He couldn't imagine things could get worse after the past few tumultuous weeks, but they just did.

He tried his best to stay calm and think rationally. It had to be in the house somewhere. He probably lost it in the scramble to leave. He had to go back to find it, but not with the kids in the car.

* * *

They arrived a short while later at the hospital. Jace threw on his hood and ran to the hospital entrance with Ryan and Ava in hot pursuit. Once inside, they pulled off their hoods, but Jace kept his on, mindful of his last visit, not wanting to be recognized.

They eventually entered Sarah's room. She immediately sat up in bed with arms extended and a grateful smile. The kids proceeded with a delicate embrace. Jace followed with a gentle hug of his own.

"Thank God, you're all okay." She focused on Jace. "Why are you still wearing your hood?"

"It's a long story."

Sarah shrugged. "Is the house still standing?"

"It was when we left."

Sarah focused her attention on the TV, the news still broadcasting helicopter footage from the chaos at Granwin. "This is a complete nightmare. Some more homes collapsed, but I haven't heard any reports of casualties."

Jace nervously tapped his foot. "I'll be back later. I have to go take care of something."

"Where are you going?" Sarah asked.

"I forgot something."

"What are you talking about? You just got here."

Jace sighed, reluctant to utter the truth. Seconds of silence followed.

"Well . . .?" Sarah asked.

He pulled off his hood and tugged down his shirt collar, exposing his bare neck.

"What happened to your locket?"

"I don't know. I lost it somewhere."

"Do you have a clue where it is?"

"Yeah." He followed up with silence.

"Aren't you going to tell me?"

"The house."

Sarah shook her head with conviction. "Don't even think about going back to look for it."

"I have to."

"No, you don't."

"Look, I'm not going to sit here and argue with you. You know how important that is to me."

"Yeah, but do you also know how important your life is to us?"

"Thanks for the concern, but I already made up my mind."

"No, Dad," both Ryan and Ava said in unison.

"I promise I'll be back." He took a few steps, approaching the door.

Sarah unleashed a frigid stare. "Jace P. Valentine, if you don't sit your damn ass in that chair!"

He calmly walked over to Sarah and kissed her on the forehead. He turned to the kids, embracing them before walking away.

Sarah reached out, attempting to grab him, grimacing in pain at the sudden movement. Tears streamed down her cheeks. "Don't you dare leave this room," she said, her voice quivering. "I was sitting up, watching the news for the past hour, worried sick that you all wouldn't come walking through these hospital doors safely. And now that I have the family together, no one is leaving. Do you understand?"

Jace turned, looking at the ground. He couldn't bear to see Sarah crying at this point. She was already torn down physically, and now he had to watch this emotional meltdown. He closed his eyes, attempting to block out her plea. His eyes watered as he took another step toward the door.

"Ryan, don't let him leave," Sarah pleaded.

Ryan stepped in front of Jace, blocking his path to the

door. "Can't let you do it, Dad."

Jace felt a tug on his parka. He turned to see Ava holding his jacket.

"Me, neither," she said.

He gazed up at the ceiling, not interested in looking at his children's worried faces.

"Sweetheart, can you please let go of my jacket?"

Ava said nothing but remained holding with a firm grip.

"This is Daddy talking," he said, raising his voice. "This time, I'm not asking you . . . I'm telling you to let go!"

Jace felt her grip ease until she eventually complied.

"Thank you."

He turned to Ryan. "Now it's your turn. Just like your sister, I'm not asking you—I'm telling you."

"No," Ryan said in complete defiance with his arms folded.

Although Ryan was physically larger than Jace, he was still a boy, not yet having entered into the realm of manhood. Jace knew this, but Ryan apparently, had to be reminded.

Jace took a step toward him and extended his right arm in an attempt to push Ryan aside. Ryan grabbed hold as both their arms became intertwined. They struggled for a second, Jace using leverage to push Ryan up against the wall. He put his forearm against Ryan's chest while pinning him to the wall. Ryan's eyes were wide open, apparently frightened at this physical confrontation, and most likely surprised by Jace's strength. Ryan eased all further resistance. Jace stared at him, face-to-face, nose-to-nose.

"Now, I'm going to let you go in a second, and when I do, I want you to stand still until I leave the room. Understand?"

Ryan stared, breathing heavily before eventually nodding.

Jace eased his forearm away from Ryan's chest and, without looking back, quickly exited the room, leaving behind the soft cries of his family.

# Chapter 55

Maria stared at Malcolm's outstretched hand but didn't offer to shake.

He lowered his hand. "If you don't want to take my hand, that's fine. All you need to do is say yes or no."

She shook her head and reached into the envelope. She stuffed the bills into her pants pocket, and then threw the empty envelope on the desk.

Malcolm let out a sigh. "Please don't do what I think you're about to do. I'm truly looking to make amends for what happened between us, and I would hate to see this end on a bitter note."

The window of opportunity for him to be sincere had closed a long while ago. Helping herself to this money constituted only a small portion of what she believed was owed to her for the stress and anxiety he had put her through over the past month. She had made up her mind to keep the money and was planning to enjoy every single moment of stealing it from him.

Maria's thoughts of vindication were rudely interrupted by the reality of the present moment as she realized her bold plans would mean nothing if she couldn't flee the office without getting caught. She also didn't honestly know if she possessed the sheer brutality needed to actually stab this man if he did grab her.

She let out a massive exhale, clearing her thoughts and

focusing on the opponent in front of her in this real-life game of tag. Practice was over, and game time was upon her.

She took a deep breath and glanced behind her to make sure a clear path was available to start her sprint.

"I'm giving you one more chance, Maria, to put that money back on the table and leave this office peacefully," Malcolm said as the vertical crevice developing between his eyes would indicate his pleasant demeanor was fading fast.

*Three, two, one.* Maria twisted her body away from him and started her sprint to the front door.

"Get back here!" he screamed.

She hurdled a couple of boxes outside his office and continued scurrying, approaching the front entrance. She heard heavy footsteps not too far behind as she grabbed the doorknob but struggled to twist it open with her sweaty palm and numb left hand. She switched to her right hand, which was not as moist, and twisted the knob, running outside into the drenching rain. Afraid to turn around, she continued to her car, splashing into puddles of water. She reached into her coat pocket, fumbling for her car keys. That instant, she regretted not having a more recent car model with a keyless entry fob, although she was in no position to afford one. She hadn't a second to waste, and undoubtedly struggling to open the car door with her keys would waste more than a few, and she would find herself in the death grip of this behemoth behind her. She didn't recall if she left the door unlocked when she'd arrived, but she prayed that was the case.

She lunged for the door handle, pulling up. In one swift motion, the car door opened. She dove inside, closing the door behind her and locking it. Not more than three seconds later, Malcolm hit the door with a thud, shaking the car from side to side.

He pounded on the glass. "Open this damn door, or I swear I'll break this glass."

She jammed the car key into the ignition as the engine roared to life.

Malcolm grabbed the door handle, violently pulling, trying his best to open it.

She shifted in reverse and slammed her foot on the accelerator, just about the same time he raised his hand to smash through the glass. The car jerked backward as he grabbed the windshield wiper that broke off in his hand.

She shifted into gear, coming within inches of sideswiping him. She glanced in her rearview mirror, leaving him standing in the rain with the broken windshield wiper in hand. She abruptly stopped a few feet from the main road as several fire engines and police cars sped by. She swerved onto the route, heading in the opposite direction. She displayed a delighted grin, patting her pants pockets that were now five hundred dollars richer, but her quest was only halfway complete.

# Chapter 56

He stood in the pouring rain, watching Maria's car speed off down the road. The rain didn't seem to bother him much as he stared in anger, throwing the windshield wiper blade to the ground. He would see her again. He would get his money back one way or another.

His attention shifted to the fire engine and police cars racing west. It was unusual to see multiple emergency vehicles heading in the same direction. Must be something big.

He gathered himself and walked into the office. After drying his face and hands with a paper towel, he focused his attention on a stack of mail that he was planning to open prior to Maria crashing the party, and performing her cash grab and run routine. There was one piece of mail in particular, which garnered his full attention. It was addressed from the Environmental Protection Agency and Malcolm figured this was the long-awaited test results from the lake. Upon opening the envelope, he read through the first couple of pages and immediately let out a heavy sigh before tilting his head toward the ceiling.

His thoughts were immediately interrupted by more sirens approaching in the distance, prompting him to grab a nearby radio and tune into a local AM news station.

*"It's total chaos at Granwin Estates, as several houses have collapsed under what appears to be large sinkholes*

*that have opened up throughout the community. Emergency personnel are doing their best to evacuate and search for survivors,"* a newsman reported.

Malcolm struggled to catch his breath with this sudden horrific news. His worst fears were now confirmed after reading the results from the lake and hearing about the devastating events happening within the community.

He grabbed a blue, hooded parka hanging on the corner coatrack then ran to the back door, leaving the office in shambles. He hopped in his truck and sped out of the parking lot. He thought for a split-second to head east, in search of Maria, but he quickly doused that idea, especially with the drama unfolding at Granwin.

He made a left, heading west. He sped on the rain-slicked roads, about five miles away from Granwin Estates. He clicked on the radio, back to the local AM station giving an update on the situation.

*"Inhabitants of the community are leaving in droves as the police escort them to safety. There have been a few confirmed deaths, and this deluge of rain isn't helping the rescue efforts."*

A short while later, he neared the entrance. The police had blocked off any incoming traffic into the community. He was determined to enter in the hopes of helping with the rescue efforts. In particular, making sure Mr. Aderlee was safe. Losing Mrs. Aderlee was bad enough, but the thought of Mr. Aderlee perishing under the weight of a collapsed home made his stomach turn.

He circled back onto Coors Boulevard and drove a

half-mile down, making a left onto a small, dirt-covered road, a shortcut into the community that most people didn't know existed. He raced down the mud-covered terrain, toward his chaotic destination.

# **Chapter 57**

Jace eased up on the accelerator, creeping near the main entrance. Several police cars were parked with swirling lights spinning, piercing the dark. The evacuation was still in progress with various cars and other emergency vehicles exiting the premises. Several officers were stationed outside with rain-soaked parkas.

*This would be interesting. Everyone else is trying to flee the area, and I would be the only fool trying to enter. What could I tell them? Should I act frantic and tell them I'm looking for a missing family member? Or maybe I should just tell them the truth and see how far that gets me?* He shrugged, driving in the officer's direction.

One of the officers tapped on the windshield with the flashlight. Jace opened it halfway.

"Sir, we have an evacuation in progress," the officer said. "No civilians are allowed to enter."

Jace swallowed the lump in his throat. "What's going on?"

"All I can tell you is there's an emergency situation and all homes are being evacuated."

Jace glared at the officer. "I can't just turn around and leave my dog at home. I just left an hour ago to run an errand and left him asleep in the basement. He's probably frightened to death. I need to go get him."

"Give me the address, and we'll have someone search

the basement for your dog."

"No, you don't understand. He won't come to anyone else but me, and he's a full-grown, one hundred and thirty pound Rottweiler. If anyone else tries to go get him, no telling what he might do."

"Well, that's a chance we have to take."

*Damn! This officer is not budging.*

He was out of ideas and also ashamed of his lame-duck excuse to try to get by the officer. He peered through the front windshield and noticed there were several police cars parked on each side of the road, but more than enough space to squeeze a car through. He looked at the officer. *Is it worth it? Of course it is.* He wasn't leaving without his locket, especially if the house was in danger of collapsing — if it hadn't already.

He squinted at the parked police cars once more, nodding his head slightly.

"Excuse me, sir? I'll tell you one more time, you need to turn around."

Jace gritted his teeth and eased his foot off the brake as the car rolled forward ever so slightly before skidding forward upon jamming his foot on the accelerator.

"Hey! Get back here!" the officer shouted, banging his flashlight on the trunk as Jace sped by.

He peered through the rearview mirror. The officer stood in the middle of the road with his hands up. He could only hope, with all the commotion concerning the evacuation, they wouldn't bother trying to chase him.

He sped down the rain-slicked roads, spotting a

handful of homeowners fleeing their houses. The garage and driveway of one house had completely crumbled into the ground, swallowed by a massive sinkhole. It resembled a war zone, no longer the cookie-cutter neighborhood he remembered when they had first laid eyes on the place.

Jace navigated the Camry around the corner, approaching the house. He hoped and prayed the house was still standing.

"What the hell?" he said, smashing his foot on the brake. The car skidded and completed a ninety-degree turn before stopping.

The road before him had disintegrated, collapsed into oblivion.

"Damn!" He slammed his fist on the steering wheel.

He turned off the ignition and grabbed a mini flashlight from the glove compartment before jumping out of the car. Although he couldn't see well through the darkness and rain, he knew his house stood only a few hundred feet away.

He looked to the far right, showing a small portion of the sidewalk that remained, although the massive cracks would indicate not too stable. He neared the sidewalk, hoping it was strong enough to support him. He stepped forward, applying only half his body weight. The mangled concrete stood firm. He applied more pressure, once realizing he was in no danger of falling through.

He continued to step over the uneven pavement for another fifteen feet until he cleared the area in question. Then he ran, picking up the pace, squinting through the windswept rain. The house eventually came into view, still standing, with no visible damage to the exterior. He stepped onto the driveway, feeling somewhat giddy at the prospect of retrieving his most precious item.

He opened the door, the rain rushing in behind him, wetting a portion of the foyer's floor tiles. Closing the door behind him, he felt extremely fortunate to have made it this far.

He reached for the light switch, but nothing happened. No electricity. A cold shiver consumed his body while his rain-soaked jeans clung to his legs.

He glanced around the house, the silence now surrounding him in pure contrast to the mayhem happening outside. Only the muffled sound of the rain and wind hitting the windows could be heard.

He sighed, no longer feeling like the owner of the house, but more like a guest—a complete stranger.

He shook his head, coming back to his senses. He didn't want to be lulled into a false sense of security, fully aware the house could collapse at any moment.

He pointed the flashlight in the direction of the stairs and followed, in an attempt to retrace his steps. He shined the light on each step, looking for the chain. He eventually made it to the top with no luck.

He entered his bedroom and frantically searched the entire area. He neared the closet with the flashlight, searched the floor, and immediately stopped upon seeing a sparkle amidst the beige fibers of the carpet. He smiled with pure delight, reunited with his precious jewelry.

He surmised it must have been jarred from his neck

when he'd tripped. The clasp was bent, most likely leading to it falling from around his neck. He stuffed it in his pocket, elated the first part of his mission had been completed.

He rushed out of the room and down the stairs to the front door. He ran down the driveway that displayed a spider web of cracks, originating from the center and stretching out to the sidewalk. He approached the battered sidewalk, tiptoeing along, feeling more confident all would be fine. Then he closed in on his car and immediately froze.

The collapsed pavement had expanded, engulfing a portion of the right rear wheel.

He circled the car, afraid to get any closer. He squinted down the road. No cars or people in sight. He thought about running, but his legs were tight and struggling to keep him comfortably upright. He glanced back at the car.

"You're wasting time," he mumbled. "Make up your mind."

He walked to the car door and opened it gently. He eased himself back into the car, conscious of any sudden shift in the car's weight. With the door remaining open, he turned the ignition and shifted into gear. He lightly tapped the accelerator as the engine revved. The Camry jerked a foot forward before stopping. He applied more pressure, the tires spinning, but the car remained stationary. He eased off the accelerator and tilted his head up, sighing before applying pressure once more. He pressed the pedal just short of the floor, the tires screeching violently, kicking up a puff of smoke, but still no movement.

As he eased his foot off the pedal, the rear end of the car tilted down to the right. He grabbed the steering wheel for leverage in an attempt to propel himself out the door. His hand slipped on the slick steering wheel, prompting him to fall backward, deeper into the cabin of the car.

The earth beneath the car had given away completely, collapsing into a cavernous pit of cement and dirt.

The car eventually stopped, the front end pointing up at a ninety-degree angle. Both sides of the car were engulfed in debris with the doors sealed shut.

He held on to the steering wheel with both eyes shut. He opened them one at a time, his head and back firmly pressed against the seat, mimicking an astronaut in a space shuttle, preparing for takeoff.

He looked up at the sky, the rain relentlessly crashing against the windshield. He stared, eyes wide open, in a state of shock. He feebly attempted to open the door, but the mass of dirt and cement surrounding the door prevented it from budging. There was also no room for him to climb through the side window as the debris was pressed firmly against the side of the car. The only way out was through the windshield. He made an attempt to contort his legs over the dashboard and tried kicking the windshield. But the odd angle prevented him from mustering enough force to do any damage to the glass.

He immediately stopped and reached into his pocket to grab the locket, and held it in the palm of his hand. He closed his eyes once more, his senses numbing with each second, drifting off to that horrible day. There he was again, in the back seat, trapped in the seat belt. His brother screamed next to him in agony, bleeding from the neck. He glanced up front, his mother dangling halfway through the windshield.

His heart pounded violently, unable to move and escape the confined wreckage of the car. He swung his head from side to side, ridding himself of the horrible daydream. He opened his eyes, squinting through the rain-drenched windshield, up into the heavens. A tear rolled down his cheek as he gripped the locket firmly in his hands. This was his destiny, he imagined. Although it was thirty years later, he would suffer the same fate as his mother and brother. He felt blessed with the additional thirty years given to him on this earth. A beautiful wife, and two healthy children. What more could he ask for?

The tension in his body immediately began to ease. His heartbeat slowed to normal as a sense of peace overwhelmed him. He was ready. Ready to see his mother and brother once again. And to make it extra special, he would have the opportunity to hand deliver the locket to its rightful owner.

He rested quietly, eyes closed, a grin etched on his face, waiting for his everlasting sleep.

# Chapter 58

"Hey," someone said.

Jace thought he heard a faint voice in the background. With eyes closed, he wondered if he had made it to his final destination. *That was quick.* Also not the greeting he had expected.

"Hey? Are you okay?"

There it was again.

He opened his eyes. The rain-battered windshield revealed a shadowy figure looking down at the car.

He raised his right hand, acknowledging the stranger, although a part of him was angry. Upset that someone had dared interfere with his fate, his chance to see his mother and brother.

"We have to get you out of there!" the person screamed.

Jace scrunched his eyebrows, still trying to work his way back to reality.

"Hold on!" the person shouted then disappeared for an instant. Seconds later, the shadowy figure reappeared holding a large object.

"Cover your face," the person said.

Jace looked on, confused, unsure of what was about to happen.

"Cover your face now!" the person shouted, raising the object over their head.

Jace twisted the hood from behind his shoulders, covering his face.

The person walked over to the passenger side window and dropped the large object through the windshield. It crinkled into pieces, shards of glass showering the front seat and bouncing off his body. He uncovered his face to see a large chunk of cement resting on the passenger seat.

He squinted, looking upward to see what appeared to be the end of a jacket sleeve, dangling through the hole in the windshield.

"Grab this. I'll pull you up."

He grabbed the sleeve of the jacket.

"Wrap it around your wrist," the person continued to give instructions.

Jace obliged.

"I need you to stand up slowly before I try to pull you out."

Jace moved slowly and slid his body over to the passenger seat. He suddenly stopped as the car shifted. He waited a few seconds before continuing. With his left wrist wrapped around the jacket sleeve, he reached up with his right hand, still holding the locket, and grabbed the exposed portion of the dangling sleeve.

"Ready?" the person shouted.

Jace nodded.

The person leaned back and started pulling. Jace hung on as the jacket sleeve around his wrist tightened like a boa constrictor squeezing its prey. His head approached the shattered windshield, but the hole wasn't large enough to fit his entire body. With his right hand, he pushed around the edge of the hole, pieces of glass collapsing to make the hole larger. His head and shoulders cleared the windshield, his body slowly rising from under the collapsed cement to street level. His feet cleared the windshield, his elbows eventually touching the wet pavement. He pushed up on his elbow and rolled onto the waterlogged streets.

He lay on the ground, numb and unable to gather enough strength to stand. He felt a tap on his shoulder.

"You okay?" the person asked.

He turned to see Malcolm looking on with concern.

"Come on; we gotta get you outta here. Can you walk?"

Jace shrugged.

"Here, let me help you." Malcolm positioned his hands under Jace's legs and arms and hoisted him into the air, carrying him to his truck, parked twenty feet away. He planted Jace into the passenger seat, shutting the door behind him. Then he circled the Silverado, entering from the driver's side.

Both men sat exhausted for different reasons. Jace shivered, his clothing drenched, feeling twenty pounds heavier from the extra water weight. His hair lay flat, covering half his forehead, water droplets trickling down his face. A streak of blood ran down the side of his right temple, a result of the shattered glass opening a wound on his head. Although the outside of his body was engulfed with water, his insides were bone dry, dehydrated from the traumatic event. His lips were cracked, surrounded by a white film. Throughout the entire event, his fist remained tightly closed, still holding the locket.

Malcolm looked over at Jace. "You look a mess." He grabbed a bottle of spring water resting in the cup holder. "Drink this."

Jace grabbed the bottle, swallowing several large gulps, water overflowing his lips, cascading over his chin, and down his neck.

"Let's get the hell outta here before the rest of the street collapses and we both end up in a ditch." He shifted into gear and drove away.

Jace glared out the window, feeling like a rescued prisoner of war. Lights from fire engines and other emergency vehicles lit up the sky. They drove past several white sheets laying on the sidewalk, covering the bodies of a few unfortunate victims.

He rotated his head toward Malcolm, who was quiet for a change, looking vulnerable and afraid with the events unfolding before them. He returned Jace's gaze, his eyes appearing extra moist, almost to the point of tearing.

They arrived at the exit with more police and emergency officials continuing to stream into the complex. They turned onto Coors Boulevard, driving a few miles before the Silverado slowed and pulled onto the shoulder of the road.

Jace stared at Malcolm, puzzled as to why he stopped. Malcolm turned on the local AM station, listening to the chaotic broadcast of the disaster. He stared out the driver's side window before eventually turning to Jace.

"Do you know if Mr. Aderlee got out safely? I couldn't find him."

Jace nodded.

Malcolm puffed out his cheeks in relief before exhaling the pocket of air that filled his mouth. "Who would have thought? What were the chances?"

Jace remained silent.

"I thought I was doing folks like you a favor by selling beautiful houses in what I thought was the perfect neighborhood. Everyone was so excited to move in." He put his head down. "That's all I wanted—the recognition, more business—and more money, of course. That would make any man proud. Now all the things that could have gone wrong did go wrong. Damn Jeffries Jinx. Guess I got it honestly. Like father, like son."

Jace sat silently, still trying to recover from the recent events and trying to figure out where Malcolm was going with his banter.

"I know I took a chance, but I did my research, Jace. There was less than a one percent chance."

He eyed Malcolm, utterly confused. He cleared his throat, gathering the strength to speak. "What are you talking about?"

"I'm sorry. Can you please forgive me? I know I should have said something sooner, but I just didn't want to believe it was happening. It wasn't supposed to happen."

"What?" Jace said, somewhat annoyed at this point.

Malcolm turned to Jace, hesitating to speak. "The community was built on top of a mining excavation site, and it seems the land was still unsettled."

Jace's eyebrows scrunched in confusion. "What?" he said, not sure he heard correctly.

"The houses were erected on top of an abandoned mine."

Jace unleashed a ferocious stare as a sudden jolt of energy coursed through his body. "And all you could do was lie to my face each time I approached you. How could you keep that a secret?"

"It's not a secret. It's . . . it's public record."

"*Public*? How could it be public if I didn't know about it? Did anybody else in the community know?"

"I'm sure some people knew."

"Some people? Don't you think this should have been disclosed to everyone in the community? Was it too difficult to tell everyone when we met at the realty office?"

Malcolm sighed. "I didn't want to cause any unnecessary panic. I still couldn't confirm at that time what was causing the problems."

It was all now coming together for Jace. The cracks in the foundation were all preludes to the sinkholes. Jace was no mining expert, but he imagined the empty mine shafts were filled with massive amounts of soil, which apparently was not too stable. The rain must have softened the soil further, eventually leading to its total collapse and giving birth to these sinkholes.

Jace pondered further. "What about the water? How do you think it got contaminated?"

Malcolm continued to stare straight ahead and did not

offer Jace any eye contact. "Based on the report from the EPA, the lake was contaminated with acid mine drainage. It's some form of acidic discharge from the abandoned mines that still existed in the soil. I imagine this seeped into your underground well tank and . . . you know the rest of the story."

"And when the hell were you planning to tell us about the water results?"

"I just found out about this literally a couple of hours ago. I swear I would have told you and the rest of the residents about this today, but obviously didn't get a chance with all this now going on."

Jace struggled to ingest this news all at once and keep his sanity in check at the same time. "So, if the mining site was supposedly public information, don't you think someone in the community or city who knew about this could have warned us?"

"But you can't just evacuate the entire community based on a scenario that had a less than one percent chance of occurring."

Jace cupped his face, tempted to grab Malcolm by the neck, but he had no physical energy to propel his body. He looked at him once more, flashing back to all the drama that had occurred since the move.

"What about my wife? She's in the hospital, suffering for something that could have been avoided. And we can't forget about Mrs. Aderlee's death."

Malcolm turned with eyebrows scrunched. "We still don't know what killed Mrs. Aderlee. Could have been something else."

"Well, we sure know what happened to my wife, and it's all your damn fault, and whoever else knew about the risks."

Malcolm pursed his lips with a tear rolling down his cheek. "Don't you think I'm suffering enough? If I wasn't such a concerned person, I would have sold the houses and not cared about the risks. But I took time to research and figured it was safe to sell homes in the community. Can you at least give me a little credit for that?"

Jace shook his head, not fazed by Malcolm's melodramatic attempt for sympathy.

"Did you know the first house that collapsed on the news was the first one I sold in the community? It was to a lovely couple, like you and Mrs. Valentine. They had three kids and a dog. A perfect family. Well, unfortunately, before I found you, I was informed the mother was killed, along with two of their children." He looked away from Jace. "Now that I think about it, no telling how many people died back there. Don't you understand? I was just trying to save my business. It was either try selling the homes, or pack up the business."

"So, you chose to risk the lives of innocent people for the sake of a few dollars to save your business."

Malcolm slammed his fist on the dashboard. "The chances were a million to one this would happen. Who wouldn't take that chance? Most people would have done the same thing."

"Guess I'm not most people."

Malcolm leaned back against the headrest, closing his eyes. "Just when things were starting to turn for the better. I was all ready to move forward and restart my sorry-ass life, looking forward to new beginnings. I knew this was all too good to be true," Malcolm said, cupping his hands over his face. "I can't deal with this guilt any longer. I can't deal with my life any longer. It's been a tragedy ever since my childhood. And this is just the icing on the cake."

With his head tilted down, he continued, "You know, my doctor told me something recently that stuck with me, and I only wish this advice was given to me sooner. Accept what is, let go of what was, and have faith in what will be." He turned to Jace. "I'm just paying it forward in the hopes it's not too late for you to live by this message." He leaned forward, lightly tapping his head against the steering wheel. Then he turned in Jace's direction. "I guess there's only one thing to do."

Jace glared at him, still stewing over his recent confession.

Malcolm cut his eyes toward the glove compartment. Jace followed his eyes, flashing back to the only other time he was in Malcolm's truck. His heart rate quickened. He pivoted his head back to Malcolm, his anger quickly morphing into a fit of nervousness. Malcolm continued to stare at the glove compartment. Jace shrugged, as if confused by his gesture, but he knew deep in his mind what he wanted.

"Go ahead . . . open it," Malcolm said.

Jace's senses became numb, hypnotized by the

moment. His arm said no, but his brain complied, unwillingly.

He reached, pulling the tab, opening it gently. There it was—the cold black steel, resting among the loose papers and other miscellaneous items.

"Can I have it, please?"

Jace sat in disbelief. He shrugged in a feeble attempt to play dumb.

"Come on, Jace. You know what I want."

Jace struggled to move as a sudden wave of mental and physical paralysis took hold.

Malcolm leaned toward the glove compartment. "Guess I'll grab it myself," he said, reaching for the gun. He placed the gun in his lap, staring out the front windshield with no discernable expression.

Jace wanted to speak, but his fear rendered him mute, helpless, and only able to communicate through body gestures.

Malcolm reached for the gun in his lap, opening the revolver. He spun it around, looking at the six bullets resting in each chamber.

Jace's mouth opened slightly, trying to force the air through his voice box to make a sound—any sound. A short monotone grunt escaped his lips. It wasn't a word, but it was a start.

He breathed in deeply, his hands trembling. "P-plea," he mumbled, his voice gaining steam. "Please take me to my family." He swallowed hard. "I . . . I won't tell anyone what you just told me."

"It doesn't matter. I already made up my mind." He started to empty each chamber, resting the bullets on his lap until there was only one still in its place.

Jace gripped the locket, shaking his head in disbelief. "I promise, if you let me go, I won't tell a soul."

Malcolm glared at him with a cold stare. "Let's play a game."

Jace shook his head. "N-no. Don't do this."

"Don't worry; it'll be fun. It's a sick, twisted game I learned from my father. Ever heard of Russian roulette?"

He spun the chamber before closing it and lifting the gun off his lap. "As you can see, I emptied five bullets, leaving one in the chamber. Now the object of the game is to avoid blowing your brains out, but it's all about luck. The odds are sixteen percent against you and eighty-four percent in your favor. Pretty solid odds, don't you think?"

Jace continued to stare out the front, his senses numb, unable to utter any more words.

"Are you listening?" Malcolm said with a hint of anger.

Jace didn't acknowledge him.

"That's okay. You don't have to look. Maybe it's for the better." The truck cabin became quiet before Malcolm continued, "Next step is to aim the gun at its target and pull the trigger."

Jace clenched his fists, adrenaline giving him a sudden jolt of energy. He thought for a quick second to reach for the door handle and jump out but figured that would be a mistake. By the time he reached for the door and opened it,

Malcolm would have already pulled the trigger.

He closed his eyes, hoping and praying for a miracle.

"Let's count down from three," Malcolm said.

Jace's eyes were shut tight, tears squeezing between his eyelids, eventually cresting them and falling harmlessly onto his cheeks.

"Come on, Jace. We can't do this with your eyes closed."

He slowly opened his eyes and glanced over, wondering if his blurry vision was deceiving him. The gun wasn't pointed at him but pressed against Malcolm's temple.

"Now, are you ready to count with me?" Malcolm asked.

A quick and instant sigh of relief flowed through his body, realizing he was never the intended victim. But now he had to deal with potentially being a witness to this brutal act that Malcolm threatened to afflict on himself.

With a sudden burst of energy, he wet his lips and said, "Don't do it. It's not worth it."

Malcolm sat calmly with the barrel of the gun firmly pressed against the side of his head. "I appreciate your concern, but I have no choice. My life has been filled with disappointment, and I can't take it anymore. Besides, who's to say the bullet is in this chamber? I'm only going to pull the trigger once."

"You can't take that chance." Jace reached out, his hand still trembling. "Just give me the gun."

"Okay, let's make a deal. I pull the trigger once, and if

nothing happens, it was meant for me to remain on this earth and I'll give you the gun. Now count down with me."

"No! Give me the gun," Jace said, his voice getting stronger.

"Three . . . two . . ."

"No!" Jace shouted, making a feeble attempt to lunge for the gun, but his strength and energy were still depleted.

Malcolm pushed him aside with his massive arm, Jace recoiling back into his seat.

"Don't ever do that again!" Malcolm shouted.

Jace remained slouched in the seat. That sudden thrust of movement had zapped whatever bit of energy he possessed.

Malcolm repositioned the gun against the side of his head. "Let's try this again, and this time, when I start counting, I'm not stopping."

He realized there was nothing he could do to stop this. With his physical strength completely gone, he sat in shock, unable to do anything else but watch and pray luck was on Malcolm's side. He closed his eyes as Malcolm started again.

"Three . . . two . . . one."

# Chapter 59

With his eyes closed, Jace remained still, his heart pounding at a frenetic pace. A part of him hoped it was a bad dream, but his senses were proving that theory wrong.

A soft ringing permeated his ear canal. The burning scent of gunpowder smoke infiltrated his nostrils. With eyes still closed, he felt warm liquid running down the side of his forehead and cheek. *Could be moisture from his hair*, he thought, but deep down, he knew that wasn't the answer. He remained facing forward with his eyes closed. He reached up to his forehead, wiping it with his fingers. He held his fingers in front of his face, opening his eyes. There it was, the crimson-red liquid dripping from his finger.

He peeked down at his yellow parka, viewing a splattering of red droplets, resembling some sort of abstract artwork. He continued to stare forward, far from interested in turning to the driver's side of the car. His five senses provided enough evidence to know what had happened. His peripheral vision allowed him to see the body slouched in the driver's seat.

Throughout this entire ordeal, he continued to grip the locket firmly in his left hand.

He reached for the door handle and opened it. Without looking back, he pushed himself out of the car, his legs wobbling once they initially touched the ground. He threw on his hood with the rain continuing to fall, but not as heavy. He stepped away from the pickup, closing the door. He took one step, and then another, meandering down the side of the road.

More emergency vehicles roared by with sirens blaring, heading toward the chaos. He continued his slow march, down the road, miles away from the hospital. The thought of being reunited with his family kept him going. He walked about half a mile down the road as the bloodstains were eventually washed from his jacket. Fortunately, he was able to hitch a ride to the hospital from a Good Samaritan.

***

He entered the hospital doors with the thought of admitting himself from exhaustion, but he had to get back to his family. He struggled up the stairs and stumbled, nearing the room. His legs trembled, struggling to hold his body weight. He entered the room, collapsing on his hands and knees.

Ryan and Ava rushed to his side. Sarah sprouted tears of joy, happy to see him alive. She paged a nurse, asking for immediate help.

Jace collapsed, sprawled out on his back against the cold tiled floor. He mustered a half-smile and held up his left hand, displaying the locket dangling from his grip.

He wet his lips and cleared his throat. "Told you I'd be back."

# Chapter 60

"Final call for gate ten, express bus to Juarez, Mexico," the voice said on the loudspeaker.

Maria rushed through the terminal, approaching the gate. She boarded the bus, exhausted from running and carrying a thirty-pound duffel bag filled with clothes. She shuffled down the aisle, the front, and middle filled to capacity with travelers. She glanced to the back, spotting a couple of vacant seats, and made her way to the last row, next to the bathroom. She dropped the bag on the seat next to her, too tired to put it in the overhead compartment. A few minutes later, the bus departed.

She stared out the window as the bus traveled down the highway. This was a bittersweet experience. She had wanted to live the American dream, but it hadn't worked out as planned. Her eyes watered upon thinking about Sabrina, someone whom she barely knew, willing to help her during her time of need and hadn't expected anything in return. That act of unselfishness had put Maria's trust back in mankind. Her friendship with Sabrina might have been short-lived, but well worth it. It might have been the only thing to convince her to stay in America, but that was a moot point now.

She looked up toward the heavens, hoping and praying Sabrina would recover from the devastating accident. Last she'd heard, she was still in a coma, but she was positive, with Sabrina's spirit and feistiness, she would pull through.

She had realized it was time to move on, back to Mexico in search of her family and the old life she had once known.

She looked down at her lap, patting a black briefcase, running her fingers over the large, chromed initials *M.W.* Her quest was now complete and her pot of gold had been found.

She smiled, closing her eyes for a well-deserved nap.

# Chapter 61

It started as faint, mostly inaudible noises. But with each passing moment, the noises became stronger and eventually translated into a familiar language.

Darkness was replaced with a hint of light. A light that became brighter with each passing second. Interesting shapes came into view; blurry at first, but clearing after a short while. It developed into a lovely vision of humans in white clothing, gliding around the room.

One approached with a smile. "Welcome back," she said.

Sabrina's eyes fluttered to adjust to the light. Her journey back to the living world was complete.

# Chapter 62

Six months later, Jace stared out the office window at a familiar scene. The gateway arch stood tall and proud near the Mississippi River.

He had been successful in getting his old job back and moving the family back to St. Louis. With the insurance money received from the disaster at Granwin Estates, they had been able to purchase a large condo, ten minutes outside of Downtown St. Louis. He was also part of a large class action lawsuit against the builders and real estate companies that were involved with Granwin. And through the information contained in the various court filings, the full name of Malcolm's old family business was finally revealed as *Robert Jeffries Construction and Mining.*

***

At the end of the day, he packed his briefcase and approached the hallway, pausing as he came upon the elevator bank.

He smirked. "No. I think I'll take the stairs," he whispered.

He eventually made it to the parking lot, approaching a new silver BMW 5 series that he had purchased a week ago. He sat in the driver's seat, listening to the Sade classic "Cherish The Day" tapping his fingers on the steering wheel to the rhythm.

He exited the parking lot, driving east on Interstate 70.

It was late spring, the sun still bright in the sky, a few hours from sunset. City life was in full bloom.

Jace slowed down with traffic backing up on the highway. He rolled down the window, taking a deep breath. He rubbed the center of his chest, feeling the comforting lump. This was home. This was where his mother and brother had lived and died. The same place he planned to be when he took his last breath. Until then, he beamed fondly at his new lease on life.

He planned to live every day to the fullest and stop living in the past. His future was full of possibilities, and he was eager to explore each and every one of them.

He craned his neck, getting an eyeful of the surrounding city.

Home is where the heart is, and his was in St. Louis.

# Epilogue

Sarah made a full recovery from the burns, besides some permanent scarring around parts of her body. She still fought to control her jealous rages, which had become less frequent over time. For the most part, she realized Jace had no intentions of leaving her, though a small part of her couldn't help but leave that open as a possibility. Her headaches mysteriously subsided, allowing her to go back to work part-time.

Ryan rejoined his school baseball team, on his way to becoming an all-star.

Ava found a new lease on life, cherishing every day with the family and no longer at war with Ryan . . . or at least not as much.

It was determined from an autopsy that Mrs. Aderlee's death was due to a stroke and not the consumption of contaminated water. Mr. Aderlee was unable to cope with living life alone and moved in with his son in San Francisco.

After three months in the hospital, Sabrina fully recovered from her accident, except for a slight limp. She resumed long-distance contact with the Valentines and confirmed with them the information she had found out about Granwin was, in fact, related to the land being a former mining excavation site.

She also remained in contact with Maria, which allowed them to continue their budding relationship, although convincing Maria the accident was never her fault had become an ongoing challenge.

Maria started a new life in Mexico. She married a kind and caring gentleman and added a daughter to her family. She found work as an administrative assistant at a construction business in Mexico City and, during her off hours, she volunteered as a domestic abuse counselor, following in the footsteps of someone near and dear to her heart.

-------------------------------------------------------------------------

-----

"Accept what is, let go of what was, and have faith in what will be." - Unknown

## Acknowledgments

"Ambition is the path to success. Persistence is the vehicle you arrive in."
Bill Bradley

This quote personifies my journey with writing this novel from beginning to end. Believe it or not, it started with an idea over two decades ago, born from my desire to simply tell a story. Little did I know this would lead me through a twisted journey full of detours, roadblocks, speed traps, and the ultimate deterrent on anyone's path to success — self-doubt.

I would first like to thank God for giving me the creativity, imagination, and determination to push through this journey of becoming a published author. I would have never succeeded without your abundant grace and mercy.

A huge thank you to my wife, Debbie, for encouraging me to continue on this journey of becoming a published author. This book stayed hidden on the hard drive of my computer without any movement for years, and every once in a while, she would nudge me to finish what I started.

Through her encouragement, I finally dusted the book

off, and proceeded to make the necessary edits needed to complete the manuscript, and push forward with the self-publishing process.

I would like to thank my now young adult children, Justin and Kiana, for being patient with me, and not thinking I was crazy for being stapled to the office chair as I mercifully pecked away on the keyboard for all these years. I also want to give a special nod to my daughter for offering a suggestion, which I did incorporate into this novel. She knows what I'm talking about.

I would like to thank my brother, Ken, for offering advice based on his self-publishing journey. I also owe him thanks for connecting me with, Eldar, who provided important additional insight into the self-publishing world, which led me to connect with the individuals noted below.

A special thanks to, Kristin, who helped with the editing process for this book, as well as, Mihai, who was the graphic designer that created the book cover.

And I can't end without thanking my mother, Barbara, for supporting me throughout these years, giving me encouragement when I needed it, and cheering me on along on the sidelines as I navigated this journey of becoming a published author.

www.ingramcontent.com/pod-product-compliance
Lightning Source LLC
Chambersburg PA
CBHW030730310726
48969CB00005B/1162